Escaping Circumstances

Out of Darkness Book Two

by

Gloria Joynt-Lang

Out of the Darkness

Escaping Circumstances

Cover Art by *The Wild Rose Press, Inc.*

The Wild Rose Press, Inc.
PO Box 708
Adams Basin, NY 14410-0708
Visit us at www.thewildrosepress.com

Publishing History
First Edition, 2024
Trade Paperback ISBN 978-1-5092-5340-1
Digital ISBN 978-1-5092-5341-8

Out of the Darkness
Published in the United States of America

Dedication

To John, who supported my aspirations, and to Ms. Smookie, who begged for attention while I crafted this book. You are a persistent diva, Ms. Smookie. And you are a patient soul, John.

Chapter One

He kicked the broken bricks from the path and stomped toward the corroded sign. Blazing sunshine, harsh winters, and overall neglect had faded the address on the rusted plate. He wedged his hand into his pocket and pulled out a crumpled note. His fingers clenched the paper, preventing the wind from stealing the address. Mother Nature and the universe had screwed him enough. Not even a tornado would ruin this opportunity. He scratched the grime off the metal with his pocketknife. As he thought, the number was an *eight* and not a *three*. This was the place. Her fate was now in his hands.

A warm breeze blew across his face. Clouds were drifting from the north. A summer storm was on the way. New York's heatwave would end.

Good.

He had donned his last clean T-shirt and had no time for laundry.

Ignoring the broken liquor bottles and used condoms under his steel-toed boots, he charged toward the apartment building. On the outer wall hung an intercom. Loose wires sprung underneath the device, creating a hazard to any polite users. He squeezed the door handle, not the least surprised the door opened. He stepped inside. A pungent, musty odor accosted his nostrils. If city workers weren't so overwhelmed, the place would be condemned. He climbed the narrow stairs two at a time. The baseboards creaked from his body weight. He reached the top floor and trudged through the hallway, scanning the numbers on the walls.

He stopped dead, his boots scuffing the stained linoleum in front of apartment two-ten. He drew a breath. His chest rose. Two years of repeated roadblocks would soon end. A horrible metallic taste, like an Allen key wedged in a cavity, rose in his mouth. He sucked a breath. This was not how he pictured confronting her. He lunged his fist and pounded the door. Paint peeled under his knuckles. He wasn't the first to bang the battered wood. A chain-clasp door clanged behind him.

"Fool," he grumbled.

Flimsy chain locks were useless. They gave people false security. With minimal effort, he could bust through the nosy stranger's door. And if he did, not a soul would stop him. Hell, he could torch the place without any interference. People were intimidated by his bulging biceps and towering six-and-a-half-foot frame. And if his backside didn't frighten the neighbor into submission, he'd turn around and give them a hardened glare.

The door behind him squeaked closed. The rubbernecker chose personal safety over curiosity. Even if the occupant gave a damn—which was doubtful—they wouldn't dial the cops. Alerting the authorities risked disclosing their own identity. Those stuck in this shithole lived in the shadows, hiding from their own sins.

He struck the door. "Dammit, Carly. I know you're there."

Silence followed.

He struck the door again. "I'm done with your

bullshit games." Blood rose to his clenched fists. "Fine, don't answer. I'll kick my way in." The threat was real. He would smash his boot through the wood.

Shuffling came from inside. He stilled. Footsteps clicked near the door. He stepped aside, bracing for one of Carly's boyfriends to crash through the doorway. He had learned not to count on Carly. She wouldn't do a damn thing if some asshole ran out and shanked him with a blade. The woman hated him. She never wanted him around.

Fine by him. He sure the hell didn't want her in his life. He waded through rush hour traffic on a stinky hot afternoon for one reason—the child.

The deadbolt unlatched, and the door creaked open. Mere inches separated him from the woman. He stared at her sunken eyes, brittle, bleached blonde hair, and crooked mouth. She was in her mid-forties, but thick eyeliner and deep facial creases made her appear older.

"What are you doing here, Marion?"

She used his given name—a name he despised.

"It's Eliot," he snarled, "and I'm here for her."

She smacked her crimson lips, her teeth stained from the waxy lipstick. "Who?" she drawled.

Rage grew in his belly. He didn't know the child's name. The only detail he had was the kid's location.

Carly crossed her arms. "Not that it's your business, but I'm alone." Her nasal voice annoyed him almost as much as her game-playing.

Eliot charged past. The putrid stench inside the tiny apartment intensified. The smell reminded him of his childhood—filthy dishes, soiled clothing, and the noxious odor of men's shame.

She trailed behind him. "You can't just storm

through my home."

"Right," he scoffed. This wasn't a home. It was a hiding place.

He yanked a half-hinged door. A makeshift bedroom appeared. The windows were boarded with plywood. He adjusted to the dark and spotted an old mattress. A dirty syringe rested next to a one-eared teddy bear.

"What the hell's the matter with you?" He continued berating her—four-letter words fired from his mouth like an assault rifle.

"Are you done?" the woman asked. She treated him like a toddler having a meltdown in a grocery store.

Eliot bit his cheek, swished a mouthful of blood, and swallowed. He'd come too far to lose control. Ignoring the woman's comment, he marched down the narrow hallway. He ripped open another door, banging it against the wall. Cockroaches scurried. He stomped his foot and crunched the slower ones. Except for a sweater on the floor, the tiny coatroom sat empty.

Pain throbbed in his chest. Had the girl been there, his rapid, violent insect slaughtering would have terrified her. He clenched his teeth, straining his jaw muscles. No one should live in a roach-infested apartment, but what he discovered went beyond filth and poverty. This was a crime scene—though charges would never be laid. The woman who lived here manipulated the authorities. She was crafty. She was also a liar, an utter waste of skin…and his *mother*.

Unable to avoid her hapless mug, he aimed a visual dagger into her skull.

Pointless.

His contempt had no bearing. It never did.

"I'll find her," he yelled, spewing saliva.

She dared to smirk.

"Screw you," Eliot shouted. He raced down the stairs. His chest tightened with every pounding footstep. He rammed his shoulder against the metal exit door. He squinted against the daylight and gasped. The fresh air offered no comfort. He clamped his mouth over his fist. No way would he scream and allow Carly the satisfaction of hearing his anguish. He braced his body against the building's wall. A warm, scratching burn of stomach acid crept through his throat. He closed his eyes. Strangled by memories, he hurled his breakfast.

****

Quinn's frizzy hair fell over her eyes. The humidity had declared war upon her tresses. "I can't," she said to her friend Gabby.

"There's no reason you can't join Kiefer and me."

"I have a deadline on a piece." Lingering guilt followed the teensy white lie.

"You always make your delivery dates."

Quinn tugged the wrapped elastic from her hair and redid her ponytail. "In case you forgot, I'm moving next week." She grappled the bottom edges of the corrugated cardboard and lifted it. Pain radiated through her shoulder. Noticing the minimal floor space, she stacked the box on two others. She longed for a break but pictured a hot bath, not a dingy bar.

"Why are you moving? You love this place," Gabby said.

"What I love is being able to afford rent *and* groceries."

"Yeah, point taken. I'm lucky I live with Kiefer, or I'd be sleeping outside."

"No," Quinn corrected, "we'd be bunkmates." She survived twelve long months crammed into a shoebox apartment with her gregarious friend when they arrived in the Big Apple. Living together proved challenging, but she'd do it again if needed.

"Thanks," Gabby mumbled. As an unemployed actress, she landed bit parts but never a permanent gig.

"Where are you guys going tonight?" Diverting to Gabby's social life would rekindle her friend's festive mood.

"Neon Nights in Queens. Even the name is amazing."

No. It sounds like a retro disco full of sleazy old men reliving their youth.

"Oh, and the best part. Kiefer knows the bouncer. We won't have to wait in line. You can wear those high heels you bought last month and not get callouses."

"I'm not going."

"Oh please, girl, we'll have fun. Kiefer's friend Logan is going. Did I mention he's a drummer? He's fricking unbelievable. Boy, can he bang it."

Quinn stifled a groan. Logan could bang his drums all he wanted, but he wouldn't get a chance to bang her. She hated setups. How could her best friend believe she'd be okay with this—and at a bar, moreover? There would be alcohol involved. It didn't matter whether it was whiskey, beer, or tequila shots, for she'd stick to soda water. But this Logan fellow might pound back the drinks. And no matter how devoted Gabby was to their friendship, she became flighty around Kiefer. The two lovebirds would take off and leave Quinn alone with Drummer Boy. If she said yes to going out, a dark corner, a secluded alley, or a vacant washroom lurked in her future. "I'll pass," she said, keeping a long-ago promise to avoid bad situations.

"I'm offering an exciting night out, not a pizza with anchovies."

Quinn threw her arms up. "Look around. This place is filthy. If I expect my deposit back, I need to clean. Sorry, but I'll be battling dust bunnies tonight."

Gabby countered with puppy dog eyes and a pout. Even at her most annoying, she was endearing.

"How about brunch on Sunday?" Quinn suggested. "Your favorite place."

"*La Fleur Mignonne*?"

"My treat."

"Okay, but it's not healthy shutting yourself off from men. I wish you had never met that man."

Sweat glistened on Quinn's forehead.

"Chad was a horse's ass."

She let out an exasperated sigh. For a second, Quinn feared Gabby would mention Michael. "I'm staying in because I'm busy."

Gabby swung her purse over her shoulder. "I'll give you one week to settle into your new place, and then, no more excuses."

Quinn escorted Gabby to the door. "Go. Have fun. Enjoy dancing with Kiefer." She gave her a quick hug. "I'll text you the details for Sunday."

Once her friend left, Quinn settled into work, twisting a metal cage around a light fixture. She was an art school dropout who landed a job upcycling with Beloved Re-Creations. When first hired, her sole responsibility entailed scouring junk yards, garage sales, and trash cans. She spent long days collecting materials for other designers. Digging in back-alley dumpsters and apprenticing under talented artists had paid off. Now she had her own signature line. A line which she aptly named Resilience.

Her success was a godsend. Her salary tripled. Though far from wealthy, she no longer panicked when the utility bills were due. And best of all, her increased wages allowed for a better neighborhood. Soon she'd live in a building with non-rattling pipes and where the neighbors held legitimate jobs. Not that she minded Neil, the low-level weed dealer down the hallway. He never bothered anyone. But one day, Neil might vacate, and a new tenant would arrive and open shop to dubious clientele.

She was excited about the new apartment. The place came with ample square footage and a working thermostat. She could shed the winter blankets and boot slippers and blast the AC on sweltering summer days. Maybe she'd meet a nice guy in the new neighborhood.

Jeez. Gabby's persistence was wearing her down. She didn't need any more heartbreak and upheaval. Besides, she wasn't without male companionship. She had Hudson. Sure, his breath smelled like roadkill, but her beloved dog would never burn her trust to ashes.

Chapter Two

Marion *Eliot* Traversini scrolled through his phone and added bed, clothes, and toys to his shopping list. He had no idea what a five-year-old girl would like, but these items were essential for any child. He typed princess dolls and sports equipment, placing a question mark behind each.

"Hmm," he said, considering dinosaurs. Their gigantic heads and tiny, strange arms might scare the tyke. He'd ice the T-rex for now.

He added *books*. Internet experts stressed the importance of reading to a child. He would seek inspiring stories with happy endings. Hansel and Gretel weren't welcome in his household. An evil witch preying upon children hit too close to home. He tapped a few more keys and created a new grocery list. The first addition was *kiddie food.* He'd swapped protein drinks for milkshakes or, better yet, juice boxes. A parenting blog suggested healthy foods shaped into animals.

How the hell do I shape broccoli into a kitten?

There was a lot to figure out. Though becoming a guardian unnerved Eliot, he'd manage. But what terrified him more than child-rearing was failure. What if Carly won, and his sister grew up in that hellhole? Losing the kid for good would haunt him forever.

He grabbed his wallet. If he hurried, he could make it to the furniture store before closing. He locked the door and turned. Cardboard boxes lined the hallway.

Great, a new tenant. He better not be a creepy old guy.

New York was full of sickos searching the internet for young girls. God forbid if a guy ogled his sister. He'd deal with them—and not by society's rules.

He imagined the kid's teen years and scowled. *What if she's rebellious?* He wasn't expecting perfection. He just didn't want his sister to be like their mother…or him. He stomped through the hallway, frowning at his boots. *Please let her be a sweet five-year-old.*

He noticed a shadow and peered up. "Look out," he hollered.

A large cardboard box rammed his midsection. A high-pitched voice squealed. Tiny colored glass shards flew into the air, hit the ceiling, and landed on the carpet. A woman lay at his feet, her red bra strap exposed.

He extended his hand. "You okay?"

The sweaty, dumbfounded woman straightened her T-shirt and stood. Her frizzy, auburn curls rebelled against her haphazard ponytail. Half her hair had escaped their elasticized captor while the other half was ready to bolt. She stared, scrutinizing him in an all too familiar and accusatory manner. He withdrew his dark shades, hoping she wouldn't panic.

The woman inched back as if encountering an arctic musk ox. She continued her odd, receding shuffle until she gained ample distance.

"Sorry," he said, apologizing for the woman striking him.

Ignoring him, she sat. She leaned forward, collecting the broken pieces with her bare hand.

"What the hell are you doing?" he hollered,

grabbing her wrist.

She jerked her arm free. She had the reflexes of a goalie snagging a soaring puck.

"Don't," she warned.

Most women love my touch. He held back the wisecrack and stopped himself from being an asshole. "You'll hurt yourself. I'll get a vacuum."

"It won't cut me."

He had enough of her snootiness. "You're no superhero. You'll bleed like the rest of us mortals."

She pursed her lips and stared.

Trust me, princess. You don't want to play the intimidation game. One angry scowl and she'd hightail her sweet ass home.

She zeroed in on the inked viper encircling his neck and frowned. There were always women who loved the badass tattoo, but not this lady. The snake appeared to offend her as much as his superhero barb.

The woman motioned toward the glass. "Touch it." Her voice was hesitant yet bossy.

"Uh, no." He wouldn't cut his hands to prove a point.

She set her palms on the scattered glass pieces and pushed them across the worn carpet. He yanked her hands to his chest. "Are you crazy?"

She flinched. An *f you* glare shot from her eyes.

Eliot loosened his grip. The woman slid from his grasp and showed her palms.

"It's not glass. They're rubber sprinkles," she said.

"Huh?" He hadn't the foggiest what rubber sprinkles were or why the weird woman had a whole box of the strange item.

"They're an art supply. Though movie studios

employ them to simulate glass." Her voice rose as though excited. "I use them in my work. Harmless, but a hassle to clean."

"Right," he mumbled, glancing at the thingamajigs on her yoga pants. "There's some on your—"

"Leave them alone," she growled.

"Chill, lady." He had no intention of touching her inner thighs. He moved fast, but he wasn't a creep. He waved his hand toward the line of boxes. "I'm guessing you're moving in."

He took her bobbing head for a *yes.*

"I'm Scorp." He earned the nickname from his platoon mates after he fought with another Marine. He showed the other soldier what it felt like to be stung by a scorpion. He pointed toward his apartment. "I live here."

She remained quiet.

Being cautious of strangers was smart, even admirable. Too bad she couldn't be subtle and less offensive.

"Hey, Sprinkles, I'm trying to be nice."

Giving her a nickname was fine, but mentioning *nice* was probably a mistake. When you have to state your intentions, you best wrap up and go. But dammit, he wanted to help, even though she didn't want his assistance. He avoided subjecting himself to angry women, but there was more to this woman than an infuriating glare. Vulnerability seeped from her pores. She was beyond wary. She was terrified. And that alone bothered him more than it should have.

"How many more boxes are there to haul?" he asked.

"A few."

"Good. You collect these sprinkle things, and I'll

fetch the rest."

"I'm fine," she responded, refusing his offer.

Eliot held back a smirk. The woman was definitely fine. Compact, curvy, and loaded with attitude. "I'll bring your stuff upstairs and leave them outside your door." *I promise I won't infringe upon your sacred kingdom and steal your cat figurines.*

"Thanks," she murmured.

He grinned. He had won her over.

****

A quiet neighborhood with better tenants was Quinn's plan. But instead, a tattoo-infected Neanderthal lived across the hall. A possible drug dealer. Not a benign low-level pot dealer like Neil from her old building, but a notorious gang leader. Who else would have all those tattoos, including a hideous serpent wrapped around his neck?

She knew a lot of inked people. Okay, four. Five if she counted Gabby, though the tiny star on her ankle resembled an enlarged mole. But regardless, they weren't like the fellow across the hall. Unless the guy was an artist who used his flesh as a portfolio, he was bad news.

Without all the graphic tattoos, he'd still make her uneasy. The guy was massive. He towered her five-and-a-half-foot frame by a good foot. Pure muscle exploded from every part of him. His thighs were like tree trunks, his biceps nearing the size of her waist, and a sharp, hard protrusion bulged in his pants. Yes, there was no doubt about this. A gun was tucked inside the man's waistband.

Message received. Avoid the dodgy neighbor.

But his insistent plea to help was confusing.

Is it plausible the guy's being considerate? Or does

he want something? And how will he react when I refuse his personal and intimate request?

“Quit it,” she mumbled. Overthinking the situation was unhealthy. But darn it, the guy made her anxious. Her icy vibe was rude yet deliberate. She didn’t want him coming around to borrow her lasagna pan.

Thank goodness she had a dog. Though far from vicious, Hudson would alert her to danger. She debated bringing Hudson along on moving day, but why risk tripping over him? Instead, she sent him to the kennel and collided with her disheveled neighbor—like a scooter ramming into a tanker truck.

He introduced himself as Scorp. Surely the name wasn’t legit. Celebrity parents seeking attention opted for better than Scorp. It had to be a street name. Two things were certain. He wasn’t a Wall Street guy or a man who owned a tie.

However, he did have a decent smile—nice, were it not for his scraggly beard. Once he knocked off the sarcasm, he seemed genuine, not smarmy. But what did she know? She once considered Chad sincere.

Ruminating over her neighbor’s intentions was a waste of time. She checked the front door, ensuring the deadbolt was locked. She shook the chain clasp, ensuring the device caught in the track. The added security eased her mind. A single woman living alone ought to be careful.

Chapter Three

Eliot closed his eyes and shuddered. He swore hundreds of toothpicks jabbed his skull. He rang the wretched, loud buzzer and waited. The door squeaked open. A slender, silver-haired woman lurched forward for a hug. He waved her away, protecting her from the stench of cheap whiskey.

The woman shook her head. "You'd have to stand across the road for me not to notice."

"Can I come in, Paula?"

She whacked his arm. "You know better than to ask. You're always welcome."

He followed her into the cramped apartment.

"Saturating your liver is not the answer for whatever ails you."

"Yeah," he mumbled. Paula was right, but he grew tired of chasing dead leads. Getting stupid drunk or having meaningless sex dulled his anguish. Last night, he chose the bottle—twenty-six ounces of liquid gold. His drinking had become too frequent, but once he found the child, he'd quit…or so he promised himself.

Paula motioned to the living room. "I'll bring you coffee."

Eliot sank into the worn recliner. Before Carly regained custody, he had kept it together. He got drunk, but not as often. And when he tied one on, he stayed clear of Paula and Malcolm Wilson. He respected the couple.

They were his confidants. They knew his secrets—most of them, anyway. They treated him like family and loved him like a son. The only son they now had.

"Where's Malcolm?" Eliot shouted toward the kitchen, wincing at his voice.

"He took the car for an oil change. He'll be back soon. Stay for dinner and visit with him."

"Thanks, but I can't." He loved Paula's cooking, but if he ate, he'd hurl.

Last night's binge proved brutal—only equal to the bender after Ty's death. His childhood friend—Paula and Malcolm's beloved son—died in combat. Eliot was fourteen when he met Ty. The guy was his first and, for years, his only friend. Both had been angry teens, though their reasons were different. When Paula learned her son's friend lived in an abandoned train tunnel, she offered her home. Eliot hated rules and boundaries, but he loathed charity more. Desperate for shelter and food and without options, he conceded and moved in with the Wilsons.

Paula and Malcolm proved different than other adults he encountered. Paula went ballistic when he skipped school, but she never stayed angry. And Malcolm never once raised his hand.

Paula strode into the living room and gave him his coffee. "I'd insist you stay for dinner, but you best sleep off your wicked night. I'll put together a care package. Shepherd's pie and some banana bread."

"Thanks." He wrapped his monstrous hands around the oversized coffee mug. "You're a saint for putting up with my sorry ass."

"Shush. You're family, and we love you." She kissed his forehead and sat.

She remained quiet while the caffeine jolted him to life.

"What did Carly do this time?" she asked after his fourth sip.

Paula stopped referring to Carly as his mom ages ago. The woman who birthed him never wiped away his tears; instead, she caused them. He never imagined dealing with Carly again, let alone initiating the contact. But he never imagined her having another child.

He rubbed his knotted neck muscles. "Why can't I catch a break?"

"What did you learn?"

"Still don't have a name," he grumbled. "Carly gave me nothing other than a bitchy attitude." He avoided outright calling his birth mother a bitch. Paula tolerated a few cuss words but drew the line at demeaning women. Her influence prevented him from being a total dickhead toward the opposite sex.

"You're sure she has the girl?"

"Yeah, and now Carly has bolted." Yesterday, when he realized she had vanished, he headed straight to the bar. "Visiting her was a mistake, but I thought the kid would be there." He dropped his head. "I can't let this happen again."

"Don't beat yourself up. We all agreed to the dentist and his wife adopting the child. If only we had known."

The vein in his neck throbbed. "Typical abuser. Mr. Nice guy to the neighbors while beating his wife behind closed doors. At least we found out before he touched the kid."

"Yes, thank goodness. Malcolm and I should have stepped in. We could have raised her like a daughter, but back then—"

"She's my blood," he snapped. "Signing up for a second tour was selfish. And it's not as if things changed for the Iraqi people."

"Don't you dare say Iraq was a mistake. You made a difference. Ty made a difference."

He rose and hugged her. "You're right. I'm sorry."

She grabbed a tissue and blew her nose. "The girl is my kin too."

Although the Wilsons weren't blood, they always treated him like family. Naturally, they'd extend the same to his sister.

"I'm an asshole," he mumbled.

"Forget it, Eliot." She patted his hand. "You're doing all you can. You left the Marine Corps for your sister."

He remembered the day he visited his Commanding Officer and asked for a discharge. He loved being a Marine. He was good at it. Hell, his skills went beyond good. He was Special Ops. Exposing his dysfunctional upbringing had been tough, but he refused to let shame hinder helping the child.

Paula poured him another cup and shoved a plate of cookies his way. "How's work? Any interesting cases?"

He ignored the treats. "I'm headed west for a few days."

"Hmm…west of New York. Well, that whittles it down to anywhere in the nation."

He gave a weak smile. Only a few close colleagues knew where he was going. "It sucks leaving, but I don't have a choice."

After downing his third coffee, he went to his Prospect Heights apartment. He moved into the Brooklyn two-bedroom place last year. An obvious tough sell with child protective services, he worked hard to become a suitable guardian. Yes, he had a job, but his work had drawbacks, including irregular hours. And without a spouse, let alone a girlfriend, he'd be on his own. He couldn't even say he sucked at relationships, for he never had one. He was the king of one-nighters, a choice he made long ago—a decision that wouldn't go over well with the authorities.

"Being a guardian means serious life changes," Malcolm had warned him. Paula, however, had been blunt and crass. "Quit the booze and keep the banana out of the fruit salad," she had said. Due to her ill-phrasing, he avoided the black-spotted bananas on his kitchen counter.

Eliot had changed. He was less of an asshole than he was a few months ago. He even achieved two months of sobriety. Unfortunately, self-restraint ended when Carly vanished. Disappointed about falling off the wagon, Eliot refused to be consumed by failure. He had made bigger mistakes than too many whiskey shots. Besides, once the kid was safe, he wouldn't need to get drunk. Sure, other problems would arise. Balancing work and raising a child would be challenging but not impossible. His vices were nothing more than a crutch. Solving life's problems with babes and booze never worried him. What woke him up at night—provided he slept—was knowing his sister was in danger.

Time was running out. Carly had already relocated. To find the kid, he'd need help—a favor that carried enormous risks.

****

Eliot set his empty mug on the table and scowled. He had spent five dollars on mediocre coffee with no free refills. His colleague suggested the trendy café, calling the restaurant a quiet meeting spot. Expensive, crappy coffee guaranteed people stayed away. He checked his phone. Omeir Talebi was fifteen minutes late.

He had known Omeir for eight months. They met on assignment. Five minutes after their introduction, Omeir despised him. Trying to charm the formfitting pants off their female colleague Safia El-Moudawi had been Eliot's first mistake. In his defense, he wasn't aware of Omeir's infatuation with her. All he saw was a hot woman—aka., a potential conquest. Another colleague, the legendary Zak Ahmadi, intervened and prevented an outright battle. Challenging Eliot would have been a disastrous move on Omeir's part. Eliot had fifty pounds of pure muscle on Omeir and could throw a wicked punch. But when a lovestruck guy is obsessed with a woman, adrenaline takes over. Maybe Omeir would have claimed victory. Yeah, if he let him.

By the end of the first mission, Eliot became friends with Omeir. He was still baffled by how Omeir stayed true to Safia, a woman who continually chucked him into the friend zone. His buddy was more sucker than saint.

He likened Omeir to those storm chasers—fools addicted to a force capable of destroying them. But Eliot kept his opinions quiet. Who was he to judge? He also placed himself in harm's way, though his actions were more calculated than careless. And as far as his interactions with the ladies, women were more apt to shoot him than shatter his heart.

Omeir busted through the diner's door. Eliot's shoulders sank. Safia had tagged along. Obtaining Omeir's cooperation had now decreased tenfold.

The woman settled into a chair. "I hope you don't

mind me being here."

"Nah, it's fine," he lied through gritted teeth.

He considered shooing her away, but Safia wasn't the dismissible type. She'd kick up a fuss. Paula's scoldings were child's play compared to this woman's wrath.

"Omeir said you needed to meet right away." Her voice turned gentle. Her soulful eyes and encouraging smile were powerful weapons.

"Scorp, are you in trouble?" Omeir asked.

"I have a problem, and I need your expertise."

"Sure."

He agreed without knowing the details. Omeir was a better friend than he deserved.

"I need you to find someone."

"Give me a name."

"I don't have one, but I know who *she's* with."

"Is this related to what we're working on?" Safia asked.

"No, but it's important."

Safia slammed her coffee mug on the table. "This isn't what we do."

She was as difficult as she was attractive. "What isn't?"

"Tracking people for no good reason. Omeir won't be coerced into finding you a woman. If you want a date, then pay for a service."

"I'm not looking for a date."

She leaned forward. "I know. I'm being kind. But since you clarified, I'll be blunt. Locating a woman you want to—"

"Safia," Omeir barked, "let Scorp finish."

Though pissed, Eliot couldn't blame Safia for

assuming the worst. His reckless lifestyle was common knowledge. More ladies frequented his bedroom than a free yoga class.

"I'm trying to find my sister." He shifted in his seat, focusing on the green-stained tablecloth—*first overpriced coffee and now dirty linens. The shitty restaurant is likely a front for money laundering.*

"You don't know your sister's name?" Omeir asked.

"No, I've never met the kid. Her birth…my biological mother…the situation is complicated."

Safia tilted her head. "How so?"

"My bio mom is a…" The words crack whore lingered on his tongue. "She's a sex worker."

"Seriously?" Omeir said as if waiting for a punchline.

"Yeah," Eliot mumbled. With no other choice, he spilled the particulars.

Safia and Omeir remained silent, their empathetic faces bordering on pity.

"You can imagine what it's like for a kid, especially a girl, stuck in such an environment."

Safia rubbed Eliot's clenched fist. His gaze shifted to Omeir, concerned he would misinterpret the compassionate gesture.

"We'll find her," Omeir reassured.

"Our jobs are on the line if you get caught hacking," Eliot warned.

A cocky smirk flickered across his friend's face. "Don't worry. I've got this."

****

"No need to fret, Dad. Gabby and Kiefer came over and helped." Quinn pierced another scallop and twirled the pasta around her fork.

Her father, Tom Merrick, suggested the Italian restaurant. He often entertained clients at the upscale Midtown Manhattan eatery. Although pretentious, the place had phenomenal pasta dishes. The vegan fettuccine Alfredo was heavy for lunch but more satisfying than a mixed green salad.

"Who's Kiefer?" her father asked.

"Gabby's latest boyfriend. Her one true soulmate," she replied, using air quotes.

"You don't like him?"

She shrugged.

Tom set his water glass on the table. "Should I be worried?"

"No, he's not a sleazebag," she responded, reading her father's mind. "Gabby met him at an audition. He fronts an indie band called Intense Apathy. I'm guessing he's the moron in the oxymoron." She chuckled. Her mother, an English teacher, would have laughed. "Kiefer was a last-minute replacement for a pianist suffering from food poisoning. Undercooked chicken wings resulted in Gabby finding true love for the fifth time this year."

Her father frowned. He worried about Gabby almost as much as he worried about her. Luckily, Dear Dad wasn't around when she ran into her new neighbor yesterday. Though the encounter put her on edge, she didn't need her father stressing and paying for an expensive apartment. Providing the Ballsy Brute stayed on his side of the hallway, there'd be no problem.

Her father rested his elbows on the table. "I hate that you didn't ask for help. I could have hired movers."

"That's why I didn't mention the moving date. I didn't want strangers coming into my home."

"I could have adjusted my schedule, flown out, and hauled the furniture myself."

"Yes, but there was no need. Gabby and Kiefer were there." *And Mr. Muscles.* The man lifted three heavy boxes in one trip.

"Okay, but if you need anything, you call."

She appreciated his concern, but not informing him until after she moved was for the best. His heart attack two years ago forced him into several lifestyle changes. Now, he bragged that he was as fit as a professional athlete, an exaggeration she left unchallenged.

"I'm not an old man. I go to the gym," Tom said when she didn't respond.

"I know." Treating her father with kid-gloves annoyed him, but she couldn't bear losing another parent. Except for a few distant cousins, her dad was all the family she had left. "When you visit next, I'll have you over for dinner."

He sliced into his grilled chicken. "I'd like that."

She lifted a large parcel from the floor. "Before I forget, I made this for your office."

He opened the box and lifted the object out. "Wow, honey."

She had attached a vintage camera to bent birch wood, creating a unique desk lamp.

He kissed her cheek. "It's gorgeous, like my brilliant daughter."

"It's from my new collection, Resilience by Quinn Merrick."

"I'm sure it will be a best seller. Soon you'll be running your own business. You could set up shop in Chicago."

She let his comment slide. Although she hated

instilling false hope, she couldn't bear to crush him. Brief visits to Chicago were all she could handle.

Her father set his fork down. "I'm pleased your career has taken off, but don't waste all your time working."

She delivered a placating smile. Her father had worked twelve-hour days since her mother's passing. "No worries. My hours haven't changed, but I'll get to work more from home. Louise appreciates how important Lights Out is to me. She hired more employees to handle the workload."

She suspected her father wasn't referencing Lights Out, the inner-city boxing gym where she volunteered. She worked in the center's office but set aside the paperwork and sparred with the younger teens once a month. The kids learned a variety of skills, including assertiveness techniques. The owner did his best to protect teens from the cruel world. And Quinn Merrick understood humanity's dark side better than most young women.

"Glad you're enjoying the gym," her father said, "but maybe it's time to date again. They're not all like Chad."

"Whatever happens, happens." A safe non-committal response was preferable to presuming most men were like Chad…or, God forbid, Michael.

Chapter Four

"Hell, yeah," Eliot screamed, slamming his fist against the kitchen table when he got off the phone. Omeir Talebi had delivered on his promise. Within forty-eight hours, Omeir had circumvented a weak security system and accessed the database of a charitable organization that offered inner-city children free preschool. Using limited—and illegally obtained—information, Omeir found a possible address for Eliot's sister.

Eliot scanned Omeir's email. He winced at his sister's legal name—another sign of Carly's horrendous parenting skills. Edna Lorraine sounded like an eighty-year-old woman, not a five-year-old girl. And the last name was even worse. Hiscock. Rage shivered through Eliot's veins. Carly used her warped humor to ridicule the child.

"Good," Eliot said, reading about the preschool teacher who shortened Edna Lorraine to Raine. He'd switch the girl's surname to Traversini as soon as possible.

Now to rescue the kid. But how? He couldn't storm into the preschool and grab her. That would be outlandish. Though he had done a lot of crazy shit in his life, obeying the law was essential this time.

The situation called for a police raid. Smart-talking Carly wouldn't be able to con child protective services if caught using. In addition to drug felonies, the authorities would nab Carly for child endangerment.

He clenched his teeth. Although Carly deserved multiple charges, he couldn't bear Raine's presence during the raid. A tactical squad pounding down the door would scare a young child. Arresting Carly while Raine was at school was the only acceptable strategy. But, for this to happen, he'd have to tell one more person about Mommy Dearest.

"Ugh," Eliot grunted. He'd have to wait until tomorrow.

He paced his apartment, itching to celebrate. Obtaining his sister's name was a big win. He stopped and stared at his hands. *Dammit. No.* He had committed to sobriety. Since last week's bender, he succeeded and stayed off the booze. Instead, he burned his toxic energy by bedding a hot aspiring model. Once he gained custody of Raine, the revolving door of women would stop.

****

Quinn awoke to Hudson whimpering. Squinting against the daylight streaming through the curtains, she checked the time. It was midmorning. She had slept in.

Her dog let out a bark.

"All right, Hudson."

Loosening her feet from the tangled blankets, she rolled out of bed. Though the closet contained clean clothes, she threw on yesterday's yoga pants and hoodie for expediency's sake. She paused at the bedroom mirror and ran a hand down her head, taming her wild mane. "Argh," she grumbled and strode to the front door. She leashed Hudson and hurried into the hallway.

What in the world?

She rubbed her eyes. Her neighbor stood at the end

of the corridor, accompanied by a humongous toy giraffe. He stomped forward. The giraffe's foam-filled head grazed the ceiling. The plush animal and the man occupied the hallway's entire width. She retreated past her doorway, allowing him access to his apartment. Hudson let out a sharp bark.

Her neighbor cocked his head around the giraffe's neck. "Hey, Sprinkles, I didn't know you had a dog."

"Didn't know you had a giraffe."

He let out a deep, hearty chuckle. "Mind if I ask a question?"

"Depends on the question." Her tone was bitchier than intended but justified. Carting around a large toy didn't make him any less dangerous.

"Do little girls like giraffes?"

"How old?" she asked, normalizing the odd conversation.

"She's five."

"Hmm…I'd guess it shouldn't scare her."

He stepped forward.

How dare he encroach upon her side of the hallway.

"Does the pooch have a name, or should I nickname him too?"

"Hudson," she muttered into her hand, blocking her stinky morning breath.

"Sorry, *Huds*. I didn't mean to get in your way. I bet you're eager to go outside." He set the giraffe down and glanced at her dog. "I know, buddy, it's large and intimidating, but it's harmless…like me."

She waited for a growl, hoping Hudson would do her dirty work. Hudson stayed silent. The man inched closer. Her throat muscles tightened. The guy lowered his hand and stroked Hudson's ear. Her disloyal baby nuzzled the man's leg. Quinn glared at Hudson. There'd be no extra treats today.

The guy smirked and returned to his giraffe. Digging into his jeans pocket, he grabbed some keys. He unlocked his apartment and stuffed the toy through the doorway. "Later, Sprinkles," he said and disappeared into his home.

She walked Hudson along the busy street and mulled over her encounter with Scorp. Maybe her neighbor wasn't so scary. He bought a toy for a kid. *His kid.*

But what dad didn't know whether his daughter would like a giant giraffe? *A deadbeat father, that's who.* The toy was a paltry bribe to win over a child.

Hmm. Perhaps the kid isn't his.

Maybe his single-mom girlfriend was moving in, and he bought the toy to gain her child's acceptance. Regardless, the guy couldn't be too bad. Her traitor dog, who disliked strangers, didn't snarl. But relying on Hudson's impression was foolhardy. He ate pizza from the garbage.

What in the world am I doing? Scorp was not a guy to befriend.

She had temporarily forgotten about the concealed gun from the other day. But he wasn't armed now—other than with a terrestrial animal and a dazzling smile. The only protrusion was his rippled abs and hardened biceps.

Hudson tugged the leash, snapping her back to reality.

Allowing her neighbor to occupy her thoughts was ridiculous. He wasn't handsome—well, not celebrity crush hot—though he had a rugged appeal. It was cute how his forehead wrinkled when he smiled. And what woman wouldn't be affected by all that testosterone oozing out of his massive, rock-solid body? It was impossible not to notice the man's unique attributes. The snake tattoo drew attention to his neck, and from there, her gaze fell to his long-sleeve thermal shirt, accentuating his near-perfect physique.

I didn't gawk, she told herself. *I observed like any wise person would do when a stranger speaks to them. It's not my fault he happens to be a physically appealing stranger.*

Her smile faded, and her scowl returned. *Don't be silly. The man's face is hideous.* He was sprouting an awful beard—a mangy sasquatch meets a used kitchen scrubby. *But darn it. That prominent Adam's apple and broad shoulders are hot.* Regardless of his extremely masculine attributes, he called her Sprinkles. Nicknaming a stranger was arrogant and rude. Her smile returned. At least it wasn't condescending like *darling* or *honey.* And the longer he talked, the less annoying he became. His eyes, a shade of hazel that bordered on blue, brightened, and the untamed facial bush became insignificant.

Hudson barked and pawed her leg.

"Sorry," she muttered and collected the dog waste. She was seldom distracted by men, and never had she been pre-occupied by an egotistical, obnoxious, and dangerous man.

Chapter Five

The elevator opened, and Eliot stepped out.

"Good morning," a young man greeted.

"Morning," he grunted back. The cheery disposition of new guys seldom lasted.

Eliot sank into a worn vinyl office chair and gulped his lukewarm coffee. Men and women hurried between workstations carrying manila folders. Each one figured their assignment was more important than the next. Not in his wildest dreams did Eliot imagine he'd land here.

Throughout his childhood, Carly told him he'd amount to nothing. She predicted he'd end up a wanted man. He wasn't nothing, but she was right about being wanted. The police hunted him down, but not the way Carly envisioned. Returning stateside from Iraq, Eliot was summoned to this precinct.

The recruitment team never delved into his education or his experience. Though his vetted military file revealed he despised orders, they were impressed by his skill set. Not graduating high school wasn't an issue. His interview lasted a minute, with the recruiters asking one question. *Will you follow command?*

"Yes," he had lied. Employment with the NYPD allowed access to information, particularly child protective services files.

Motivated, he graduated from the police academy. Two years later, he made detective, but his actual goal remained unfulfilled. He ran into repeated roadblocks, unable to uncover his sister's whereabouts. Bureaucracy sucked.

He kept trying. Weeks became months, and months grew into years. Then one day, he received a call from a court worker. The civil servant broke with departmental policy to save a child. Although appreciative of the tip, he feared what the information meant. Carly had wormed her way back into the picture. Playing the victim card, she convinced the authorities she was now clean. Carly, the sociopath, preyed on the biased belief that a child belongs with her mother. The fact that a court worker risked her job disclosing confidential information validated what Eliot already knew. Carly was incapable of changing.

Eliot set his coffee mug down and flipped through a few files. He hated the paperwork that came with the job. "Dammit," he grumbled and stood. There was no way around this. He marched to his boss's office. The door was open, signaling the occupant was alone. Eliot stuck his head into the room. "Sir, got a minute?"

The paunchy middle-aged man waved him into his office. Lieutenant Pratt scribbled in a notebook before dropping his pen. "Don't stand there making me crank my neck. Sit."

Eliot eased into the lone empty chair. The old wood creaked from his body's weight. Like most of the precinct's furnishings, it needed replacement. Completing a requisition form for a new chair was a waste of his lieutenant's time. People would park their asses for too long if they were comfortable.

"What's up, Scorp?" Pratt despised idle chitchat. He juggled too many priorities to roll out a welcoming mat.

"I need a warrant for a drug bust."

"What case is it related to?"

Eliot shifted in the rickety chair. "It's not."

"Then contact the responsible precinct." Pratt hated having his valuable time stolen by mundane tasks. He spearheaded undercover operations. Run-of-the-mill drug dealers held no interest.

Eliot stared at the screaming eagle on his wrist—an earlier tattoo whose color had faded. "The woman who lives in the drug house…I…I know her."

"What the hell is the matter with you?" Pratt barked. "Not enough decent women for you to screw."

He gritted his teeth. Being pissed served no purpose. "The woman holed up there is Carly Traversini."

Pratt's neck darted forward. "Traversini, as in—"

"She's my biological mother."

Lieutenant Pratt paused, seemingly absorbing what Eliot said. "Dammit, Scorp. If your mom's there, she'll be arrested too."

"Good. I want her locked up."

Keeping his tone even, Eliot disclosed the details. Although it was Carly's filth, shame loomed over him. His childhood had been shitty. He lived in dumps with junkies hanging around. He had no toys, no clean clothes, and no love.

"I'll get the raid done," Pratt assured.

"During the day when the kid is at school. She mustn't experience a drug bust atop the crap she's gone through."

"We'll do it right, son." his lieutenant promised. "Have you talked to child protective services?"

"Several times. They ramble about how little girls need their mother and how Carly's now clean. I've heard their bullshit."

"The system isn't perfect, but when this goes down, you'll want the authorities on your side."

"Right," he grumbled, still shocked the social worker believed Carly's lies.

"Now, let's discuss work. I want all pending reports completed and on my desk by morning."

So much for knocking off early to assemble the kiddie bed. He'd be stuck at the precinct until midnight.

"You hear me, Scorp? No excuses, no exceptions."

He nodded. He dared not speak and let resentment seep from his voice. The guy was doing him a favor by conducting the raid when Raine wasn't there. Cops hated kids being around when they stormed in, but waiting for the perfect opportunity wasn't realistic. The city had too much shit going on and insufficient resources.

As Eliot proceeded to leave, Pratt cleared his throat.

Great, what next?

"HR will send you forms. Fill them out. It takes a few weeks to process paid leave, but I'll expedite them. I'm guessing two months should give you ample time to get the kid settled." Pratt rolled back his chair and stood. "Get out of my office and go do your paperwork. Don't make me haul you back early."

Eliot stifled a grin. Underneath his lieutenant's hard-ass exterior was a good man.

****

Eliot stared at the stupid and expensive plush giraffe. What was he thinking? Sprinkles *guessed* a five-year-old would be okay with it, but Raine wasn't your average kid. Children raised by addicts never are. While other children learned to ride a bike, young Eliot learned not to walk barefoot. *You only get jabbed in the foot with a syringe once before you keep your shoes on.*

And even if the enormous stuff toy didn't freak his sister out, living with him would. His body was covered with terrifying ink. He made the woman across the hall uneasy. Surely, he'd horrify a little girl.

The giraffe he could exchange for a comforting plush lamb, but the kid was stuck with him. He was no teddy bear. Yesterday's haircut and shave weren't enough to soften his image. Long-sleeved shirts could cover his arm and chest tattoos, but not the viper wrapping around his neck. Wearing a turtleneck in New York's sweltering summer heat wasn't practical.

Eliot opened his laptop and started browsing for a preschool. He hadn't a clue where to find one. The landmarks he paid attention to were bars. He knew where to find good whiskey, cheap vodka, and a cold pint at three a.m. Luckily, he had Paula and Malcolm. They volunteered to babysit Raine when his hours got erratic. She'd like the Wilsons. They connected with kids. Their son Ty got into some trouble as a teen, but he became an honorable man thanks to his parents' solid moral foundation. And the Wilsons did their best to guide Eliot, but he was already too jaded.

The Marine Corps curtailed his rebellion. A bit of attitude remained, but Eliot stopped infuriating his superiors. He listened more. Sometimes, he took advice. With Raine, he'd learn as situations arose. But what if he screwed up big time? He didn't know shit about kids, let alone how to deal with a girl disappointed by her family.

He typed child care and found several within walking distance. He clicked on one of them. They offered a Montessori program. It sounded like an extinct dinosaur. He tried the next one. The place was called an academy and required three references. He wanted the kid to finger paint, not polish her résumé for NASA. He clicked again. The day home had a ratio of one staff member for every three children. Perfect. He scrolled to the bottom.

Are you insane? Three thousand dollars a month. He logged off the computer. A drink would take the edge off. Too bad he had poured every ounce of alcohol down the kitchen sink. Luckily, his other vice remained accessible. A fifteen-minute stroll and he'd be surrounded by sexy women, but it meant sitting in a bar. He couldn't remember the last time he drank soda when beer was available.

He smirked. Across the hallway was the answer to his dilemma. He still didn't know Sprinkles' real name, but she had warmed to him. Yesterday, she cracked a smile. And Hudson had succumbed to his charm. A simple neck scratching had the mutt whimpering in delight.

Hey. I *won over Huds. Sprinkles' dog trusts me, so maybe my kid sister will too.* "Not a chance," he grumbled. Kids weren't dogs. Besides, his neighbor's dog had likely been showered with love since puppyhood. Raine's life was devoid of affection. He had made a grave mistake letting her fall into the system. Plagued with a horrible mother, the kid also had a selfish dickhead for a brother.

He shelved the self-loathing. Regrets would lead to tapping the bottle when what he ought to tap was his neighbor. She'd make him feel good. Real good…at least for an hour. Hell, he'd settle for a few minutes of quick and dirty. Whatever the woman was willing to offer, he'd take. But bedding her might be difficult, for Sprinkles wasn't like his usual pickups. The uptight ginger wouldn't fall for flattery. Complimenting her hair or luscious lips would either piss her off or terrify her. A subtle approach was required, like asking her opinion on children's books and suggesting chatting over coffee—or tea—whatever Ms. Prissy would fancy. Maybe she preferred not to talk about kids. Maybe her likes ran toward current events or stupid-ass poetry. No worries. He just had to appear interested no matter how boring she was.

He crossed the hallway and rapped on her door. He needed this. Not specifically Sprinkles, but a warm, feminine body. Her petite, curvaceous figure more than fit the bill.

"Answer," he mumbled. Sprinkles was wasting his time. Didn't she know he had to smooth talk her, buy her a coffee, and then make his move?

He struck the door with more force and determination. Again, no answer, not even a bark from Hudson. Perhaps if he drank expensive whiskey at a trendy lounge, he could limit himself to one.

"Scorp, are you looking for me?"

He jerked his head. Sprinkles marched toward him, her red waves bobbing in sync with Hudson's tail. Baggy denim coveralls hid her curves but not her cuteness. Hell, if she lightened up, she'd be sexier than those coeds at the corner bar.

A sharp ring shot from his pocket. He stalled and then lifted the phone. "Yeah?" he grumbled.

The caller said three simple words.

A smile engulfed Eliot's face. "I'm on my way," he said. He hurried down the corridor, his boots pounding against the floor.

Chapter Six

Eliot's mouth became dry. The girl was tiny, smaller than he expected. He stuck his trembling hands in his pocket. Children's height-weight ratios weren't in his wheelhouse. An expert could tell him whether she was malnourished. He frowned. He hadn't yet found a doctor for the kid.

Pediatrician. I mustn't forget. Or is that a foot doctor? He doubted the kid's medical issues included toenail fungus or heel spurs.

He searched his sister's face for a family resemblance. A massive mop of hair hung over her lower lashes. The honey-colored corkscrew curls overwhelmed her small frame. Her strands starkly contrasted his dark hair, which was the same shade as Carly's when she didn't bleach it god-awful yellow. He inched forward. The thud of his boots made her peer up. Her eyes were the same color as his. Millions of unrelated people had hazel eyes, but it didn't matter. The one similarity was enough. And thank God her eyes weren't blue like her mother's. Carly's cold, cruel stare remained forever etched in his memory.

He smiled. The girl dropped her head and retreated behind her springy curls. Mesmerized by her fragility, Eliot blinked and swallowed the lump in his throat. Carly, who caused nothing but chaos, had created this precious little girl. Undoubtedly, his sister's existence was from an accidental pregnancy. But her origins were irrelevant, for the girl would never be unwanted again.

Eliot endured the pain of the world. Seeing the worst of humanity made him cynical, but he didn't lose hope. He cared about children in war-ravaged countries but didn't let their suffering consume him. Yet nothing could prepare him for the sound of his sister's broken cries. They pierced his heart like a knife.

The naïve social worker, Alisha Ruttan, motioned him to leave her office. He complied. Raine required a stable, calm, dependable adult. The kind of man he vowed to become.

He entered the hallway. "Can I talk to her?" he asked, pleading.

"Yes, but I'll fill you in first." Alisha closed the door and peered through the window, monitoring the child.

Eliot stepped back to avoid towering over the woman.

"The authorities arrested her mother for drug possession and prostitution."

No shit.

"When we spoke earlier, you indicated you'd care for her. Did you mean it?"

"Why else would I be here?" he snapped.

"Sorry for asking, but you wouldn't believe how often circumstances change."

He ran his hand through his hair, forgetting he had cut it short. "I get it. To you, I'm a big lug. You question if I'm capable of raising a child. Can I be gentle and patient with a kid who's gone through hell?"

"I assure you. I don't judge people based on their appearance. What matters is—"

"The child's happiness."

"Yes, and her safety."

"I swear I'll do right by that little girl. I lived with Carly for more years than I ought to have." His voice became brittle. "I'll give Raine a permanent home and stable life. She'll never be abandoned again."

"I believe you, Mr. Traversini."

The woman probably believed in the Easter Bunny. He corked the sarcasm and nodded as if her endorsement mattered. Lieutenant Pratt was right. He needed the social worker's cooperation.

"You're approved for guardianship, but this isn't permanent."

"Huh?" *What kind of lunatic is this social worker? Carly's a heroin-addicted prostitute.* Sure, street people turned their lives around, and he had issues too, but Carly was beyond redemption.

"Please, let me finish."

"Go on," he grumbled.

"Returning your sister to her mother is not an option."

"Good."

"The courts decide permanent guardianship. A scheduled hearing won't happen for a while. So, in the meantime, I'll follow the department's placement process. I'll conduct home visits and monitor how she adapts to her new environment. All decisions and recommendations concerning your sister are made in her best interests."

"Come by anytime." Hell, he'd give the social worker an apartment key if necessary.

"I've put together a package on what to expect. We're not sure what Raine has experienced. She's pretty close-lipped. She utters a few words when asked a direct question, but she won't volunteer information. It's normal in these types of cases."

He nodded, feigning patience. He understood clamming up. If he could have found Raine by himself, he never would have disclosed his shitty upbringing to his colleagues.

"There's a parenting course. Attendance is mandatory. I understand you work shift work. I hope it won't interfere."

"I'll be there."

Most sessions shouldn't be a problem, thanks to Lieutenant Pratt. Once Eliot returned to work, he'd ask his colleagues to cover his shifts. They owed him a few favors. And once he depleted their generosity, he'd beg for more. If all else failed, he'd charm Alisha and shirk the compulsory classes. It wouldn't be hard considering Carly conned the woman several times.

****

Quinn stared at her closed door. *What did Scorp want?*

She was unnerved yet intrigued by her neighbor's trip to her apartment. She ran into him several times but during daylight, not at night. And although their conversations were light and brief, they never ended with him running off as he had just done.

The guy had cleaned up his appearance. Though she welcomed the change, she was shocked by the drastic transformation. He had gotten a decent haircut. And with his beard shaved off, she discovered he had dimples. The large facial dents softened his rough edges. He no longer resembled a horror movie villain, but he still exhibited an element of danger. Any sensible woman would stay clear of such a man in a darkened alley…and banish him from their dirty thoughts. Sensible women also wore comfortable shoes, ate broccoli, and had no fun.

Tonight, her neighbor's hands were empty. Every other time, he was hauling kids' stuff. First, the giraffe, then clothing, and a few days ago, he carried a large box with the words *hot rod* emblazoned across it. He asked if girls preferred princesses over sports cars.

"Cars," she replied. She had no idea, but why have him fret?

All those kiddie items got her thinking. Maybe he wasn't buying the affection of his girlfriend's child. Perhaps he cared about the kid.

Funny. No woman ever accompanied him. Perhaps she had the situation all wrong. The guy might be a single dad expecting custody of his kid. A man who battled to raise the girl. A guy who liked children and who'd want more. Another man longing for a truckload of kids with his features.

Mini Scorplings. She shuddered, imagining tattoo-covered tykes.

Regardless of his connection to the child, his presence at her door was odd. His bare rugged, handsome face betrayed his usual air of confidence. He seemed on edge, not irritated but nervous. And his whole expression changed when he answered the phone. The caller made him bolt. He took off like he won the state lottery.

"A late-night booty call," she huffed. Of course, sex would be the ultimate prize for a man like him.

She checked her phone. The time was two a.m. Scorp still hadn't returned. She wasn't stalking him. She wasn't a weirdo lurking by the stairwell or peeking over the begonias. The hallway floors squeaked. The man wore work boots. Sneaking home without her hearing was impossible. Her theory must be correct. He came to bother her about a child-related question. When the phone rang, his attention diverted to the female caller. Eager to get lucky, he ran off.

Quinn headed to bed. The man wasn't worth a second thought.

Chapter Seven

Eliot followed Alisha back to her office. The kid looked up, her eyes big and feral as he leaned against a metal filing cabinet. The child's gaze darted to the social worker. Eliot recognized the silent plea. His presence often had an impact on others. Women stiffened when he entered an elevator, and children ran when he took a shortcut through a back alley. This, however, was worse.

Sweat trickled down his back. Removing his leather jacket was not an option. Alisha stated she wouldn't judge him, but Raine sure the hell would. The fanged viper slithering over his collar was enough shock for one day.

Focus on my head, kid. Stare at my nose. Having spent his youth fighting, he was proud he never broke the old schnoz.

He curled his lips into a smile. His face was more adept at scowling than conveying kindness. He cleared his throat. "I'm…your brother."

He almost muttered *Scorp*. Work colleagues, one-night stands, and Sprinkles—the cute ginger from his apartment building—knew him by his nickname. But a name with violent origins had no place in a child's world.

He tapped his finger against his chest like a zoo trainer teaching a chimp sign language. "I'm Eliot."

"Well-eee-it," she said.

Close enough.

Alisha lowered to her heels. "You'll be staying at your brother's place," she said to Raine.

The child's forehead creased. Alisha whispered to his sister. Neither the woman nor Raine looked happy.

Alisha stapled her business card to a folder and shoved it into Eliot's hand. "Call if you have any questions. There's a twenty-four-hour hotline for emergencies."

"Yeah," he replied with the confidence of a cat trapped in a vending machine.

"Go ahead," Alisha said to the girl.

Eliot offered his hand. Tiny fingers clenched his pinkie. Though his sister likely acted in fear and resignation, Eliot was grateful.

Arriving home, Eliot carried the tuckered-out kid into his apartment. He settled the child on the car bed, letting her sleep in her juice-stained leggings and T-shirt. He dropped to the floor, leaned against the wall, and watched the air trickle from Raine's fragile body. Every so often, her eyelids fluttered. She deserved pleasant dreams—a place with no villains. No doubt, Carly had robbed Raine's childhood. He remembered the sickening feeling when left alone and the sheer panic when men visited.

"No more," he whispered into the night. At last, his sister was safe.

****

Morning sunlight peeked through the window. Eliot awoke. Pain radiated through his stiff back. He hadn't slept on the floor since Iraq. Leaving Raine to sleep, he strolled into the kitchen. Tiptoeing around his apartment was odd. His schedule had always been erratic. Different shifts, different women, and now his whole life would be upended. Rough seas were on the horizon. A two-bedroom apartment in a decent New York neighborhood had squeezed his finances. And added to the monetary strain was the stress of raising a kid—*a female child.* Not to say a boy would be easy, but they had common ground. He knew nothing about girl stuff. As if facing pedicures and teddy bear-picnics weren't bad enough, he'd also have to contend with the horrors of puberty. He snickered at those poor schmucks hiding feminine hygiene products behind beer at the grocery checkouts. Sooner than he'd like, he'd drop his credit card for flavored lip gloss and tampons.

He shook his head, remembering Alisha's comment about taking one day at a time—vague advice which meant nothing in the real world.

He yanked the lid off the blender. "Dammit," he grumbled and slid the appliance into the corner. Raine was still asleep. His morning protein shake would have to wait. He grabbed an apple and chomped until the seeds were exposed. Tossing the core in the trash, he brewed a pot of coffee, scowling when the coffee maker sputtered too loud. After each cup of java, he checked on Raine. On the fourth bedroom visit, her eyes were open.

"Mornin'…" *Sis* lingered on his tongue, but the word felt foreign and too personal. He had known the girl for only a few hours. "You like pancakes?" he asked.

She stayed mum. At least she didn't cry.

"After we eat, we'll head to the park."

Raine nodded.

Did she agree to breakfast, the park, or both? Regardless, she had communicated, a first in what he hoped would be several breakthroughs. He crossed the room and opened the closet door, eager to show her the adorable outfits. Although some were big, he was confident she'd find one in her size. He visited three stores to ensure a rainbow of bright colors—greens, yellows, blues, and a pink shade resembling a flamingo massacre.

He stepped into the small walk-in. "You coming?" he shouted. He stuck his head around the doorway. His smile collapsed, his hands balled into fists, and a barrage of four-letter words shot from his mouth.

Raine was in the back corner of the bed, cowering like a frightened animal.

As a kid, Eliot would duck into a bedroom when johns arrived. But often, he was locked in a musty, dark closet. After Carly completed business, she'd let him out. But if strung out, she'd forget about him. Terrified of the dark, Eliot bawled the first time his mother left him overnight in a closet. As he grew older, Carly let him be. It was then he learned there were worse things than an empty, unlit room. Darkness never hurt him, but the men on the door's other side did.

"It's okay," he said, softening his voice. "I'm not locking you in a closet. Not now nor ever. I wanted you to check out your new wardrobe. How about I bring them out?"

Silence.

He edged closer. Tears flowed against her red cheeks. She refused to look at him. Instead, she focused on her tiny, shaky hands. He stared at his own hands: big, calloused, and useless. He peered at Raine. She stopped quivering and sat still, like a rabbit afraid of a wolf. He squeezed the bridge of his nose. No bloody way would he cry. He never wept when bombs exploded around him or when terrorists opened fire. No, he moved his ass and tackled the problem.

But what the hell could he do?

Paula would have suggested he hug Raine, but no way. Physical contact would make matters worse. Although blood-related, he remained a stranger, a scary man who had no business raising a child.

He left the room and returned within seconds, holding a screwdriver. He shoved the tool into the hinges and went to work. A few minutes later, he carried the heavy panel to the curb. Screw the landlord. He'd buy another door if he ever moved.

With curly hair and a cherub face, the girl appeared perfect. But underneath, she was as broken as he had once been. Seeing Raine's sheer terror when he opened the closet door dug a hole into his chest. His hatred for Carly became a runaway roller coaster, twisting and accelerating through his veins. Swearing before a tyke was wrong, yet he couldn't control himself. His sister's trauma ran deep. She needed far more than pancakes and a doorless closet.

Continue to dialogue, use a calm voice, and let her come to you. There are no miracles. Alisha's mantra, which she wrote on her business card, rang through Eliot's head. Boy, was he screwed.

Frustrated, Eliot wandered into the kitchen and started cooking bear-shaped pancakes.

"Breakfast is ready," he announced minutes later.

Raine drifted into the kitchen wearing green leggings and a purple-striped T-shirt. Eliot suppressed a grin and placed the flapjacks on her plate. She nibbled one little bear, the ears mangled because he flipped too soon. As far as he was concerned, eating and not crying was progress. He left the dishes in the sink and took his sister to the park.

"Go ahead," he said, hoping she'd join the kids on the playground.

She neither budged nor spoke.

He took a few steps toward the swings. "It's safe here." He could have been standing in the city's most crime-ridden section, and his words would have been true. No one would ever harm this child as long as he was around.

Nearby parents glanced from their phones and glared. Although sleeves covered most of his tattoos, the viper's blood-soaked fangs remained visible. Soon, the playground became vacant.

Assholes. The adults were more interested in their social media accounts than their kids, yet they dared judge him.

"Wanna try the swing?"

Raine shook her head.

"Yeah, me neither." His teasing comment fell flat. "Hey, let's walk around."

They meandered like two lost basset hounds. Finding an empty bench, Eliot parked himself and motioned Raine to sit. She climbed up without assistance and stared at the swimming ducklings. He had listened to Alisha, Paula, and several child-rearing videos. None worked. The jerks from the playground would mock his directness, but honesty was all he had left.

"I've screwed up numerous times. I say words a kid shouldn't hear, and I mutilate pancakes. Though more mistakes will come, I promise I'll get better at being your big brother. I'll always be your protector. No one will ever lay a hand on you again, and you'll never have to live with Carly. You'll stay with me until you get old and want your own place. And even then, I'll keep a room for you." He waited for a response. None arrived. "I'm aware I frighten people." He grazed his fingers along his neck. "The snake is ugly, but it can't hurt you, and neither will I. I'm a teddy bear, not a grizzly." *Enough with bear analogies. She'll be terrified of the zoo.* "You can tell me anything. I promise I won't get upset."

Again, no response.

"I'm good at fixing things, but you have to say what you want fixed." He was unsure if what he said made sense to an adult, let alone a kid. "If you hate pancakes, we'll have cereal or eggs. Just not cake." He paused. "If I scrape the icing off, I reckon it's a breakfast muffin." He'd deal with nutrition later. "I'll paint your room whatever color you want. Orange. A mural of rainbows. Or large green polka dots. Whatever makes you happy."

Her face remained deadpan.

He heaved a sigh. "I get you're scared. As a kid, I lived with Carly. I know."

Raine tilted her neck. "I like bear pancakes," she said.

Alisha, the social worker, was wrong yet again. A miracle had happened.

Chapter Eight

"Sprinkles, wait." Eliot hurried down the hallway, ensuring he didn't tug Raine's hand hard.

Quinn spun around. "Oh, hi, Dash."

"Huh?"

"Don't you deserve a nickname?"

"Dash as in dashing. I like it."

"I'm referencing how you race off whenever I run into you."

He choked back a chuckle, amused by her sharp response. "I have someone I want you to meet." He touched his sister's shoulder. "Sprinkles, this is Raine."

She lowered onto her heels. "Hello. You can call me Quinn."

He imagined his neighbor as a Juliette or an Olivia, something delicate, feminine and proper, but Quinn was also suitable. One-syllable names were bold. He favored hot women in short skirts, but there was nothing wrong with adorable and determined—especially in the bedroom.

"So, Quinn," he said, retreating from the sharp cliff of desire and confirming he heard her name, "I haven't seen you in a while."

She rose and straightened her posture. "I've been busy."

Busy, my ass. She stayed home, lurking behind her door and spying. For a small person, she was rather heavy-footed running to her door.

"Doing what?" Eliot asked.

"I'm an artist."

"Right, you work with those rubber sprinkles."

"Yes, along with wood, metal, and other mediums."

"Shouldn't you be at work?"

"This is my studio. I put in more hours than people who commute."

She was testy. He liked that about her. His best sex had been with strong-willed women. He benefited greatly from their explosive outrage.

"Hmm. Long workdays. You're due for a breather then."

"I took a vacation last year," she huffed.

He chuckled. "I'm suggesting a coffee break, not whisking you off to Paris. If only my jet weren't in the shop."

Her face flushed. "I thought you were mocking me for working hard."

"What you do with your time is your business," he replied, flattered she watched him through a peephole. "Raine and I are headed for ice cream. Take a break and join us." He flashed his best smile. He was itching for adult company. Raine was great, but she didn't carry a conversation. Not that he ever had long chats with women, but he was determined to lessen Quinn's fears. He was no threat. "So what do you say?"

"Er…I…"

"The shop's nearby. Ten minutes on foot. We'll be back within the hour." He considered adding that it was broad daylight, and the streets were crowded. After all, only weeks ago, she had treated him like a serial killer.

Frustrated that she didn't respond, he kneeled beside

his sister. "Raine, wouldn't it be great if our new friend came along?"

"Don't," Quinn sniped.

Her quick response signaled she had a backbone. He liked women who stood up for themselves. Hell, he liked a lot about the opposite sex, but this one was especially interesting.

He glanced up. "Nothing wrong with ice cream in the middle of the day." Toying with the feisty ginger was fun. "C'mon, live dangerously."

"Don't manipulate me."

Her reprimand was different than Paula's. She sounded like a hot librarian reaming him out for an overdue book.

Fricking celibacy. It made him stupid *and* delusional. "Raine and I have an agreement," he said, shifting into damage control and moving his mind away from the library's *friction* section. "We tell each other the truth, don't we?"

"Um-hum," his sister said.

"So should we buy this nice lady an ice cream cone?" He waited, knowing he would be stuck with Raine's decision. A lot of work had gone into urging Quinn. Getting his cone dipped had never been this taxing.

His sister nodded.

He swallowed a victorious grin. Gloating would annoy her. "It's settled. You're officially invited. It's cool outside, so grab a jacket."

"Thanks, guys, but—"

"Please," he mouthed.

"I'm lactose intolerant."

"What?"

"Dairy and I are mortal enemies. Anytime we meet, there are dire consequences."

"Fine," he grumbled, cringing at his desperation. "We'll go for coffee. There's a shop nearby that sells those fancy ones."

Quinn's gaze diverted to his sister. "You might want to rethink the double espresso."

He glanced at Raine. Her lower lip quivered. "No, no," he reassured his sister, "We'll get ice cream. I'm sure the place serves coffee; if not, we'll grab one on the way."

Quinn squatted. "Okay," she said to Raine, "let's get ice cream with your daddy."

"Weliot," Raine squealed.

Quinn peered at him. "What?"

"She said Eliot. Scorp's a nickname. And I'm not her dad. I'm her brother."

"Oh, I assumed you were her father because of the resemblance, but brother makes sense."

He grinned, pleased she noticed not only his sister's hazel eyes but his.

****

"You're in a good mood," Gabby commented, removing an old magazine from a shelf in Quinn's apartment.

"I'm always cheerful."

Gabby settled into the bright turquoise sofa and flipped through the vintage edition of *Cabin Decor*. "You're extra bubbly today."

Quinn plopped into her favorite chair, brushing her hands against the soft velour armrests. She was glad she didn't pick the yucky tweed on sale at the upholstery shop. "I'm relieved to have unpacked. Now I can concentrate on my work."

"It's nice you're so relaxed. I was worried about the guy who creeped you out."

"What guy?"

"Your neighbor. You mentioned him when we chatted on the phone."

"Oh," she said, remembering the conversation. "There's no reason to fret. Besides, he didn't creep me out. I was taken aback by…" She paused. His inked arms caught her off guard, but so did his playful smile and audacious masculinity. "I'm sure running over me in the hallway was an accident."

"Okay, but if the man gives you any problems, you call me."

"You'll be my second call."

Gabby threw the magazine on the coffee table. "Who would you phone before me?"

"The police."

"So, you are worried."

"No, I'm teasing."

Her friend's phone buzzed.

Gabby's frown transformed into a grin. "Kiefer's texting. I better respond."

While Gabby sent heart emojis to her boyfriend, Quinn fetched fresh lemonade from the fridge. Halfway through pouring, a knock sounded.

"I'll get it," Gabby yelled.

"No," Quinn hollered. "I've got it." She hurried and swung the entrance door open.

Raine stood in the hallway dressed in a bright floral dress, her eyes peeking from underneath a sunhat. Her elfin fingers encircled her brother's enormous pinkie finger.

"Hey, Sprinkles, you and Huds wanna join us at the park?"

She eyed Eliot. A faded long-sleeve T-Shirt covered his muscular torso and broad shoulders. The fabric looked soft and inviting. "Thanks," she said, stiffening her hands before dropping them to the side, "but I—"

"You've got company," he said, finishing her sentence.

She turned, bumping into Gabby.

Her friend brushed past her and shook her neighbor's hand. "Hi, I'm Gabby. I'm Sprinkles' BF."

"And I'm Eliot, the BN."

"Bad news?" Gabby responded.

He snorted a laugh. "Best neighbor."

"Yes, of course. Quinn mentioned you."

Quinn gritted her teeth.

"Is that so?" Eliot commented with a smug smile.

She had developed a love-hate relationship with those dimples.

A tiny voice shouted, "No come?"

Quinn welled with embarrassment. She had forgotten Eliot's sister.

"Hi, sweetie," Gabby said, addressing Raine. "I'm leaving, so Quinn's free to join you guys. Can you give her time to throw on lip gloss?"

"We'll come back in ten minutes," Eliot responded.

Quinn shut the door and whacked Gabby. "What's wrong with you?"

"Oww," Gabby wailed, rubbing her arm. "Why didn't you tell me?"

"Tell you what?"

"That the man's melt-your-panties hot."

"For gosh sake, Gabs, he's my neighbor."

"Crusty old Mr. Snippet lives beside me, and you get Mr. Muscles. Not fair."

"What happened to your rocker boy? Don't tell me Kiefer no longer completes you?"

Gabby waved her hand. "You're not dodging this. The man likes you."

"Don't be ridiculous."

"He gave you a pet name."

"I have no idea what you're talking about," she lied.

"Okay, *Sprinkles*, but answer me this?"

"What?" she snarled.

"Is there another set of dimples on his perfect tushy?"

Gabby loved baiting her. "Thanks to you, he knows I talk about him."

"Big deal."

"He'll get the wrong idea."

"Let him. I met him once and already have many wayward ideas."

"Gabby," she scolded.

"Hey, he seems nice."

"With ten thousand adjectives in the English language, you use nice?"

"I suppose with all the kick-ass ink along his neck, there's an edge to him, but he can't be too bad. His daughter is a darling."

"She's his sister."

"Aww, it's so sweet for a guy his age to hang with his kid sister."

"She's living with him," Quinn clarified.

"Why? Where's her mother?"

"How would I know?"

"You're aware he's raising the kid." Gabby pursed

her lips. "Hmm…interesting."

"What is?"

"He gave you a pet name, and you're spouting intimate details about him." Gabby paused and glared. "Did you go out with him?"

"No," she snapped.

Gabby circled her finger. "Quinnie girl, what aren't you telling me?"

"His sister invited me for ice cream, and he tagged along."

"You went to his place?"

"No, of course not. He's a stranger. We went to a parlor."

"Parlor? A time machine transported you to the eighteenth century?"

"The neighborhood ice cream shop is called…"

"Called what?"

"Paradise Parlor."

Gabby exploded into laughter. "Oh, my God. I usually don't get to Paradise Parlor until the third date."

"Ha, ha. Very funny." Quinn's patience was deteriorating like discount toilet paper.

"Admit it. I busted you."

"Okay," Quinn stammered. "But it wasn't a date. We discussed kids."

"Wow, aren't you moving fast?"

"You know what I mean."

"No, I don't."

"He asked for my opinion. What books kids like, and what toys he should buy. You know, basic parenting stuff. And no, I have no idea why he assumes I'm an expert other than I have a vagina."

"I'm sure he's quite pleased you do."

"Look, all I know is that he has an adorable sister."

"And?"

"I, too, noticed the resemblance and thought he was her father."

"The dimples?"

"Yeah, but hers are more subtle. Anyways, I ran into him in the hallway last week. When he found out I worked from home, he asked if I wanted to take a break and go for ice cream."

"And you let him waffle your cone?"

"I told him I'm lactose intolerant."

Gabby grabbed her arm. "You did what?"

"Well, I am."

Gabby shook her head. "When a hot guy asks you out, you go. You don't mention getting all gassy with dairy."

"Do you want to hear what happened?"

"All right, I'll shut up."

"I went because his sister wanted me to go."

"Aww, you're my hero, sacrificing your precious time to make a kid happy. And here I thought you were indulging in hard cream. Oops, I meant hard ice cream."

Quinn sputtered a laugh. "Are you done?"

"You will text me later and tell me how he kisses?"

"For the umpteenth time, it's not a date." She gave Gabby a quick hug and nudged her out the door. Hurrying, she swooped her wild hair into a ponytail and dabbed her lips with pink gloss. She faced the mirror before leaving the bathroom. "Heck, why not?" she said, applying mascara and brightening her cheeks with blush. This wasn't a date, but it was the best offer she had from a man in a long time. She smiled, thinking how wrong her friend was. Eliot wasn't so hot that your panties melted. He was so hot that your panties spontaneously combusted.

After an hour stroll through the park, they ended up at the same ice cream joint near their apartment. This time, because they had Hudson, they ate outside.

"Does it taste like broccoli?" Eliot asked Quinn as the ice cream melted against her tongue.

"Why would it?"

"Isn't vegan stuff flavored with vegetables?"

She laughed. "They substitute cow's milk with coconut milk."

"It tastes normal?"

"Yep. Can't tell the difference."

"Hear that, Raine. We, too, can be vegan…up until dinner."

"There are plant-based burgers. You'd be surprised how delicious they are."

"Nope. I love meat with my vegetables. Not gonna ruin good food by adding chemicals and running it through a blender. How's the strawberry?" he asked his sister.

She smiled in approval and chomped her cone.

He slid a dish toward Raine. "Thanks for getting a bowl," he said to Quinn.

It was near impossible for young kids to eat a cone without losing chunks of ice cream. How did he not learn this from last time? She paused judgment. So what if ice cream dribbled over Raine's clothes? That was what washing machines were for.

Quinn rested her back against her chair. She wasn't gawking, she was observing, and when it came to Eliot, there was a lot to observe. His hair was dark, thick, and inviting. And those eyes. He had the most curious and beautiful eyes. He had a gift for making her laugh and putting her at ease. He had a charm that drew her in and a smile that made her weak. This bad boy had a heart of gold and a physique a Greek god would envy. But beneath his playful demeanor and carefree attitude was a troubled man. He had felt a need to carry a gun in public. Why would anyone go after the guy? You'd have to have a death wish to tangle with him. And although he no longer walked around armed, he looked over his shoulder a lot. Eliot no longer scared Quinn, but she'd be a fool not to be cautious. But his hardened edges had been replaced with vulnerability. He practically pleaded with her to join him and his sister. Not exactly a tough guy move. He seemed more like a man who locked away his true feelings, who put on a brave face and hid his scars. A person so like her that it scared her. As long as she didn't wander into his bed, she'd stay safe. She was here as a friend to Raine. Nothing more.

And when it came to raising his sister, Eliot did a great job. He may not know much about kids, but he understood what mattered. He appeared to spend a fortune on toys and kid clothes, yet he didn't just toss cash at Raine. He took her to places. In fact, he never seemed to go anywhere without his sister.

Except for crunching her cone with her teeth, Raine remained quiet. A child so silent wasn't right. At the park, Raine was ambivalent about the playground. She acted as though she spent a lot of time around adults but not fun ones. And she appeared overwhelmed by all the flavors. She was nervous, as though choosing strawberry over chocolate would have dire consequences. And when other customers drifted near, she scooted toward her brother.

Quinn intended to ask about Raine's parents, but Eliot sidetracked her with kid jokes. They weren't funny, but his slow and painful delivery made her laugh.

Scorp's the type of man who owns a Komodo dragon and wrestles bears, while Eliot writes poetry and cultivates bonsai plants.

A different name wouldn't change anything, but hiding in her apartment and avoiding him would be foolish. Besides, ice cream with a five-year-old and her brother was no big deal. Today's outing was as innocent as a church picnic. But now, thanks to Gabby, she couldn't stop thinking about his dimples, seen and unseen.

****

Despite their frequent hallway encounters in the past few weeks, Eliot never hit on the curvy ginger. Not that he didn't want to, but he behaved himself for his sister's sake and Quinn's sake. Just because he stopped drinking didn't mean he had become a decent guy. Speaking to Quinn's face and not her boobs wasn't difficult. He could be a jerk without being a pervert. Though he couldn't lie, he had checked out her ass. But what guy wouldn't? She had a great body. But the only time his jeans tightened was when he was alone and daydreaming. Surprisingly, his favorite fantasy wasn't where she answered the door wearing see-thru lingerie, though it was a close second. His favorite was her naked in his kitchen, making him a turkey sandwich. Yeah, he was a sexist jerk in these daydreams, but if she ever actually showed up naked, he'd make her lunch.

Though his inner voice told him to go for it, he wouldn't dare. Pursuing a casual sexual encounter spelled disaster. He couldn't bed her and then return to hallway chats. Besides, Sprinkles was smart. She'd shoot him down.

He kept the conversation light whenever they talked, discussing Quinn's old neighborhood, sushi bars, and parks with playgrounds. The irrelevant topics mushroomed in interest whenever she smiled or laughed. Other than the time she called him out for manipulating, which he was *guilty* of, she didn't interfere with how he raised Raine. Quinn remained supportive. She offered practical suggestions, like returning the pricey giraffe and creating a college fund.

Enormous toys ought to have warning labels. Even with a nightlight shining in Raine's bedroom, the thing freaked her out. Eliot kept the giraffe in his room for a few days hoping Quinn would accompany them to the department store. She always had an excuse. If it weren't weird for a grown man to have a giant stuffed toy, he would have given up.

"Enough," he muttered. Towing both Raine and the giraffe across the hallway, he knocked on his neighbor's door.

Quinn's dog barked, and a moment later, her door opened. Eliot petted Hudson, his new canine friend.

"Hi there," Quinn said, greeting his kid sister.

"Get your coat," he grumbled at Quinn. "We're going to the store."

"I'm in the middle of something."

He peered past her shoulder, relieved she was alone. Sprinkles was good for his baby sister. He didn't need some guy ruining their arrangement. He leaned the giraffe against her doorway. "Every day without a refund is one less day of that compounded interest you spoke about. I don't want Raine scrubbing toilets for rich people when she's older because there's no money for college."

"Huh?" Raine asked.

He tousled her hair. "Don't worry. You're a Traversini. You can do anything you want when you grow up."

Raine angled her head. Once again, he confused her.

"Hey, Quinn, Huds' fur feels like a scarf of bunnies. Did you bathe him?"

Quinn's eyes bulged in horror. "Did you say—"

"It's soft," he interjected, realizing how frightening a scarf of bunnies would be. "Hey," he whispered in Quinn's ear, "If I don't return this, I'll be stuck with it forever."

"Well, go. You're a big boy. You don't need hand-holding to cross the street."

"No, but I need you to hold Raine's hand. It's impossible to carry a giant zoo animal and not lose her in a crowd." He wasn't exaggerating or manipulating. People lost their children all the time. Often, they were found safe, but two years ago, he had to tell a father his son was never coming home.

"Okay," she huffed, "but I have to walk Hudson and change."

He shoved the giraffe into her apartment. "We'll take care of Huds. Go get ready."

An hour later, he stood in the department store's toy section. When he explained how the night shadows from the gigantic toy frightened his sister, the sales lady pressured him to exchange it for an equally large unicorn.

"The horn looks like an ice pick," he argued.

"Sir, you purchased this a while back, and our

policy—"

"Here," Quinn said, marching up beside him. She removed a smaller version of the unicorn from a bag. "I bought this." She smiled at the difficult sales associate. "So, this isn't a refund but an exchange."

"But you already bought this," the woman said.

"Then I'd like to return it and get a refund. And afterward, we'll exchange the big giraffe for this little stuffy. Seems like unnecessary paperwork, but if that's policy."

The sales associate grabbed the receipt from the counter.

"Thanks," Eliot mouthed to Quinn.

She was as savvy as she was sexy. She'd be perfect if she could see beyond the blood-thirsty serpent circling his neck and not ask about his past.

He wore long sleeves almost as much for himself as for Raine. The women he bedded sometimes asked about the tatt's meaning. He responded with bullshit stories. But with Quinn, he preferred not to lie. Though she might view hiding the truth as wrong, it was warranted. The sleeves provided protection, like sunscreen for the soul. His skin wasn't adorned with cartoon caricatures or poetic words. Etched into his flesh were darkness and violence—reminders of his origins.

Quinn handed Raine the plush toy. His sister leaped into Quinn's arm, snuggling against her neck. Raine had never hugged anyone besides him. He considered asking Quinn for one of those warm, lingering embraces, but why ruin a friendship by being a selfish ass.

Chapter Nine

"We're having pizza later," Eliot said, exiting his apartment and catching Quinn hauling a bag to the garbage chute. "Why don't you come over and watch the ballgame?"

She joined them at an Italian bistro a few days ago, but now he was shifting the venue to his apartment. The closest she came to entering his place was hanging around his doorway. Staying near her apartment, she chatted while trying to peek past him. He blocked her view, letting her imagine his home as a dingy man cave.

He dropped his sister's hand and took the bag from Quinn. Not long ago, he spent leisure time lifting weights and chasing women. Now he hauled garbage and read bedtime stories of dancing fairies. Domesticity had trampled a victory dance over his sacred bachelorhood.

"So, pizza and ball tonight?" he repeated.

Quinn smiled at his sister. "You like baseball?"

Raine glanced at her feet. "I like the mascots," she said.

"Did you know not all teams have mascots?"

Here we go again. Quinn had changed the subject, stalling while figuring out how to say no. *Fine,* he grumbled to himself. He'd employ his own effective tactic. Yup, he'd beg. Pleading would be demeaning, but what other option was there? He longed for adult company. He also longed for sex, but that ship had sailed and sank.

"I made a deal with Raine," he said to Quinn. "I agreed to watch cartoons, providing she watches sports with me. Last week, due to a doubleheader, I binged through a series on smack-talking reptiles." He winked. "Don't tell anyone, but those dudes are hilarious."

A laugh escaped her lips. His charms were working.

"So, you in?"

"Baseball's not my thing."

His smile dropped. No way he would watch a sappy chick flick. Sprinkles would have to be butt-naked on his sofa for that to happen.

She opened the garbage chute. "I prefer contact sports like hockey and boxing."

He pushed the bag down the shaft. "Right."

"Can't beat the sweet science. I belong to a boxing club." She walked toward her apartment.

He hurried behind her. "You're messing with me."

She huffed and turned. "Not all women inside the ring wear bikinis and carry cards. There are many successful female boxers."

His dimples exploded. "You spar?" He pictured Quinn in a plunging tank top with tiny, tight shorts hugging her perfect ass.

"Absolutely." Confidence coated her voice. "If you don't believe me, I'll show you pictures."

"No," he stammered when she whipped out her phone. He'd love to flip through the photos, but not here in this hallway with his sister and not while wearing thin sweatpants.

"I'm pretty decent at it."

"I'll be mindful you're able to kick…" He paused and glanced at Raine. "My butt," he finished saying.

"Now, getting back to my question, will you join us for the game?"

"Pizza with lactose-free cheese?"

"You bet," he said, eager to please her.

****

He didn't need detective skills to figure out what was happening. Her mannerism spoke volumes. Before she stepped into his apartment, she scanned the place, checking for danger. But homicidal psychopaths didn't leave chloroform and chains on their coffee tables. They used puppies to lure children and offered roofied appletinis to unsuspecting women. He'd love to say, *don't fret*, but that was the sort of thing a creepy dude with a van would say.

Raine bounded into the room, resolving his predicament. His sister squealed and raced to hug their neighbor. The tension dropped tenfold from Quinn's shoulders.

If his instincts were right—and often they were—what happened wasn't personal. Quinn wasn't just scared to be alone with him. She was afraid to be alone with any guy. Somewhere in her life, she encountered a bad man. Jerks who harmed kids and women were society's bottom feeders. He erased his scowl. He couldn't alter his past. Likewise, he couldn't change hers.

"Here, this is for you." Quinn shoved a lemonade bottle into his hand.

He accepted, understanding the bottle's dual function—as a drink and a weapon. He wished he could say, *It's fine. I plan to keep my hands to myself. You won't need to bash my head and escape.* But that wasn't the icebreaker he aimed for.

"Can I take…" He glanced, noticing she wasn't wearing a coat. She came from across the hall, not blocks away. He stuffed his hands in his pockets and backed away, allowing her space to move about. The women who came to his apartment never needed a large pathway. As soon as he unlocked the door, they were on top of him. "Shit," he hollered. He ran off, disappearing into the kitchen.

"Is everything okay?" Quinn shouted.

"All good." His voice strained with emotion.

He returned a moment later and found Quinn seated at the dining room table, coloring alongside Raine. "I forgot to lock the butcher knife in the drawer," he confessed.

Raine rolled her eyes. "I'm not a baby."

"Yeah, I know." His sister had become comfortable voicing her opinion. "I'm not good with age-specific abilities," he told Quinn. "There's loads of information on the internet. It's hard sorting the BS from the truth."

Quinn rose and wandered through his living room. Eliot followed her.

"Raine's a bright kid," Quinn said as she stared at his sofa.

Did she expect rusted camping chairs and a table made from empty beer cases? "She is, but I should know better than leaving sharp objects around. Accidents happen. Raine likes you. You're a natural with kids."

Quinn gazed at the plush toys on the coffee table. They were arranged in a circle with plastic teacups in the middle. "I never envisioned your place like this."

"I might have gone overboard on the kid stuff."

"No, it's great." She grabbed a cushion and squeezed it. "Panda bear pillows are a hot décor item this year."

He shot her a playful sneer. "Want a glass of that lemonade you brought? I have three kinds of milk and apple juice as well. Sorry, but I don't have any booze."

"I don't drink."

"Me neither." *At least not since my last shit-faced episode.*

"The lemonade's fine."

When he returned with her drink, she was again seated with Raine. He peered over Quinn's shoulder. She had drawn an elaborate tree house beside his sister's lopsided butterfly.

You love coloring, don't you, munchkin?" Eliot asked.

Raine lifted her chin.

"Maybe you'll grow up to be an artist," he said, addressing his sister. "They tend to be antisocial, but once you get them to interact, they're fun."

"What's *aunty socal*?" Raine asked.

"It means *choosing* to be alone," Quinn replied.

"Oh," Raine said and resumed coloring.

Eliot grabbed a notepad and joined them. He drew a stick person with a yellow crayon, wrote Quinn's name below, and slid the paper to Raine. "Pretty good, huh?"

She glanced up.

"Right. I missed something." He took the drawing and drew two more figures, one small and the other more prominent. He pointed to a bold long line. "That's me. The smaller, prettier ones are you and Quinn."

A rosy hue spread over Quinn's cheeks. He loved making her blush.

The doorbell buzzed. Raine jumped. Unexpected noises still made his little sister uneasy, but she no longer cried. "It's the pizza guy," he announced and strode to the door.

"Wow. You ordered a lot," Quinn remarked as he hauled three large boxes to the table.

"I didn't know what you like, so I got two with weird vegan cheese and Raine's favorite."

"As long as there's no dairy in the cheese, I'll eat anything."

"You're good with olives and spinach?"

Quinn scrunched her nose. "Eww, I'm not a monster."

He flipped a box open, tossed a pizza slice onto a plate, and slid it to his sister. "Eat up, little Frankenstein."

Quinn's jaw dropped. "You like olives and spinach?" she said to Raine.

She nodded and stuffed the crust's edge into her mouth.

After dinner, Eliot coaxed Quinn and Raine into the living room for the ballgame. Raine carried her crayons and a sketch pad to the coffee table. Quinn sat next to his sister and began drawing.

"Who's that?" he asked during a commercial break, pointing at Quinn's caricature, which he bore a close resemblance to.

"He's the sidekick from the turtle cartoon."

Raine ruined the lie by giggling. Her infectious laugh led to Quinn snorting.

Eliot started to feel like an adolescent boy. His stupid heart skipped a beat whenever he was in the same room as Quinn. Her smile was so damn pretty that he couldn't take his eyes off her. And now that weird snort made him want to kiss her. There was no end to the agony of celibacy.

By the fifth inning, both girls were heavy-eyed.

"The game will pick up," he reassured, stifling his yawn.

At the top of the sixth inning, Quinn undid her ponytail. The innocent act drew attention to her dark waves cascading above her breasts. Breasts he ought to ignore.

By the seventh, Raine had fallen asleep. He glanced at his sister snuggled beside him, her blonde ringlets dangling on his lap.

He ought to wake her and send her to bed. But Raine would want a story like she did every night, and Quinn would head home. He enjoyed hanging out with a friend, especially one with a beautiful face and dangerous curves. Sprinkles was a minefield for a man intent on making good decisions.

Now the bottom of the eighth, Raine hadn't stirred for ten minutes. He inched toward Quinn. Her enticing aroma filled his lungs as he breathed. Waves of desire washed over him. He had encountered many women who soaked themselves in heavy perfume. This was delicate, like a shampoo or a body lotion. For a moment, he was speechless.

"Hey," he whispered. "I'm putting Raine to bed. I'll be right back."

"I'll go."

"C'mon, Sprinkles, stay for the rest of the game."

"It's late."

"It's not even eight. There's one inning left. Baseball is all about the ninth. Pitches whizzing across the plate. Bats swinging. Players sliding into base. You don't want to miss the action."

"Okay, but if this game doesn't pick up, you'll have another person falling asleep on you."

He smirked. Carrying Quinn to bed—his bed—would be a hell of a lot more fun than baseball.

Stop before you drool, fool.

With his little sister in the house, he better stick to a PG-rated script. Besides, casual sex wouldn't be Quinn's MO, and relationships weren't his.

Eliot carried Raine like spun sugar. Although resigned to a chaste evening, he still yearned for Quinn's company. Raine crawled into bed. He covered her with a soft blanket.

"Snuggles," his sister mumbled.

He glanced around the room and found Snuggles, her toy unicorn. He tucked the stuffed animal beside Raine and kissed her forehead. Though his sister was damn near perfect, being responsible for another person was hard. He lost count of how many times he screwed up. Often, he headed to bed exhausted.

He clicked on the nightlight and switched off the lamp. "I'll do better tomorrow," he whispered.

He returned to the living room and found Quinn yawning. He loved a good ballgame, but this wasn't one. He plunked down on the sofa, sitting in the same spot as earlier.

Quinn straightened in the armchair and tucked a leg underneath her bottom. "Raine seems to sleep well."

"Yeah, for the most part." He remembered how he awoke to his sister's screams every night for two solid weeks. Her horrific nightmares still occurred, but they didn't happen as often. "It's okay she didn't brush her teeth tonight?"

"Of course. Cavities don't happen suddenly."

He glanced at Raine's room.

Quinn leaned over and tapped his arm. "You're doing good." Though brief, her touch was like a blanket on a chilly night.

"I'm trying, but I still screw up."

"You're too hard on yourself. I'm sure Raine doesn't expect you to be perfect."

He smiled, appreciating Quinn's kind words. He strove for excellence, not because of pride or ego, but because his sister deserved a good life.

"Thanks for sticking around. Raine's awesome, but occasionally I get tired of kid stuff. I don't get much adult time, and frankly, I'm unsure what I'd do if I did."

"What did you do for fun before Raine came along?"

He flashed a mischievous grin. Seeing Quinn's frown, he decided not to go there.

"I shouldn't complain," Eliot said. "Watching the same cartoon over and over makes Raine happy. I need to be patient. She's been through a lot."

"Why are you raising your sister?"

His gaze shot to the postgame analysis. "Wanna watch something else?"

"Eliot," her voice softened, "what happened to Raine's mother?"

"She's sick," he mumbled. He wasn't lying. Carly was one sick woman.

"I'm sorry. Will she get better?"

He grabbed the TV remote and flicked through the channels. "How about this?" he asked, referring to a nature show with a lion chasing a wildebeest.

"Where's your dad?"

"It doesn't matter. He's not Raine's biological father." He kept his tone even. "My sister's dad, whoever he may be, has never been part of her life."

"Oh, I assumed you had the same father but not the same mother. You're—"

"Old?" He chuckled, easing the tightness in his chest. "There's a twenty-four-year difference between Raine and me."

"Your mom must have been—"

"Too young. She was sixteen when she had me and forty with Raine. I'm twenty-nine now, and Raine's five. Enough with the math lesson. So how did you end up in New York? You're from Chicago, right?"

"After I left college, I moved to the Big Apple with a friend."

"A male friend?"

"Gabby. You met her a few weeks ago."

"You plan to stick around?"

"I like it here."

"Yeah, my apartment is nice."

"I like New York," she clarified, stone-faced. "I returned to Chicago when Mom's cancer metastasized but left after she passed. Dad's still in Chicago. He travels a lot for work. He's in New York once a month, so we visit then."

He turned off the television. "I'm sorry, Sprinkles."

"It has been a rough year. Having a creative outlet helps. I'm fortunate to have a great job. What about you?"

"You saw my stick drawings. I'm not the artsy type."

"No, not that. The other day, you said you would return to work in September."

"Yeah, my boss gave me the summer off. I'm not sure how Raine will adjust. She's starting kindergarten this year. I'm concerned about how she'll do with the other kids. She's still anxious around new people."

"Where do you work?"

"Did I mention I found a kindergarten school a few blocks away? I'm taking Raine for a tour and orientation next week. I'm not sure how she'll adapt, but I checked their website and—"

"Eliot," she snapped, "I asked about your job."

"Why are you pissed?"

"Why are you so secretive?"

"I'm not," he lied.

Quinn eyed the door. "I noticed the bulge when we first met."

He sputtered a cough. "The day you ran me over in the hallway?"

"Yes," she barked.

"You bent over to gather the rubber sprinkles. What can I say? I loved the view."

"I'm done." She rose, cringing as she bumped the coffee table with her leg.

"Don't go." He regretted his asshole remark. "I'll answer your question."

She rubbed her knee. "I'm not comfortable staying."

"I'm sorry about the stupid comment, but please let me explain."

She marched to the hallway door, opened it, and waited. She was no fool.

He stayed where he was. "You're right. I was carrying a concealed weapon." He took a deep breath. "I'm with the police force."

Her mouth dropped. "You're a cop?"

He stepped around her and closed the door. "Detective," he clarified.

"But why didn't you say so?"

"I'm with the Counterterrorism Bureau. It's not something you go around telling people."

"Jeez, I'm sorry, Eliot."

"Don't be."

"I would never have imagined—"

"Yeah, I get it. I don't look the part."

"Are the tattoos part of your cover?"

"If you're asking if they scrub off, no. They're permanent." Wrinkles spread across his forehead. "I'm sorry about the smart mouth."

She waved her hand as though she wasn't bothered by what had happened. Quinn was far more gracious than he deserved.

"I'll make you the same deal I made with Raine," Eliot said. "She, too, was unsure about me." A nervous laugh escaped his mouth. "Okay, that's an understatement. She was terrified. I tried being patient, but little changed after several weeks. Her cowering when I got near her tore me apart."

"What did you do?"

"First, I took her little hands." Eliot settled his fingers over Quinn's chipped nail polish. Her soft, delicate hands trembled under his touch. He stared into her whiskey eyes. How had he never noticed the gold hue around her pupils? For a moment, he imagined confessing all his secrets. Would his burden be lessened, or would he feel like he jumped from a cliff-bound car only to be hit by oncoming traffic? He shoved the unsettling thought aside. "Dear, Sweet Girl," he said, lowering his husky voice. "I'll always tell you the truth, no matter what. I swear I'll never hurt you, and if anyone makes you cry, I'll destroy them."

Quinn gulped. "Those were your exact words?"

"Yeah, except I didn't say destroy. But you get the gist. This goes for you too." He inched closer. "You'll always be safe when I'm around."

The air thickened. Their lips were mere inches apart. Tasting paradise was a sliver of wind away. He dropped Quinn's hand like a burning log. "We're good? Still friends?" he asked.

****

She threw herself onto her bed. *What in the world happened next door?*

She was always careful of her surroundings. Except for walking Hudson, she didn't go out alone at night. She would never have gone to a man's apartment, and technically she didn't. This was his sister's home too. She ensured Raine was there before she entered the place. She had accepted Eliot's invitation for pizza by convincing herself he worked as a bodyguard, perhaps for some celebrity. A studio executive hired him to protect an obnoxious teen star. But when he evaded her questions, her stomach knotted. She was trapped in a stranger's home with a man who might be a mob enforcer or a drug lord. But then the truth came out. Her jaw dropped, darn near denting the floor. Not once did she ever picture Eliot as a cop. Thankfully, he wasn't perturbed by the silent accusation etched on her face. He apologized for his stupid joke about his bulging pants. And he went beyond atoning for the remark when he said he'd never hurt her and would always tell her the truth. She had heard such declarations before, but this time, the man delivering the words seemed sincere. When Eliot clasped her hand, she felt the frost on her heart dissolve, and a fiery sensation ignited her flesh.

Her attraction toward him began weeks ago, but she didn't do bad boys, so she shoved her emotions aside. But now, learning he was a police officer, she could no longer ignore the chemistry. She wondered how it would feel to caress his cheek, to press her mouth against his, and melt into his embrace.

She swore she caught him stealing glances during the ballgame. Perhaps there was a desire on his part too.

Sure. The desire to stop a silly-assed woman from fleeing like a roadrunner on amphetamines. And what was she thinking? Fleeing would be stupid. He knew where she lived.

But Eliot wasn't interested in chasing or locking her inside his apartment. He simply wanted to talk. And boy, did he. How he spoke—and what he said—tingled inside her belly. But before she could swoon, he dropped her hand like a greasy sledgehammer.

She had made the situation weird with her stupid little fantasy. Holding her gaze meant nothing. Eliot wasn't interested. Desperate for adult companionship, he would welcome a crazed cat lady into his home if she were willing to chat. The reason she received an invite was a matter of availability. Her social life sucked.

Why not be Eliot's sidekick?

Hanging with him was better than being the third wheel in Gabby's life. Eliot loved boxing and hockey, and she could learn to enjoy baseball. There were other pluses too. He didn't drink, he liked dogs—including her disloyal hound—and he made her laugh. *A perfect friend.* If only she could stop visualizing her hand following his snake tattoo down his body.

Chapter Ten

"Hey, what's this?" Eliot asked, holding the floral-wrapped package Quinn had shoved into his hand.

"A present."

"Why?" The only people who gave him anything were Paula and Malcolm—a gift card for his birthday.

"Do I need a reason?"

"I'm not the kind of guy who randomly receives presents."

"Yeah, and I bet you don't normally play with dolls, but you do when Raine asks you to."

"Bite your tongue, woman. Princess Gwendolyn of the Golden Shire is an action figure, not a doll."

She giggled. "Then this is a peace offering and not a gift."

"I didn't know we were at war."

Her gaze dropped.

"Quinn, what's this about?"

"I feel awful for jumping to conclusions last week. I treated you like…well, I wasn't very nice."

"And neither was I, so let's forget it."

"Okay, but you're still getting the present."

"You don't have to."

"I want to. Go ahead and open it."

He glanced at her. A big, gorgeous grin engulfed her face. He reminded himself to make her smile more often.

"If you don't like it, give it back."

Right, and hurt your feelings. He was stuck with whatever it was.

"Remember, you promised you would always be honest."

Shit. He was stuck with the truth.

He ripped apart the tape. The wrapping fell to the floor.

Her hands flew to her hips. "Well?"

She had the patience of a toddler.

He brushed his hand over the object, letting the tiny bumps graze his fingertips. "It's that fake broken glass."

Quinn had glued colorful rubber sprinkles into a pattern. It resembled his tattoo without the blood dripping from the viper's fangs—a friendlier version of the ink on his neck.

"You hate it. The colors are too bright. I should have made a desk lamp, but you don't have a desk here. Do you have one at work? I'll take this back and—"

"It's effing badass."

"Seriously?"

"Yes."

"But you're not smiling."

Shock prevented his face from cracking. "I didn't know you were this good and…"

"And you have no use for it."

"Hush. I'm keeping it." He laid the art piece on a nearby table. Considerable thought would go into where he would hang it. "I'm not good at this sort of thing."

"At what?"

He straightened his back. Having a female friend outside of work was strange. "You're a good person, Quinn."

She slugged his arm. "You're sweet."

Women had punched him before, but never in a teasing manner.

"Help," a tiny voice screamed.

Eliot bolted to the kitchen. He found his sister stuffing school supplies into a Supergirl knapsack. Relieved, he hugged her. "You scared me, Raine."

"It won't fit," she said.

"Here, let me see." He took the bag and moved into the eating area.

Quinn rushed over. "What's wrong?"

"The zipper won't close," Raine said.

Eliot dumped the knapsack's contents onto the table. "Let's see what we got." He hated seeing Raine upset, but at least he could fix this problem.

"Wow," Quinn said, standing beside Eliot. "This is a lot of stuff. I don't remember all these supplies when I was a kid."

"I grabbed a few extras," he confessed.

Quinn lifted the graphing calculator. "I doubt she'll need this on the first day…or the first ten years."

He took the calculator from her and hit a few buttons. "I have no idea what this does."

"If you kept the receipt, you could return it. By the time Raine learns trigonometry, this baby will be obsolete."

Quinn sat beside Raine and began sorting the supplies.

Raine grabbed the colored pencils and handed them to Quinn. "Weliot's taking me to school next week. You come too."

"Thanks, but I'm sure your brother—"

"I could use the help," Eliot mouthed and handed Quinn a glue stick.

"Please," Raine begged.

"Sure, I'll tag along." She leaned across the table. "She'll be all right, Eliot."

And with Quinn coming along, so would he.

****

Eliot managed a somewhat regular schedule returning to work. He finished the mandatory parenting courses and even learned a few things. For instance, a single father suggested putting your kid on rollerblades to ensure they hold your hand.

Thanks to Quinn, Raine's kindergarten orientation was a success, and now several weeks later, Raine was adapting well to school. Paula and Malcolm pitched in, babysitting when Eliot's workday ran late. They adored Raine. She was the grandchild they would never have.

Tonight, Eliot's apartment would be empty when he got off shift. Paula had insisted on keeping Raine for a few more hours. He had battled against the idea. His sister was his responsibility, but Malcolm had spoken gently but firmly. "It has been years since Paula has enjoyed a child's laughter. Don't ruin my wife's joy by hogging Raine to yourself."

Message received. Eliot relented and headed home.

Plodding through his apartment hallway, he didn't know what to do with a night off. He stopped and stared at Quinn's apartment door. She wouldn't be home tonight. Dinner with Gabby was on her agenda. He pictured her all dolled up, wearing a short, colorful dress with her red hair dangling between her firm breasts. Frankly, he didn't know how firm or jiggly her boobs were, but they looked perfect in that white T-Shirt she had worn the other day.

"Celibate fool," he grumbled. Cold showers weren't

working. Barring electric shock therapy, he didn't know how to brush his forbidden neighbor from his mind.

He unlocked his door and went inside. Sticky jam fingerprints adorned the interior wall. The once comfy bachelor pad was now a kid's playground. He kicked off his boots and headed to the kitchen for a cleaning rag.

"Clean home, healthy child," Paula had told him and tossed him a container of disinfectant wipes the last time he visited.

After removing the print marks, he went to the kitchen to tidy up. Halfway through unloading the dishwasher, he heard a knock. "Coming," he hollered.

He peered through the peephole and swung the door open. "Weren't you meeting Gabby for dinner tonight?"

"Yes," Quinn snapped.

"Is everything okay?" His gaze flickered to what she was wearing. It wasn't a dress, but instead a tight yellow T-shirt. He imagined how it would feel to touch her, to peel off her shirt and reveal what was underneath.

"No. I mean, yes," she stammered. "I'm annoyed."

He dropped his grin. "With whom?" Unless she had secret telepathic abilities, she wouldn't know about the mental striptease.

"With friends who don't keep their word."

"Did Gabby stand you up?"

"No. She invited Kiefer."

He jammed his large hands into his pockets. "Who's that?" he asked, aiming to sound nonchalant.

"Her boyfriend."

"You don't like the guy?"

"That's not the problem. Kiefer brought along Cody, and Gabby didn't warn me."

Dammit. Her friends were trying to hook her up with

some guy. He remained quiet, waiting for her to rattle on.

"Gabby should know he's not my type." Information rolled from her tongue like a paid informant.

"He's homely?"

She glared.

"Isn't that what women mean when they say he's not my type? Or is he scrawny? Toothpick arm Cody. Oh, I know. The guy's hairy like a chimp. Take it easy on the dude. Evolution isn't for everyone."

Her hands swung to her hips. "Women aren't shallow."

"Aha—" He chuckled. "—the man is homely."

"He's attractive," she huffed. "He was a model."

"Yeah, yeah. It's New York. Half the population claims to have strutted down a runway."

Her face scrunched, highlighting the cute freckles on her nose. She was sexy and adorable.

"Then why isn't pretty boy your type?" *Perhaps men with scary tattoos who teased her were more to her liking.*

She bit her lip. A quirky little habit that signaled she was uncomfortable with the conversation. He had gone too far.

"Hey, no sweat. If you don't like the guy, he must be a jerk."

"That's not it. Cody's boring and obsessed with making money. I don't give a monkey's butt about the financial markets, dividend growth rates, or the formula used to…" She peered into the room. "Where's Raine?"

"She's at Paula and Malcolm's. They're dropping her off at nine."

"Oh…" she said, clamping her bottom lip between her teeth.

“Did you forget what today is?” he asked, sensing her nervousness about being alone in his company.

“Friday?”

He grinned. “Yeah, it’s Friday.”

“Oh…I’ll get going.”

“Why?”

“I’m sure you don’t want me hanging around when your date arrives.”

He chuckled. Getting laid no longer happened on Fridays…or any other day. However, she could be the one to change that. He bit into his cheek. *Wrong time, wrong woman.*

“What’s so funny?”

“Nothing.” There wasn’t a thing wrong with Quinn. His past was the problem, not her. “I’m not waiting for my date to arrive. I’m waiting for the puck to drop. Hockey season starts tonight. Did you forget?”

“I guess I did.”

“Since neither of us is spending the evening with a hot model, grab a chair and enjoy the game. I won’t bore you with commodity prices. Instead, I’ll impress you with goalie stats.”

“Two point four one,” she said, gliding past him in that wicked T-shirt.

“Huh?”

She plopped down on the armchair and snatched the remote from the coffee table. “It was the goals-against average for my team’s number-one goalie last season. Yours had a 3.42, but I’m sure I’ll be higher this year. The defense on your team is weaker than a newborn.”

His grin widened. Quinn understood the game. He wouldn’t have to explain offside or icing. She might even school him.

Eliot stretched across the leather sofa while she flicked on the television. Cody's misfortune was his gain. Every so often, Eliot snuck a glance. The adorable hair-twirling thing Quinn did was far more interesting than the game.

They bantered about their teams. Hanging with Quinn was fun and effortless. Three hours later, the final buzzer sounded. She did a dorky victory dance in her chair and giggled. Hers was the most ridiculous display of gloating he had ever seen and the hottest.

"You want to come to the gym this week?" she said. "It'll be good for you."

Until she added the last part, he thought she was asking him out on a date.

He settled his hand against his heart. "Ouch."

"What kind of response is that?"

"You're indicating I'm flabby and need to work out."

"Jeez, like you don't know."

He smirked and inched his head forward. "Go on, tell me."

"Don't be absurd. You're in great shape. I'm asking because last week you mentioned you've been too busy to work out. Bring Raine along. I'll watch her while you work out, and then we'll switch. The owner of Lights Out is a great guy. Walter lets you train for free if you volunteer a few hours a week with the kids."

"So now I'm a chiseled, hot gladiator who needs handouts?"

"I didn't say hot. I said you're in decent shape."

"Uh, no. You didn't say decent; you said great. There's a difference."

A pink tinge rose to her cheeks.

Teasing her had become his favorite pastime.

"Look," she said, "I'm not questioning your ability to afford a gym, but why not check out the place? There's nothing wrong with saving a few dollars. You can add more money to Raine's education fund."

Being a high school dropout, he recognized a formal education led to fewer struggles. "I'll volunteer, but I'll get Paula and Malcolm to babysit Raine. I won't subject her to men dropping f-bombs and flipping each other off."

"Walter doesn't tolerate rudeness. And since the gym means everything to these kids, they obey his rules. However, you, bad boy, might struggle."

"Dash and now bad boy? Your name-calling sucks," he responded, longing to show her how bad he could be.

"Anyways, the bottom line is that you can relax about Raine."

"Sprinkles, I know the drill. I've attended enough boxing gyms to realize it's full of testosterone junkies. Even if the guys aren't cursing, they're disrespecting."

"What in heaven's name are you rambling about?"

"Men in gyms. Between lifting weights and grunting, they stare at women's bodies and make lewd comments. I bet they spend more time glaring at your ass…" He abruptly halted. "um…glaring at your assets than working out."

She laughed. "My assets are safe. I've never been harassed at Walt's. And I'm sure more testosterone bounces off the walls here than at the gym."

He playfully flung Raine's plush unicorn. "Some testosterone cave this is."

Quinn picked up the toy. "So, it's a yes to the gym?"

"Fine, I'll go. Gotta maintain this great bod you've

been drooling over."

She shook her head and tossed the unicorn to him.

****

Quinn poured herself a cup of herbal tea and kicked off her shoes. She was perplexed by what had occurred next door. Not that anything had actually happened, but she sensed some weird chemistry in the air. Though Eliot teased his way through questioning her about Cody, he took a jab about him being a model. A man as built as Eliot wouldn't be jealous of any guy, let alone a guy he had never met. *Right?*

But there were other signs, too. Eliot kidded her about admiring his body. Of course, she had fantasized about him. What woman wouldn't? But admitting such would make things awkward between them. And then there was his comment about men staring at her ass which made her wonder if he had been one of those guys. And if he was, did he like what he saw?

Get serious. The guy's not into you. He likely teased a lot of women—young, old, married, single, attractive, not so attractive. But what if he didn't? What if he was flirting? She couldn't exactly confront him. *Hey, do you like me? Oh, I see. You meant nothing. No worries, I'll hide in my apartment and stop myself from further humiliation.*

And if he did miraculously like her, what would she do? *Jump his bones?* Sure, sex with Eliot would be spectacular, but what would happen when he lost interest? Living beside him would be a nightmare.

Why in the world did I even go over there? Right. To lend a hand with Raine. Not that he needed any help, but she figured he could use a break. Though she had no first-hand experience, she imagined caring for a young child was tiresome. Besides, she had nothing to do, and playing with Raine would elevate her foul mood. Her night with Gabby had been a bust, thanks to Kiefer bringing Cody along. If she wanted a man, she could find one on her own—one who wasn't fixated on making money. Men were everywhere. New York had millions of guys. And even if she eliminated the obnoxious jerks, there were still lots to choose from. But how many of them were single and interesting? Well, other than the fine specimen across the hall?

She plopped down on the sofa. Her tea spilled over the edge and onto her baggy sweats. She frowned, not because of the stain but because the thick cotton pants did nothing for her figure. She had changed into them and an old T-shirt before she headed to Eliot's place. She didn't want to be running around after Raine wearing a dress and heels. If she hadn't been so frumpy, she might have received a clear signal from Eliot. Cody liked her dress. He said so. But Cody's glance left her cold while Eliot's gaze heated her.

Inviting Eliot to the gym would allow her to spend time with him, though that wasn't her intention. Lights Out could use more volunteers. The kids would benefit from his presence, and provided Eliot didn't curse up a storm, Walter would appreciate the help. And, of course, she'd enjoy watching him flex his muscles. Seeing the guy's naked torso would be far better than an appreciation certificate. What a well-deserved reward for all those hours volunteering at the gym.

She took a sip of tea. "Ouch," she screamed. The beverage burned her lip, reminding her that with hotness came danger.

Chapter Eleven

Quinn checked her phone's clock. She had given Eliot ample time. "Are you ready?" she hollered.

"You're sure it's okay to take Raine?" Eliot yelled from his sister's room through the thin apartment walls.

"Yes."

"What should she wear?"

"Jeans and a T-shirt. We're going to a gym." *If it's still open by the time you're ready.*

There was no need for Eliot's fretting. She wasn't as naïve as he thought. Her innocence had been obliterated long ago. She'd never knowingly expose his sister to inappropriate behavior, yet Eliot kept blathering, reminiscing about a boxing club he frequented years ago.

Raine bounced into the living room wearing gray leggings and a knee-length flared ivory shirt. A cute fedora hat with a red flower completed her stylish outfit.

Quinn crouched down and straightened Raine's hat. "You ready to learn what punching like a girl means?"

"Um-hum," Raine said.

"Is she dressed okay?" Eliot whispered to Quinn.

She winked her approval. "Your selection of kid clothes is amazing."

"I'm not the one who picks them out."

She glanced at Raine. "She chooses these outfits on her own?"

"She has good taste. After all, she picked you for a

friend. But when it comes to her clothes, we frequent this kids' store in Park Slope. There's this friendly sales lady who pulls the outfits together for Raine. Monique has a great eye for fashion. She's French."

A man built like Eliot attracted attention. No doubt, the friendly sales associate would bend over backward to help.

"We'll swing by the store after the gym," Eliot said.

Quinn glanced at her yoga pants and hoodie. She would have gone home and changed if they had not been running late.

****

"How do you know Quinn?" Walter asked, holding the heavy bag.

"We're neighbors," Eliot replied between punches.

"You two dating?"

Everyone at Lights Out gave him the once over, and Walter was no exception.

"Nah, we're just friends," he said, wishing it wasn't entirely true. He ached for her touch, her kiss, her skin against his. He dreamed of being her confidant, her supporter, her lover. But he was a damaged man in a broken world. All he could be was her buddy.

"Quinn does a lot for these kids."

Eliot kept jabbing.

Walter let go of the bag. "It's Eliot, right?"

Eliot dropped his hands. "Yeah."

"You should know…"

"Know what?"

Walter looked away. "Ah, forget it. It's not my business."

"Hey, man, just say it." Eliot hated people skirting around him because of his size.

"I don't want to see her heartbroken. Capisce?"

Eliot stared into the older man's weathered face. "Who?"

"Quinn, of course. I don't reckon you'd abandon your own sister."

"I'm not following," Eliot lied.

"I'm an old geezer, and I get…" Walter waved his hand over Eliot's body. "You're huge. But if you hurt Quinn, I'm coming after you."

Whoa. He expected the lecture but not the physical threat. Though irritated by Walter's implication, Eliot respected him for speaking his mind. He doubted ole Walt could knock him flat, but it didn't matter. He had no intention of hurting Quinn.

"You have my word; I'll treat Quinn with respect."

The older man motioned to the boxing ring. "Have you done this before?"

"Yeah, but not for years." He scanned the room. Quinn was right. The place was nothing like the old dive he had trained in. Walt's gym had new equipment and gleaming floors, and Eliot hadn't heard one curse word.

"Where'd you train?" Walter asked.

"At a hole-in-the-wall place near Vinegar Hill. The guy running the joint was an incredible strategist. His lessons extended beyond the ring. It sounds corny, but he turned boys into men."

"Not Timothy O'Shea, by chance?"

He hadn't heard the name in years. "Do you know him?"

"He's legendary. He's still training. One of his fighters made the Olympic team, and they say his new guy has a decent shot at the pros."

"No shit."

"Watch your language, son."

"Sorry, sir. I never knew O'Shea trained champs."

"If he taught you, you must be good."

"As I said, it was a long time ago. What I remember the most is what the guy taught me outside the ring. He gave us kids a place to be when no one else wanted us." Though Eliot didn't say such, O'Shea had likely kept him out of prison. "Do you ever see him?"

"He drops by every month. He pretends it's a social visit, but he's checking if I have any kids worth training. I don't mind. If he can help them, why not? I'm not here to take them to the next level. My job is to keep them out of trouble."

"When you run into him, tell him Traversini finally learned to listen."

"He'll remember you?"

"Yeah, I believe he will."

Eliot had been a jerk back then. He woke up angry and remained pissed until he fell asleep. Being abused and neglected will do that to a kid. O'Shea was a patient, tolerant man, but Eliot was a punk who pushed boundaries. One day, the man had enough. O'Shea was smaller than fifteen-year-old Eliot, but the trainer could easily outbox him. O'Shea, a former Golden Gloves champ, had technique. So, when young Eliot ranted about cleaning the toilets in O'Shea's *shithole gym*—a job Eliot incidentally begged for—the man confronted him.

"Look around. This gym is full of kids with crappy lives. Every one of these guys got a raw deal in life." O'Shea had said. "So go ahead and moan like a whiny bitch. Glue yourself to misery. Hop the wallow train to nowhere. Grow into a pathetic, selfish dick."

He snapped back. "Why you busting my balls and disrespecting me, man?"

"You want respect?" the forty-year-old had hollered. "Then show me you can rise above all the shit. Be of use. There's always someone who needs more help than you."

Eliot stormed off. Challenging the guy would get him fired, and although he hated backing down, he hated being broke more. The man's words stayed with Eliot, and although the anger didn't go away for several years, he learned O'Shea was right. Life didn't get better by sitting on his ass and complaining.

A day after his eighteenth birthday Eliot joined the Marines. Hell, if he made a difference, but he'd never forget Kasim. He saved the kid's life by preventing a bomb explosion in his village. Kasim treated him like a damn superhero. He didn't deserve the boy's adoration. Eliot simply did the job of a Marine. The kid's parents, who worked themselves to the bone, were the true heroes.

****

A chime rang when Quinn entered *Bisous pour Vous*. As Eliot strode through the children's clothing store, Quinn peeked at a price tag—two hundred dollars for a simple cotton sundress.

People were insane. No doubt, the trendy French boutique catered to wealthy parents. Only the uber-rich would pay this for clothes kids would outgrow within months.

A slender blonde lady waved at Eliot. "Monsieur Traversini *et* Raine," the attractive woman shouted, her voice sweet and melodic. Her diamond and matching wedding band sparkled across her ring finger as she drew toward them.

Quinn smiled. Monique wasn't crushing on Eliot. Being cordial to customers who spent an outrageous fortune on a T-shirt was her job.

"I'll text Monique," the woman said. "I'm sure she'll hurry back for her favorite customer."

Darn. Why couldn't this married woman be Monique?

"Don't bother her if she's busy," Eliot responded.

"Nonsense. You're Monique's favorite customer. Have a seat, and I'll bring you a latte. Raine, would you like sparkling apple juice?"

"Can I?"

Eliot nodded at his sister. "Remember to say please,"

"Pleeease," Raine said, dragging her vowels.

"And for you, Ms.…?"

"This is my friend, Quinn Merrick," Eliot interjected.

The lady extended her hand. "Nice to meet you, Ms. Merrick. I'm Trinity. Can I offer you a glass of wine or perhaps an espresso?"

Eliot dropped into a chair. "Try the latte, providing they have vegetable milk."

Trinity tilted her head.

"Non-dairy," Quinn clarified.

"Is coconut milk okay?"

"Yes. Thank you." Quinn had frequented pricey boutiques with her mother, but no sales associate ever offered them a beverage.

Eliot crossed his ankle over his knee. "Feel free to browse while we wait. "I'm not good at shopping. I'll stay here and do what I do best—drink coffee."

"Monsieur Traversini," a voice shouted. "What a delight to see you, *mon chéri.*"

Quinn tugged her T-shirt hem, regretting her choice of clothing.

Eliot rose to his feet. Quinn plastered a smile and spun around, prepared for her self-esteem to plummet. The woman was stunning and impeccably dressed. Thankfully she was also in her sixties.

The silver-haired woman kissed both of Eliot's cheeks and brushed her manicured hand over Raine's chin. Her gaze darted between Quinn and Eliot. "And you must be—"

"Their friend Quinn." With a warm, genuine smile, she shook the woman's hand.

Monique's grandmotherly kindness won Quinn over in no time. The older sales associate put together a rack of outfits for Raine to try on. All the garments were well made but pricey. Without hesitation, Eliot spent six hundred dollars on clothes one growth spurt away from a donation bin.

Chapter Twelve

Eliot invited Quinn to his apartment for takeout. As she dished up food, he thought about the gym visit. He had overheard a conversation between two guys and caught enough of the discussion to be bothered. He was also ticked with the asshole who stared at Quinn. The guy was a smarmy bastard. He used the gym mirrors to gawk at Quinn's body. Though Eliot wanted to gun the A-hole with a cold hard stare, he played stupid to the man's game. Quinn didn't need his protection, nor was she his to protect.

Quinn handed him a takeout container.

He grabbed a chicken leg and ripped the meat apart with his teeth.

Perhaps Walter would set the ignorant gawker straight. As Eliot found out, the old man wasn't afraid of confrontations. Eliot did his best to extinguish the accusations from the man Quinn adored. Although annoyed, he couldn't blame Walter's first impression. The man did what most people did, presumed Eliot would screw Quinn, figuratively and literally. The assessment would have been accurate before Eliot became Raine's guardian, but not so now. Sure, he had pictured Quinn in his bed, but he hadn't taken the lustful fantasy any further. Any man lucky enough to get her in the sack better be worthy of her.

By the time he left the gym, he and Walter were

good. He muddled through the old man's interrogation, convincing Walter of his platonic friendship with Quinn. At the time, Eliot half-ass meant it. But after repeatedly hitting the heavy bag and listening to his own guarded responses, he realized the truth.

He didn't just want a physical connection with Quinn. He wanted something more profound. That's why he couldn't stand it when the young jock checked her out. To Eliot, women were a game. Sure, there was competitiveness but never jealousy, that is, until today.

Drenched in vulnerability, he decided his green-eyed monster needed a playmate, so he deliberately boasted about the sales lady from the kids' store. Though Quinn smiled, she tensed more than a poodle on a safari.

He hadn't planned on continuing the childish charade, nor did he anticipate Monique waltzing through the door, bellowing, *moan cherry.* He wasn't sure what the French words meant, but he figured whatever she said was sweet. Not revealing Monique's age was a jerk move, but Quinn's reaction proved she cared.

His plate slid from his sight. He looked up. Quinn was clearing the table. "You're done, aren't you?" she asked.

His gaze flashed to the bones on his plate. He had devoured what looked like an entire chicken. His ears reddened, embarrassed by his caveman table manners. "Shopping makes me hungry."

"I see that. Why don't you tuck Raine into bed while I finish cleaning."

He glanced at Raine. She was doing helicopter spins with her head. "You don't mind?"

"It's just loading the dishwasher and wiping the table. Besides, it's only fair. You fed me a free meal."

"Okay, but don't leave. I want to ask you something."

Ten minutes later, he strode into the living room. Quinn was flicking through the television channels.

She tilted her head. "Is everything all right? You zoned out at dinner."

Her skin was flawless. She never wore much makeup, but after showering at the gym, she left her face bare. Her lashes were naturally thick, and the freckles across her nose were more pronounced. He bet she woke up beautiful.

Quinn waved her hands at his face. "Earth to Eliot."

"Sorry, Sprinkles, it has been a long day."

"I guess that's my cue to leave."

"Stay. At least for a bit longer." He sat, propping his feet on the coffee table. "Thanks for taking us to the gym. It wasn't what I expected."

"Told you."

"Yeah." He laughed. "A boxing club that allows little kids, let alone welcomes them, is rare."

"What were you and Walter discussing?"

"If I knew you were checking me out, I would have flexed a few more muscles."

She scrunched her face in disgust. "I saw you guys from the office window. You both looked serious."

"Lurking like a peeper, were you?"

Quinn's cheeks grew red. Eliot had pushed too far.

"He knows this guy who mentored me as a kid," he said, omitting being threatened by the senior citizen.

"Well, are you willing to lend a hand? You'd be a great role model for the kids."

A choke sputtered from his lips.

"I'm serious. The adolescent boys would benefit

from a strong male presence."

Unconvinced, he kept quiet.

"What do you say? Are you in?"

"Sure, Sprinkles."

"I'll call Walter tomorrow. He'll be excited."

Until he discovers I'm doing this to hang out with you, then he'll sucker punch me. "Seems like I caused a stir when I showed up with you." He'd ease into the conversation.

"Oh, don't take it personally. The guys size up all the newcomers. You know, seeing who they'd like as a sparring partner. And let's face it, not one is in the same weight class as you."

"That's not what I meant. They think you're engaged. Are you?"

"Er…no. I don't even have a boyfriend."

His brow arched. "Quinn, what's going on?"

"Okay. I might have mentioned a fiancé."

"You lied?"

"No. I was engaged."

He glanced at the television. A tampon commercial was playing. The silence grew awkward. He clenched his teeth as the cringy ad continued and waited for Quinn to explain.

"Here's the thing," she said. "I dated Chad for a few years. He proposed, but it didn't pan out. We split over a year ago. I saw no need to update my relationship status on the gym's bulletin board. I go there to work out and help the kids. I didn't want…" she paused, examining her cuticles.

He turned to the television, relieved to find a heavy-duty truck commercial. "Go on," he muttered.

"I didn't want any of the guys assuming I was

available. It probably wouldn't matter. I'm sure I'm not their type, but in case someone did ask me out, I had a fiancé. I presumed Walter knew. I stopped mentioning Chad except when someone spoke his name." She sighed. "I sound like a loser with a fake boyfriend. But unfortunately, Chad was real."

He took his feet off the table and leaned forward. "You made the right decision. Guys are dicks around pretty women."

She blushed.

He hadn't intended to embarrass her, but she should know she was a catch.

"El, can I ask you something?"

She had never called him El. It sounded intimate, like something she would whisper after sex.

"Uh…yeah." He hoped he'd have no regrets.

"Do you buy all of Raine's clothes at pricey boutiques?"

"Most are from the place we went to today. Why? Don't you like the clothes?"

"I love the adorable outfits you bought for Raine, but it's…umm…"

"Too girly?"

"Hush, there's no such thing. The store is expensive. She'll outgrow those clothes after wearing them a few times. The department stores have nice and reasonably priced children's stuff."

His dimples retreated.

"Forget I said it," Quinn said. "How you spend your money is your business."

He searched her face for judgment or pity. Seeing neither, he said, "I grew up with thrift shop clothes, and although what a kid wears shouldn't matter, it did. Rich kids are pricks. They pick on you for not having a cool brand. Raine shouldn't have to go through that, but I also don't want her feeling her worth is about designer labels and other superficial bullshit."

"Raine's lucky to have you."

He ignored the compliment. "I hate bugging you. You've done a lot for us, but I could use your help. Where do I go? I have no clue. What colors match with what?"

She bumped her elbow against his arm. "I always have time for a friend."

He took her hand and squeezed it. Flooded with emotion, he considered taking a leap of faith and kissing her. Instead, he rose to his feet. "I have an early morning. I should get some sleep."

"Call me when you want to go shopping."

She left, leaving him with a bulge in his pants and, for the first time, an ache in his heart.

Chapter Thirteen

A loud, angry voice hollered in the hallway. Curious about the commotion, Quinn marched to her apartment's door.

"Open up," a female voice yelled.

Quinn squinted through the peephole. A woman stood by Eliot's apartment. Quinn stilled. This wasn't her business.

The enraged lady pounded her fists against Eliot's door. "The sooner you talk to me, the sooner I'll leave your life."

No one was home. Quinn had seen Eliot leave for work this morning.

"I ain't leaving 'til we talk," the woman shouted.

Quinn cracked her door open.

The woman spun around. Her eyes were as wild as her hair. "You," she hollered, "you live here?"

Quinn staggered back. The stranger's pasty complexion didn't bother her, but her micro-mini jean skirt and the overworked push-up bra did. Clearly, this woman made her living horizontally, but why was she at Eliot's door?

Scurrying back into her apartment would be a wise thing to do. Unfortunately, she remained where she was, her curiosity surpassing good judgment. She plastered a pleasant smile across her face. "Can I help you?" She adjusted the locking mechanism, ensuring the door would lock if she needed to slam it.

"You know the worthless piece of shit who lives here?"

"No," she lied.

"Massive guy. Tatts all over his arms and neck."

"I work long hours and keep to myself."

The woman looked past Quinn's shoulder. "It's a narrow hallway, so I can't see how you haven't run into him."

"I'm new to the building."

"When you see the guy, tell him he better pay up. Traversini can't just grab what he wants and vanish."

Her stomach knotted.

"You deaf, girl?"

"No, I heard," she snapped back, her bravery exceeding common sense. "Who should I say dropped by?"

"He'll know."

Leaving the woman to scowl, Quinn disappeared into her apartment. She latched her door and sank to the floor. The stranger used Eliot's last name. There was no mistaken address nor innocent explanation.

She hadn't felt this nauseated since the fiasco with Chad. But Eliot wasn't her fiancé. He had no obligation to her. Eliot could do whatever he pleased. Except he shouldn't. Eliot had risked his job and his sister's welfare for quick, meaningless sex. Hiring a hooker and not having the decency to pay her was mighty low. She never imagined—at least not since she'd gotten to know him—that he would be a john.

****

The third period began. Eliot paced around the living room. His queasy stomach had nothing to do with the puck bouncing off the defensemen's skate into the net. Not running into Quinn today was disappointing and worrisome. He had no definite plans with the pretty ginger, but she often dropped by. And with his team playing this evening, he figured she'd be there to point out all their weaknesses.

With his luck, she'd be on a date with Cody or some suit with a doctorate in sweet-talking. By not making a move, he risked running into a smug SOB leaving Quinn's apartment in the early hours. But changing the basis of their relationship meant letting her into his world and disclosing his past. His memories were too painful to remember, let alone share. And if she found out about his biological parents, she wouldn't be his friend, let alone anything else.

He stared at the drawing on the fridge. The trees were pink, and the grass a bright orange. Raine had colored the picture alongside Quinn. His sister had grown close to his neighbor. Quinn was great with kids. She'd be the type of woman who'd want a commitment and a house full of babies. One frightened the hell of him, and the other he couldn't give.

He stormed into the hallway. *Dammit. Where the hell is she?*

Eliot raised his hand and hammered the door. Hudson barked.

He counted to three and pressed the buzzer. The poor mongrel yowled. It was odd for Quinn to be gone for so long. Surely, she'd never leave Hudson alone overnight.

Barring ramming the door, all Eliot could do was wait. Sleep was out of the question.

He couldn't go to bed without knowing she was

safe. *What if she was mugged on the subway or accosted in an alley?* The city was full of creeps and predators. He wandered to Raine's room, checking on her for the sixth time. Again, she was fast asleep. It was late. Everyone should be in bed by now. He sat on the sofa and clicked through the channels. The hockey game was tied and headed into overtime. He didn't care. A win no longer mattered.

Maybe Quinn had an accident. Perhaps she fainted, hit her head, and was unconscious in her apartment. Maybe he should break down her door and ensure she was okay. And if Quinn wasn't home and showed up later, he could say he heard Hudson in distress and went to rescue him.

"Dammit." He promised not to lie to Quinn. *Please, Sprinkles, come home.*

Just after midnight, he heard keys rattling near his door.

He leaped from the sofa and bolted into the hallway. "Hey," he yelled at Quinn, "You're out late. Everything okay?"

"Dandy," she snapped.

"Huds been barking all night." Eliot's persistent door-knocking caused the animal's yap, but that was between him and her dog.

Quinn pinned Eliot with a glare. "You're calling me out for being a bad dog parent after what you've done?"

"What are you talking about?" He's the one who was worried she was lying dead in an alley. Why the hell was she upset?

She stepped forward, nostrils flaring.

"Sprinkles." He lowered his voice. "What's going on?" The neighbors didn't need to know they were fighting.

"Stop calling me Sprinkles."

"I thought you liked the nickname."

"You thought wrong."

He was used to pissing off women, but he hadn't done anything this time. "I'm sorry I raised my voice. I was worried about you. It's not like you to be out so late."

She jabbed him with her fingernail. "Sweet self-sacrificing Eliot is such a façade. You're nothing but a sleaze with a great sister. You say all the right words, but it's all rubbish." She turned, shaking as she searched for the key.

He reached for her arm. His skin connected with hers. She spun around and slapped his hand. "Don't you dare touch me."

"What the hell, Quinn?"

"She came by."

"Who?"

"Your hooker friend. The one who wants payment."

His body stiffened. "What did she look like?"

"Jeez, how many hookers do you owe money to?"

"I don't owe her anything."

"I don't care what arrangements you made with her or the favors she's giving you. Don't you realize the risk you're putting Raine in?"

"I swear I've never been with a prostitute. Not now, not ever. I haven't even had sex in months."

"So a hooker shows up asking for Eliot Traversini because… Because what, Eliot?"

He glared at the ceiling. He hated feeling shameful.

"It's an easy question. I'm not asking you to explain the Earth's gravity," she snarled.

He stabbed his fingers through his hair and cursed.

"I'm done," Quinn shouted and turned away.

"She's Raine's mother. My mother," he hollered.

Quinn opened her mouth. A seldom-spoken four-letter word dropped from her mouth.

Chapter Fourteen

After taking Hudson around the block, Quinn hurried to Eliot's apartment. She found him muttering and pacing between the living room furniture.

She sat on the sofa and tapped the space beside her.

He plopped down. "Carly's coming for Raine."

She inched closer. "We need to tell the authorities." She kept her voice even. Her time to unravel would come later.

"Yeah, I will. But what if she doesn't stop? What if she takes her?"

"We'll hire a lawyer." She emphasized *we.* He wasn't alone. She would do whatever she could to keep Raine safe.

"She wants money. She wants to sell me Raine."

"What?"

"Yeah. It's what Carly must have meant by *pay-up.* What if she wants more than I have?"

"You're not giving her money. Your sister belongs with you. We'll call the social worker. Surely, she can do something."

"I'm a damn cop, and I can't protect Raine. Going back to Carly will destroy her."

She pressed her cheek against his chest. Eliot was splintering into pieces.

****

If it weren't for Quinn, he would have lost his mind

last night. The same redhead, livid with him hours earlier, shared his fear.

Quinn handed him a coffee. "I just got off the phone with Paula. She'll go with you to see the social worker."

Although his relationship with Alisha had improved, he still harbored resentment. After all, Carly wouldn't have been a problem if it weren't for the social worker's naivety. "Okay," he said. "I'll pick up Paula at the hotel."

"What hotel?"

"I booked Paula and Malcolm a room for a few days."

"Why?"

"They've lived in the same home for thirty years, and Carly knows the address. I don't want her threatening them." He would protect the people he cared about. "I'd prefer you go to a hotel too."

"I'm fine. Carly doesn't have a beef with me. As far as she's concerned, I don't know you. She won't bother me."

He appreciated how Quinn said *Carly* and not *your mother*. "I'm not taking any chances. I'm phoning my police buddies to come over."

"It's not necessary."

"Please, don't argue. I'd go insane if something happened to Raine or you."

His sister ran into the living room. She froze and glanced at Eliot. "Is Quinn taking me to school today?"

"No. You're not going." Promising Raine the truth, he didn't know how to explain ditching classes today. She had made significant progress. She'd regress if she knew Carly was coming for her.

"Why?"

"I'll tell you once you brush your teeth and get dressed."

After Raine slipped into the bathroom, Quinn took him aside. "Let's have a kids' party."

Had she lost her damn mind? His life was falling apart. Neither a cake nor a pinata would fix it.

"Better yet, we'll have a party for you."

"I have nothing to celebrate."

"You have a wonderful kid sister, and you've been this amazing big brother. That's ample reason to celebrate."

"Now's not the time," he grumbled and edged behind her.

She stepped into his pathway. "Now's a perfect time. Look, Eliot, you can't tell Raine the truth. Either you lie, which you promised never to do, or we have this party. Playing hooky from school isn't ideal, but it's kindergarten, and it's a temporary solution. She'll visit my place and work on the decorations. I'll keep her busy while you sort this out. Can Omeir or Safia cook?"

"Huh?"

"I'll figure something out. They can frost cupcakes or help in another way with the party. And you…" she paused. "I got it. It's a surprise birthday party for you."

"My birthday was three months ago."

"We'll celebrate you as a big brother. Sibling appreciation day, or whatever we call it. Anything that will explain why you're not around until later. And when you do show up, Carly will be behind bars."

He took a moment and mulled over what Quinn had proposed. "So, no lying? I don't mention I'm afraid Carly will abduct her. Raine skips school to plan for a party?"

"Having a child miss school for a mid-week party seems flighty, but it's all I got."

He rested his head on hers. "Thank you," he whispered, brushing his lips against her hair.

****

Raine bounded across the hallway. As soon as she stepped inside Quinn's apartment, she gasped. To some folks, an apartment is just a bunch of walls, but in Quinn's case, her home described her personality. The decor itself was a work of art.

Raine's eyes scanned the bright, bold living room curtains and pillows.

"Come on, take a look," Quinn said, urging her to explore.

Raine meandered through the apartment.

Quinn pointed at the kitchen light fixture. "I made that."

"It's *purrty*."

"Thanks."

Quinn had sold most of her elaborate pieces but kept a few earlier works that had minor flaws. Her favorite was the entryway console table—a thick maple plank screwed to an old bicycle. She was also proud of the vintage bathtub sofa seat. A rich tapestry seat cushion warmed the cold porcelain object.

"Go ahead," she said, addressing Raine, "If you can reach it, you can play with it."

Quinn remembered visiting a museum with her mom when she was Raine's age. The staff kept an eye on her, making sure she didn't cross the forbidden area. She didn't want to be disobedient, but the urge to leap the physical barrier and touch the wooden dolls was strong. Even as a young child, she despised order. Playing by rules went against her creative nature.

"I'm afraid I'll break it," Raine said.

"Don't worry. If an accident happens, I'll fix or change the object into something equally beautiful. Nothing stays broken forever."

She left Raine exploring and pulled art supplies from the hallway closet—materials they would use for party decorations.

"What do you want for breakfast?" Quinn hollered.

"Pancakes."

"Will you help me make them?"

Raine met Quinn in the kitchen. The child's company provided Quinn with a much-needed distraction. She knew little details of Eliot's and Raine's upbringing except that it had been hard. Though Eliot presented as unbreakable, she gathered he was once as vulnerable as Raine.

She startled, hearing a knock at the door and Hudson's subsequent thunderous, deep bark. Thankfully, Raine was oblivious to her shot nerves.

Quinn eased toward the peephole. "Yes?"

"It's Safia El-Moudawi and my partner Omeir Talebi."

She recognized their names. They were Eliot's friends. She unlatched the deadbolt. Raine's smile broadened when they stepped inside.

The man bent toward Raine. "I hear there's a party to get ready for." He straightened and extended his hand, "I'm Omeir. Quinn, I gather?"

"Yes, and thanks for coming over." She shook Safia's hand and exchanged pleasantries. "I guess you've met Raine."

"A few times," Safia responded.

"We had fun at the zoo, didn't we, kiddo?" Omeir said, addressing Raine.

"Yup," Raine said and lifted her hands.

Omeir picked her up and spun her in the air.

"Wheee," she said, giggling.

Safia glared at Omeir, "I don't believe in zoos."

"A lot of the animals are orphans," Omeir responded. "They wouldn't survive in the wild."

"So, how did you meet Raine?" Quinn asked Safia, sidestepping an animal rights landmine.

"Eliot and I lunched a few times. He brought her along."

"Yes, *we* had lunch with Eliot while he was on leave."

Quinn wasn't sure if Omeir stressed *we* for her sake or Safia's.

Omeir set Raine down. "Is that breakfast I smell?"

"Yup," Raine said, "I'm helping make pancakes."

"My favorite breakfast food," Omeir replied.

Safia coughed. "You already ate."

"I mixed more batter than needed. You're welcome to join us," Quinn said, attempting to deflate the rising tension.

"Thanks, but I've got a few calls to make," Safia responded.

"You can use my bedroom. It's the first door on the left."

Safia nodded and disappeared down the hallway.

"Lead the way," Omeir said, addressing Raine. "I'm going to drench my flapjacks in syrup."

After flipping the last pancake onto Omeir's plate, Quinn excused herself. She found Safia in the living room. She had ended a call and was about to make another.

"Any word from Eliot?" Quinn asked.

"I'm guessing you haven't heard anything either?"

"No. I'll text him later. Although this party is a ruse, Raine will be disappointed if he doesn't show."

"And so will someone else."

"Can I get you a coffee?" Quinn asked, disregarding Safia's comment.

"I'm caffeinated enough."

"Safia," Omeir shouted from the kitchen. "I need help in here."

"That man," Safia grumbled, "he can't do anything without me."

"I'll see what he needs," Quinn said, but she spoke too late. Safia had already stormed from the room. Feeling useless, Quinn straightened the sofa cushions for the third time today. *What the heck?* A succession of beeps came from the kitchen. It wasn't the oven timer but more like a weird ringtone.

Omeir strode into the living room, his phone to his ear. "Yeah, I understand. I'm leaving now."

"Is that Eliot?" Quinn asked.

"Lieutenant Pratt, our boss. I need to go deal with another matter."

Her tentative smile dropped.

Omeir tucked his phone in his back pocket. "Don't worry. It'll be okay. Eliot's as smart as he is tough. He'll figure this out." He grabbed his coat from the hallway hook. "Hey, Safia," he yelled. "Pratt's called me in. You'll need to bake cupcakes. Just search the internet on how to make icing."

"I can handle frosting," she yelled as the door slammed shut.

Quinn secured the deadbolt and headed to the kitchen.

Safia poked her head in the fridge. "Icing is sugar and cream, right?"

Quinn set a ready-made frosting jar on the counter. "Let's use this." She turned to Raine. "There's a wooden box on the bookcase's lower shelf. Can you bring it to me? It has edible decorations that we can use to brighten the cupcakes."

As soon as Raine left, Quinn turned to Safia. "Sorry about taking you away from real police work. I told Eliot Raine's safe here, but he insisted."

"His kid sister is important to him. And I suppose you are too."

Chapter Fifteen

"Pick up your feet," Paula yelled, "You're ten minutes late."

Eliot followed Paula up the stairs, heading straight to his apartment. At his request, Quinn moved *the party* across the hall. Raine deserved a sense of normalcy, if only for one night.

Paula knocked on the door before he could use his key.

"It's us," he shouted.

The door opened, and Raine barreled straight for him. Without a word, she handed him a glittery card. He raised her from the floor and hugged her tight. Had they been alone, he would have wept. He set Raine down and opened the card. His throat tightened. His sister had drawn a large stick man with a cape.

He kissed her tiny hand. "Great job." If only he could be the superhero she needed.

A smile spread across his sister's cheeks. Eliot glanced at his fellow detectives and Quinn. "We'll talk later," he grumbled.

He turned and ruffled Raine's hair. "You did this all for me?"

"Yup," she said.

For the next three hours, he hid his emotions. He stuffed a mouthful of food down his throat even though his taste buds were dormant. He smiled and chatted as though his life wasn't teetering toward destruction.

Halfway through her second chocolate cupcake, Raine's eyelids fluttered.

"I'll put her to bed," Paula whispered to Eliot.

"Thanks, but I'll tuck her in tonight."

Paula touched his arm. "We'll head out. Give you time alone. I'll call you tomorrow."

He followed Paula and Malcolm to the door. "Thanks," he said, kissing Paula's cheek.

She turned and wiped away a tear. Malcolm, who had one foot in the hallway, marched back and hugged Eliot. "You'll find her."

Eliot stiffened. Of all the years he had known Malcolm, they had only hugged once. The embrace, which Eliot had initiated, occurred at Ty's gravestone as tears bombarded the older man. Now was Malcolm's turn to offer comfort.

After the Wilsons left, Eliot returned to the others. "Stick around," he said to Omeir and Safia. "I'll update you."

Safia nodded.

"If you need anything, call," Quinn said. "I'll be working from home for the next few days."

He could tell caring for Raine all day had worn Quinn out. He should let her go. "I need a favor," he stated.

"Sure."

"Will you read Raine her bedtime story?" His sister was half asleep. She probably didn't mind forgoing the nightly ritual.

"I'd love to," Quinn responded.

Eliot carried Raine to her room. His sister's warm face snuggled into his neck. Reaching her bed, Eliot sat her down. He kissed her forehead and settled into a nearby chair. Raine pointed to the book on her nightstand. It was a short story with no more than eight pages. For the first time, Eliot wished his sister had selected a thicker book. Quinn read the fairy tale. When she turned to the last page, Eliot pulled the book, preventing her from saying *they lived happily ever after.* There would be no promise of eternal bliss tonight.

"Will you read one more story…in case she isn't asleep yet?" Eliot whispered to Quinn.

"Sure," she mouthed.

Hearing Quinn's soothing voice, Eliot surrendered to her comfort and laid his head on her lap. Life was hard, but just this once, he'd love for it to be fair.

****

Eliot was strong and confident, even cocky at times. They were traits that drew Quinn in but also scared her. But tonight, his strength was replaced with exhaustion and defeat.

Eliot lifted his head from Quinn's lap. "Can I ask another favor?"

"Yes, of course."

"Can you hang around for a bit more? I have to talk to Saifa and Omeir, and I might need your advice."

She gave a tight smile and nodded. For some inexplicable reason, Eliot had made her his confidante. Though she didn't get the giraffe question right, there were no dire consequences. The same wouldn't be true for major life decisions.

She sat beside Safia while Eliot briefed them on the day's events. The meeting with Alisha caused more anxiety than reassurance. Carly, although a criminal, still had parental rights under the law. Even if charged, the courts might consider the bail breach an act of love, a mother eager to reunite with her daughter.

"What about her wanting payment?" Quinn asked. "Even a lenient judge wouldn't overlook a parent trying to sell their child."

Eliot's jaw muscles twitched. "The public defender will argue you misunderstood."

"What did the social worker advise?" Omeir asked.

"The woman is useless," Eliot grumbled.

"At least the police are searching for Carly," Quinn said.

Omeir shook his head.

"Unless she is on a violent offender list," Eliot said, "the NYPD won't look for her."

Safia turned to Quinn. "Exposing a child to drugs brings a social worker to your door, not the police. Studies acknowledge the link between neglect and violence, but unless Carly assaults Raine or kidnaps her, the police won't actively track her down."

"But a beat cop may get lucky and come upon her," Omeir interjected.

"Like that will happen," Eliot scoffed.

Quinn stared at the detectives around the table. "There must be something we can do?"

"I'm not giving up," Eliot said. "I'll keep looking for her."

Soon after, Omeir and Safia left.

Eliot scrolled through his phone. "Dammit. Doesn't anyone return messages?"

"There's not much you can do at this hour," Quinn said. "Go catch some z's, and we'll start again in the morning."

Eliot glanced up. His face was a sea of deep creases.

Stress and fatigue had hammered him. "I can't sleep."

"Try resting."

She stuck around, listening to him vent. After jabbering for twenty minutes, he stretched his body across the sofa. He continued, his voice rising as he complained about how the justice system was slanted toward Carly. Now and then, he would get quiet. She'd ready to leave, and he'd start up again. Had he asked her to stay, she would have, but he didn't broach the subject. After minutes of silence, Quinn announced her departure.

****

The following morning, Quinn marched to Eliot's apartment. Safia opened the door, and Eliot waved her in.

"Any news?" she asked Omeir when Eliot left the room to get her coffee.

"Nothing yet, but Carly will turn up," replied the eternal optimist.

She headed into the kitchen and caught Eliot scowling at the coffee maker. "Stupid machine," he said, pressing more buttons than necessary.

The appliance let out a sputter. Quinn waited silently as the coffee dripped.

Raine barreled into the kitchen. "Aren't we having pancakes?"

"How about juice and cereal?" Eliot replied.

His sister frowned. "But you promised pancakes."

"I'll make them," Quinn volunteered.

Eliot handed her a mug of steaming liquid. "Thanks, but I've got it covered. After all, I make the best pancakes, don't I, Raine?"

"I like Quinn's, but she doesn't make bears."

He ruffled his sister's blonde curls. "I'll show her how to make them. Go see if Omeir and Safia want breakfast." She hurried off, leaving Eliot alone with Quinn.

"So, what's the plan for today?" Quinn asked.

"I'm headed to work. There's a break in one of my cases, so I don't have a choice."

She sipped her coffee. "What about Raine?"

He opened a cabinet, grabbed a bowl, and opened the fridge. "I called Paula. She offered to take Raine to her cousin's cabin in upstate New York for a few days, but…" he paused, his voice straining. "Sending her away is a bad idea. A few days turn into a few weeks; before you know it, we're strangers again." His frown deepened. "What if I lose Raine?"

She touched his arm. "It's going to be okay."

He pulled away. "Don't."

Her eyes moistened. His harsh tone didn't bother her, but she was exhausted and frustrated. Eliot shouldn't have to go through this.

"I'm sorry," he grumbled. "I appreciate everything you've done for Raine and me, but all my life, people told me things would be okay, and they weren't."

She understood. Chad said the exact words when her mother died.

"I have a meeting at the warehouse, but I can take Raine."

"Thanks, but you had her yesterday. I can't continuously dump my sister on you."

"I love having her around. She teaches me to view things from a different perspective. She makes me a better artist."

"Safia and Omeir are on assignment."

"So?"

"I'm nervous about you and Raine being by yourselves."

"I could reschedule my meeting."

"No, don't change your plans. Give me time to mull it over."

"Okay." She cracked an egg into a bowl. "How many pancakes should I make?"

"I doubt Safia will have any, and Omeir will down an entire stack, but I better check." He exited the kitchen.

A few moments later, Safia appeared. "I've already eaten, but Omeir will eat again. You best make a dozen pancakes, more if they're small."

Quinn whipped up the batter and mentioned her conversation about Raine to Safia.

"I get his concern. He'd never forgive himself if something happened to Raine…or you. I still can't believe Carly went to Raine's old school and obtained Eliot's address."

Quinn maneuvered around the female detective and turned on the stove. "Can you hand me the strawberries?"

"I have some phone calls to make," Safia announced, ignoring Quinn's request and left.

Eliot returned to the kitchen. He smiled softly at Quinn. She appreciated his effort to stay positive.

He grabbed a spatula and swirled the batter cooking on the skillet. "Pfft. An artist who can't make bear pancakes."

"And why do all your bears have mangled ears? Is it safe to eat mutant carnivores?"

"They have mangled ears because they fought bravely in the great pancake war. They're heroes." His face grew serious. “All kidding aside, thanks for helping out. Not only with breakfast but with everything.”

She gazed into his troubled eyes. “You’re not alone. I’m here for you.”

Safia barged into the kitchen with Omeir trailing behind.

“Smells great,” Omeir said, beelining to the food and stuffing a cooked pancake into his mouth.

Safia shoved the plate away from Omeir before he could grab another. “I’ve arranged for an off-duty officer to take Raine and Quinn to her meeting. He’ll stay outside the building and keep guard.”

“How’d you manage that?” Omeir mumbled, chewing his food.

“A uniformed officer owed me a favor.”

Omeir forked another pancake. “So, who’s the guy?”

“Perhaps it’s a woman,” Safia quipped back and handed the platter to Quinn.

Omeir fixed his gaze on his female colleague. “Who?”

“If you must know, it’s Ahmed Khoury. He’s with the nineteenth precinct.”

“That’s in Manhattan. How did you meet him?”

“It doesn’t matter,” Safia snapped at Omeir. “He’s one of us,”

Eliot stepped between them. “Good,” he said, addressing Safia. “Tell Officer Khoury I owe him one.”

****

Raine raced through the door, grinning. The tension in Eliot’s shoulders lessened.

“Here,” Quinn said, shoving a huge bubble wrap roll into his hands.

"What's this?"

"It's for dancing," Raine said.

"Sorry," Quinn mouthed to him. "A fellow artist taught Raine to line dance…on bubble wrap. She gave her this to practice."

He leaned the roll against the wall. "Glad you're not a musician. I'd hate to have a drum set."

"Can I have a snack, Eliot?"

He whipped his head to Raine. "What did you say?"

"Can I have a snack?"

"No, not that. What did you call me?"

"Eliot, 'cause that's your name."

He chuckled. "You said it perfectly. Way to go, Raine."

"Can I have a cookie?"

"Sure. Can you get it yourself?"

She nodded and toddled toward the kitchen.

"Did you hear that?" he asked Quinn.

"I did."

"Thanks for helping her with her speech. Your work has paid off."

"Raine's smart. She'll be on par with the other kids in no time."

"Yeah, providing I don't have to withdraw her from school," he grumbled. "Hey, how was your meeting?"

"Good. And your day?"

"Nothing has changed if that's what you're asking."

"Raine's welcome to stay at my place."

"I can't ask you to…"

"You're not. I'm volunteering. Now would be a good time to paint her room."

"It doesn't need painting."

"It's beige."

"What's wrong with beige?"

"Nothing if you're living in a senior's complex. Kids love bright colors. And don't worry. There's no hurry to get it done."

"Why are you so concerned with how my place looks?"

"It's a creative way of keeping Raine safe without lying to her. You said you didn't want her traveling upstate with Paula. This way, you can visit her anytime. I'll give you a key, and if you want, you could—"

"Thanks, Sprinkles," he said, worried she'd invite him to stay. Joining her pajama party was a surefire way of wrecking their friendship. He didn't have the strength to take things slow and do right by her. His greed and desire would destroy the best relationship he ever had with a woman. "I'll find out what color she wants."

As luck would have it, Raine wanted yellow walls. She already had a lemon-colored area rug, but her precious little heart desired a full sun explosion. He tried tricking her with a shade called *cookie dough*, but she realized this was simply a lighter beige.

Due to his hectic work schedule, Eliot took four days to prep the room. Though busy, he ensured he joined Raine and Quinn for dinner. The best part of the day was putting Raine to bed, though it wasn't her bed but the fold-out couch in Quinn's apartment. There was a peacefulness to the children's bedtime stories—comical heroes, determined heroines, and Quinn's presence. She became a regular in the land of make-believe. She narrated while he voiced the various characters, transforming his deep masculine voice into a shrill magical elf. Quinn and Raine's laughter assured him that his life hadn't all gone to shit.

Now he sat staring at his apartment's wall. Quinn was right. Beige was dreary. When lonely, his anger toward Carly increased tenfold. Childhood memories filled with poverty, neglect, and filth often numbed him, but now, contempt and shame blanketed him. His mouth grew dry. Eighty-proof liquor taunted him. He grabbed his coat, intent on hitting the nearest dive bar. He touched the doorknob and stopped. Raine deserved better.

Eliot sank to the sofa and dialed Zak Ahmadi. No one understood the struggle of silencing the screaming demons as well as Zak did. Eliot had met the brilliant detective last year. It was Eliot's first mission with the Counterterrorism Bureau and Zak's last. The assignment went off the rails when a notorious terrorist stabbed Zak. His friend recovered from the near-fatal physical injuries, but the man's Post Traumatic Stress Disorder intensified. These days, Zak was on the upswing. He had met a wonderful woman and got engaged. Eliot and Zak were opposite in many ways, but both had an incredible knack for reading people. Zak was the one guy who never bought his bullshit.

Eliot scrolled to Zak's number and pushed send.

An incoherent groggy female voice answered. The call had woken his buddy's fiancée.

"Lexie, it's Scorp."

"Who?"

"Eliot Traversini," he replied, unsure if the phone line cut out or if she hated his nickname.

"It's the middle of the night, Eliot. Is everything okay?"

"I'm sorry. I'll hang up."

"No, don't."

She must have handed the phone over because Zak

came on the line and said, “Give me a moment, Scorp. I’m going downstairs.”

He heard rustling, a dog barking, and Zak hushing the animal. Either the dog quieted, or he let the animal outside. Silence continued. Zak came back. “You okay, Scorp?”

“I’ll call you tomorrow.”

“No, talk to me now. What’s up?”

He told his friend about the situation with his whacked mother and confessed his desire to get totally wrecked.

“I get it, Scorp, but drinking won’t help. If it could, I would have done it long ago.”

“So, what will? I can’t keep reliving these shitty memories. I’m in peak condition, yet I get these god-awful chest pains. My life is spinning out of control, and I can’t do a damn thing about it.” Tears welled in his eyes. “Raine’s a sweet little girl. She can’t go through what I did. She won’t survive.”

“There’s nothing you can do besides what you’ve already done.”

“You’re not helping,” he grumbled.

“You can’t erase what you’ve experienced, and predicting the future is impossible. There’s plenty in life we can’t control.”

“Thanks for the great pep talk,” Eliot snarled.

“I’m not saying give up. Keep looking for Carly and find a way to manage that doesn’t complicate your life even more. And remember, different tactics work for different people.”

“So, what worked for you?”

“A combination of things. You and I have a knack for fixing problems, except when they are our own. I used to isolate myself, but I realized I needed help sometimes. You might too."

"I'm calling you, aren't I?"

"Yes, and that's why I'm on the phone with you and not in bed with my gorgeous fiancée. I know it's hard to reach out. You did good, but keep doing it. Realizing I couldn't erase my memories, I created new memories, good ones involving other people. That way, you can escape to a safe place and not spiral into a drunken hellhole."

"I struggle damn hard focusing on the positives—on my kid sister— but experience has taught me good times don't last."

"Is there a bottle in front of you right now?

"I wouldn't be chatting if I had whiskey."

"Good. Keep away from the drink. Though you may think it might help, it won't. Changing old habits is hard, especially ones that have a hold on you, but you don't have to do it alone. We're all here for you. I can't say I know what it's like to struggle with sobriety, but I know NYPD officers who have. I can talk to them. I'm sure they will be glad to help in whatever way they can. But remember you don't want an entire support system based on cops or those in recovery. You need people who help you forget about your past, even if it's for a moment. Each second, each minute, they all add up. Soon those moments become longer and longer until you end up with a good day and then a great week. It takes time, but progress will happen. Allow folks to care about you and start caring about yourself."

"Yeah. Raine gets me out of my head. She has no idea how terrified I am."

"Does Quinn?"

"Quinn?" *How the hell does Zak know about her?*

"Omeir mentioned you spend a lot of time with your pretty new neighbor."

"She helps me with Raine. She's a friend. That's all." Talking about a woman with anyone was uncomfortable, let alone with another dude.

"I once said the same about Lexie."

Eliot rolled his eyes. His buddy was on the verge of dishing out relationship advice.

"Strange, isn't it?" Zak said.

"What is?"

"We've faced situations with nerves of steel, but when a woman comes along, we fumble more than a third-string quarterback. It's ludicrous when you think about it."

"I'm not dating nor sleeping with Quinn."

"But you like her."

"When the hell did you get so personal?" Eliot grumbled.

"If you like her, get your head straight and go for it."

Yup, and there it was—relationship advice. "You really shouldn't listen to Omeir. He's as reliable as a blind lifeguard."

"According to my other source, your neighbor is attractive, single, and lives across the hallway. What exactly are you waiting for?"

"Isn't it against Safia's religion to be gossiping?"

"Work out your issues. It's not just your sister who deserves a better life. You do too. One last bit of advice, and then I'll leave you alone."

"What?" Eliot mumbled.

"Be honest with this Quinn woman. Let her get to know the real you. She'll find a big heart once she gets over your ugly face."

Zak's razzing pushed away the pressure building in his chest. "Hey, thanks for answering the phone, pretty boy. Tell Lexie I'm sorry for waking her."

"I will…and anytime, Scorp."

It was good to know Zak meant it.

****

Quinn climbed out of the shower. The hot water had eased her neck tension. She was not only stressed about Raine, but she was worried about Eliot. He was worn down, surviving on adrenalin alone. He did more pacing than a captive tiger.

There was one surefire way of getting him to unwind, but that strategy would further complicate his life. Besides, she wanted to be his girlfriend, not a convenient distraction. Though she secretly wished they were lovers, Eliot needed a friend more than a bed partner. He was full of worries as it was. He repeatedly apologized for his long work hours and for leaving Raine with her. She didn't mind. She enjoyed hanging out with Raine. His sister had transformed from a nervous and fragile child to this sweet, loving little girl. Although the daughter of a vile woman, Raine had this innate gentleness. With love and time, Raine blossomed. Meanwhile, her brother slipped further away.

Paula and Malcolm were a godsend to Eliot and his sister. Paula with her casseroles and homemade cookies, and Malcolm with his calm demeanor when everyone got cranked up about what the authorities were and weren't doing. The Wilsons took turns keeping Raine entertained, but Quinn suspected Raine missed her big brother. Surprisingly, Eliot didn't go to work this morning or hit the streets to locate Carly. Quinn couldn't tell if he was taking a break or had abandoned hope.

"Why don't you go wash up before lunch?" Eliot said to his sister upon entering Quinn's apartment. They had taken Hudson out for a walk.

Raine kicked off her dirty shoes and ran to the bathroom.

"Did you guys have a good time at the park?" Quinn asked.

He ran his hand through his hair. "Alisha called yesterday. She's worried about Raine missing school. She was behind the other kids before I pulled her. Kindergarten is more than coloring." He paused. "Not that art isn't important, but I don't want her having to repeat a grade later on."

"You're not considering sending her back?"

"Hell no. Carly knows what school she's at, but I'd hate to see Raine struggle. She's made progress, but she's still not where she should be, and her interaction with other kids is minimal. Maybe I should check out a private school that has gates and security guards."

"Sure," she mumbled. Such an education would soak up half his salary. He'd never afford it. There was, however, a way around this. *Forget it*. He'd never go for it.

A knock sounded, ending any further discussion.

Eliot glanced at her. "Are you expecting someone?"

"I bet it's Gabby. I canceled brunch, so she's likely checking on me. I'll tell her now's not a good time."

"Go hang out with her. You've spent enough time dealing with my garbage."

Before she could respond, Eliot had opened the door. "I wasn't expecting you."

Quinn hurried over. "Oh, hi, Omeir."

“Sorry for not calling, but I was in the neighborhood when the news came in.”

“What news?” Quinn asked.

“They found Carly. She’s in lockup, arrested on drug charges.”

Chapter Sixteen

After Omeir left, Eliot turned to Quinn. "I doubt we've heard the last of Carly, but her arrest is a positive first step."

"Surely her parenting rights have diminished."

"Yeah. I would think so. Hey, enough about her. Let's go out for dinner."

He had decided to take his buddy's unwanted advice and celebrate with Quinn—no alcohol, no talking about the past, just living in the present for a few hours.

"We can go to that new pizza place," Quinn replied. "Their online menu lists lactose-free choices. I'll go tell Raine."

He pulled Quinn forward. Her fingers flattened across his chest. A small gasp escaped her throat.

"Just you and me," Eliot uttered, softening his baritone voice.

Quinn stepped back. "The two of us?"

"I'm told that's how a date normally works."

The awkward silence became terrifying. How could he have misread her? He excelled at figuring people out. "Forget it," he grumbled. He wouldn't beg her to go out with him…or to like him.

She ran her fingers up his arm. A warm sensation ran down his body. A huge grin replaced his frown.

"Yes, I'd love to go to dinner with you, El."

He leaned in, his face inches from hers.

"Where is everybody?" Raine shouted from Quinn's kitchen.

"In here," he hollered, stepping away and sacrificing the kiss he had been waiting for.

Raine sprinted into the living room. Eliot kneeled to avoid towering over her. "Remember how I told you I wanted to ask Quinn out?"

"To smooch?" his sister asked.

Quinn glared at him. "You told her that?"

"No," he grunted. "Raine, spell Mississippi?

"Am I in trouble?" she asked.

He dropped the scowl. "Never, munchkin, but you shouldn't know about kissing until you can spell big words. Hey, how about hanging out with Paula and Malcolm tonight?"

Raine's eyes grew wide and watery. "You promised a movie."

Quinn crouched beside her. "What if Paula and Malcolm took you?"

Raine glanced at her brother and then at Quinn. "Will I get popcorn?"

"Absolutely." He'd give her a fricking pony if she wanted.

Quinn tapped her phone and began typing with her thumbs.

"What are you doing?" Eliot asked.

"I texted Paula. It's a go. They'll pick her up."

He chuckled in relief. Quinn was as eager as him.

****

Quinn stood by her closet, biting her lip. Her last date, if you call it that, was a year ago. Cheating Chad took her to her favorite restaurant. The expensive dinner was a pitiful tactic aimed at manipulating forgiveness.

She pushed a few hangers, searching for something suitable to wear. Eliot had mentioned a nice restaurant, but nice might mean a burger joint with table menus instead of ordering at the counter. She sucked a breath. Why the panic? Eliot had asked her out, not some stranger. She had spent countless hours with him. How hard could a simple dinner be? She squeezed her eyes and imagined all those times they went for ice cream.

“Argh,” she screamed. A date with Eliot Traversini was a big deal. It was like ordering a non-dairy cone but eating a triple fudge sundae.

She entered the bathroom, rummaged under the sink, and grabbed several bottles and boxes. Hair conditioner, facial cleanser, apricot moisturizer, she could use them all. She dropped the wax kit. Ripping out one’s hair was like home dentistry. She spotted a razor, a new one with five blades.

The doorbell rang.

Eliot promised her two hours. Why would he be here now? She padded to the door, worried he was here to cancel.

She glanced through the peephole. “Thank goodness.” She tugged the door open. “Gabby,” she shouted, “I need your help.”

“With what?”

“Picking out an outfit for tonight.”

Gabby glanced away. “Sorry, I made plans with Kiefer.”

“Good. My evening doesn’t involve you.”

“Get out,” Gabby screamed. “You’re going on a date?”

She giggled, giddy with joy. “He asked, and I said yes.”

Gabby removed her coat and flung it over the sofa. "It's with your smoldering hot neighbor, isn't it?"

Quinn nodded and marched to her bedroom. Her friend followed, beelining to the closet. "I knew something was up. You were always at his place."

"We're friends," she countered, flushing for sounding defensive. "I had no idea he liked me until he asked me out."

Gabby shook her head. "Boy, are you oblivious. The handsome hunk has been interested in you for a long time."

Earlier, Quinn fretted that dinner was Eliot's kind and innocuous way of thanking her for helping with Raine. Now she was free to freak out about the actual date.

"Are you going to help me?" She tugged her hair. "I'm a big frizz ball. I have nothing to wear. What should I talk about? I don't want to bore him with my work or babble about his kid sister. Though Raine is amazing."

"Breathe, girl. Let's start with where he's taking you."

"I'm not sure. He mentioned nice and restaurant in the same sentence."

"Okay, we'll pick out a dress. You can show off those great legs."

"You sure?"

"Didn't you tell me he didn't want to bring his sister to your boxing gym because it might be scuzzy?"

"Yeah."

"If he's protective of her, I doubt he'd take you to a dive. Now, what shall we do with your hair?" She circled Quinn, sizing up her thick mane. "We'll do an updo with a few loose curls."

"I thought maybe I'd straighten it."

"You'll look too serious. It's a date, not a court appearance. I'm in the biz. I know what guys find sexy. And don't worry about the conversation. There's a plus to dating a friend. You won't have to battle with awkward small talk. Did you know Kiefer and I hardly spoke on our first date?"

"Conversing with a tongue down your throat is impossible."

Gabby swatted Quinn's arm and giggled.

Quinn pursed her lips. "What if Eliot finds me boring?"

"Oh, spare me. Anyone can see that he's into you. You could invite him to watch smog, and he'd be fascinated. Now hurry up and get your tushy in the shower. I'll grab some dresses from your closet."

"Thanks, Gabs."

"I'm thrilled to be helping you. For a while, I was worried you'd wind up in a nunnery."

"You mean a convent?"

Gabby ignored the correction. "Remember to shave paradise valley. A trim works for sitting around the pool, but if you're going to take a plunge, you best clean up right."

Quinn stood under the shower head. The warm water failed to calm her nerves. While she averted razor burn, Eliot was probably napping.

"Aren't you done?" her friend hollered through the wall.

Quinn turned off the faucet. "Jumping out now." She toweled off and wrapped herself in a plush bathrobe.

"What do you think?" Gabby said when she entered the bedroom.

Across her crumpled duvet were two dresses—a black bodycon and a fit and flare with vibrant large flowers. “Which one do you like?”

“Floral,” Gabby responded without hesitation.

“You don’t think it’s too cutesy?” She wanted to shed the innocent girl vibe.

“Listen, I know fashion…and what goes on in men’s minds.”

Eyeing the tight black garment, Quinn lifted the other dress over her head.

“Here,” Gabby said, dropping shoes by Quinn’s feet. “Don’t forget these *take-me-against-the-wall* stilettos.”

Quinn sputtered a laugh. Stepping into the four-inch lipstick pink heels, she faced the mirror. Gabby’s suggestions were spot-on.

****

Bothered by Raine’s kissing comment, Eliot planned to speak to Paula about her television choices. But when Paula picked up Raine, he shut his mouth. He’d either sound like an idiot or piss her off. Paula had raised a child. She knew far more than him. Besides, his sister might have witnessed a couple kissing in the park. On any New York street, people locked lips. And if all went well tonight, he’d be planting several good ones on Quinn.

Eliot glanced at his phone’s clock. He wouldn’t have been crunched for time if he hadn’t taken that nap. He redid his tie for the umpteenth time. Once again, he miscalculated its length. The cloth slipped between his big hands. The length was now okay, but the knot was too tight. A man might as well wear a snake around his neck—a real one.

He dressed up for three occasions, weddings, funerals, and when ordered by Pratt. For the latter, Omeir prepped the tie like a mathematician and prevented the stupid thing from ending at his midsection like a tired insurance salesman. A lot of scrambling occurred to find a date-worthy restaurant. And were it not for Omeir, he wouldn't have secured a reservation at the rooftop restaurant overlooking the New York City skyline. Omeir swore there was no illegal hacking done. Though, *creatively rearranging things* didn't sound innocent.

His gaze darted from the video demo on his laptop to the stupid, expensive piece of silk. One more attempt, and then he would staple the damn thing to his shirt.

Eliot pulled the cloth through the knot. He stuck two large fingers between his shirt and his neck. *Good.* He wouldn't pass out from a lack of oxygen. Romantic gestures weren't his thing. He'd been with plenty of women, but they were hookups. Sure, there were sweet words and overflowing charm, but no expensive dinner or grand gestures. He sought women who understood this. He used them, and they used him. They liked his rock-hard body. Some got their jollies from making out with a supposedly dangerous stranger, and the spoiled rich girls used his bad-boy persona to piss off their fathers for withholding their trust fund monies. Everyone got what they wanted. Was it wrong? Perhaps. But it no longer mattered. He was done with being a prick.

Quinn wasn't out to gain anything other than friendship. She didn't request he behave a certain way or be someone he wasn't. Quinn had her shit together. However, being around her made him greedy. He wanted more than quiet nights watching sports or trips to the gym. He wanted her sexy thighs over his hardened body.

But that was not all. He also wanted her generous and loving heart. Unfortunately, obtaining Quinn's affection would only last until she learned who he was, for Eliot had secrets—deep, dark secrets. His skeletons were so gigantic, they ought to be housed in a warehouse, not a closet.

****

"Dang, Sprinkles, you look amazing."

Heat rocketed Quinn's cheeks. Gabby was right. The yellow and pink floral dress was perfect.

"You look pretty good yourself." A total lie. The waiter at her favorite French restaurant looked good. Eliot was smoking hot, an inferno of sexiness. She feared her veins might explode from all the tingling inside her.

Eliot extended his elbow. "Ready?"

His chivalrous behavior continued. He opened the cab's door, took her hand, and helped her exit. He had the maître d' step aside at the restaurant and pulled back her chair. She knew he had a generous heart. He did so much for his kid sister. And though he relentlessly teased Quinn, he dutifully accommodated her wishes. Last week, he sat through a chick flick—not on purpose, but he showed up midway through it. He neither mentioned the ballgame on the other channel nor complained.

Gorgeous people crowded the trendy restaurant's rooftop patio. The folks that didn't look like fashion models were with those that did. A safari of sexy women wearing skin-baring dresses circled Eliot like gazelles at a watering hole. Even their server was stunning. To Quinn's delight, Eliot gave their attractive waitress no more attention than the guy who scooped his rocky road at their favorite ice cream shop.

She gazed over his shoulder at the shimmering city

lights. “This place is amazing. I’m surprised you got a table, let alone one with this view.”

“I’ll take credit for picking the place, but Omeir helped me get in.”

“Let me pay half.”

“Whoa, what’s with you and paying for things?”

She leaned across the table and settled her hand on his, feeling a surge of warmth and electricity. The lines on his face softened, but his eyes darkened. He was too sexy for his own good. She paused, remembering where she was headed with the conversation. “I don’t mean to offend you, but you’re raising a child. Let me do my part.”

“Are you serious? You’ve already done so much. If I counted all your hours caring for Raine, I’d owe you a fortune.” He leaned forward and whispered, “You may find this shocking, Sprinkles, but I don’t frequent Fifth Avenue for haircuts, and I don’t waste money on pedicures or eyebrow tweezing. I can handle this.”

“But this place…”

He lifted her hand and rubbed her fingers. “I’m not rich like most folks here, but I have enough cash to splurge on what’s important. And tonight, nothing matters more than making a gorgeous woman happy with a lovely dinner.”

****

Although Eliot told Quinn he made decent money, and he did, dinner at the high-end eatery would never become the norm. This place was for special occasions like birthdays or anniversaries.

Anniversaries? Whoa. That’s a big stretch considering this is a first date.

But instead of flinching like a cat crossing over a hot

stove, he grinned and gladly paid the bill.

"Can you swim?" he asked, leading her from the restaurant.

"Pardon?"

"Are you able to swim?"

"I learned as a kid, although I haven't swum in years. Why?"

"I have an idea. I need to make a phone call. Give me a minute."

She glanced at her dress. "You're not suggesting we go skinny dipping?"

His face exploded with a wolfish grin. Getting naked with Sprinkles would end the night on a great note, but Lieutenant Pratt would lose his shit if his detective were caught without clothes. "It wasn't my plan, but if that's what you want."

She swiped his arm.

"Wait inside the restaurant. I'm going to surprise you. And I promise it won't involve nudity." *Worst promise ever.*

He watched her hips sway as she strolled back into the posh eatery. An older man bumped his arm.

"Watch it," Eliot grumbled, annoyed by the intrusion.

The man gave him a fleeting glance and forged ahead, treating him like an annoying speed bump.

Minutes later, Eliot entered the restaurant. The rude man from the street was chatting with Quinn. Older rich men were the worst for chasing young, attractive women. Money won over many ladies, but not this one. He strode to Quinn and locked his fingers with hers. "It's a great place," he said to the man. The guy glanced at Eliot's neck and scowled.

Asshole. You're hitting on a woman who wasn't even born when you started stealing people's money on Wall Street, and you're judging me.

Eliot turned to Quinn. "Ready?"

"Yes," she replied.

The man handed her a business card. She took it, stuffing it into her tiny purse.

"What was that about?" he asked, stepping into the evening air.

She opened her purse and ripped the card. "He claims to own a talent agency and invited me to his office. Apparently, I have great features."

"You don't believe him?"

"Do you?"

"You are striking, so he's right about your looks. But I'm sure there's a bed in his office."

"I wouldn't be surprised."

"So why accept the card?"

"I didn't want to make a scene."

He released her hand.

"What's wrong?" she asked.

"You weren't going to cause a scene, but you were afraid I would." He let out a sigh. He wasn't angry but felt compelled to set the record straight. "I may be built like a cage fighter, but I don't fight every ignorant prick that crosses my path."

"It was stupid to take his card."

"No," he corrected. "It was stupid of him to hit on you. But it's not surprising. You're an attractive woman, and guys are jerks. Providing they don't lay a finger on you, I'll sit back and let you deal with them. You're smart. You've got great instincts. How you handle idiots is your choice. If you want assistance, let me know. But even then, I won't kick ass. I might want to, but I promise I won't embarrass you."

"I'm sorry, I didn't—"

"There's no need to apologize. Just know who I am." He laced his fingers with hers. "Let's go have fun."

A short ride brought them to Brooklyn. Quinn stepped out of the cab and peered around. They were at a park. It was late, and all the attractions were closed. He smiled reassuringly and led her away from the brightly lit street and into the darkness.

"We're breaking in?" she whispered, following him through a grassy area.

A hearty laugh escaped his lungs. "You do realize I'm sworn to uphold the law?"

Reaching a sidewalk, she stopped. A man was approaching them.

"It's okay. I know him." Reaching the man, Eliot stretched out his arm. "Hey, how's it going?" He gripped the guy's hand. "Gunnar, this is my friend Quinn."

The man flashed Eliot a grin and shook Quinn's hand.

"Thanks for doing this," Eliot said.

"No problem," Gunnar mumbled and guided Eliot and Quinn down an illuminated pathway to the lake's shoreline. He halted, staring at Eliot's suit and Quinn's dress. "Take my old rowboat. It's easier to get into than the kayaks."

Quinn squinted at the wooden boat.

"I cleaned it out earlier today," Gunnar said. "Lifejackets are in the office. I don't care if you wear them, but the insurance policy requires you to take them."

"Do you want me to lock the place up?" Eliot asked.

"Nah. I've got the ballgame on inside. If I go home, I'll have to sit through a stupid reality dating show. Teenage daughter," he mumbled in explanation.

Eliot's mouth pressed into a thin line. This might be his future one day.

"There's fresh coffee in the office," Gunnar said, marching ahead. "It's decaffeinated, but you're welcome to it."

Once inside Gunnar's office, Eliot grabbed the essentials and escorted Quinn back to the lake. The docked watercraft had seen better days, but Gunnar assured him of its buoyancy. Wool blankets lay across the boat's bench. Although the night was warm, the blankets would prevent his one good designer suit from snagging on the splintered wood seats.

He crouched down and held the boat. "Go ahead."

Quinn grabbed his arm, steadying herself as she removed her heels and stepped in. "How stable is this thing?"

He removed his suit jacket and set it on the blanketed seat. "Now you know why I asked if you could swim." He gave a dimpled smirk and climbed in.

Though the boat swayed with his motion, it remained upright. Grabbing the scratched aluminum oars, he rowed into the lake, away from the silhouetted trees. Reaching the middle of the lake, he ceased paddling and rested the oars on the oarlocks. The boat drifted.

He sipped his coffee. "Still nervous?"

She laughed. "I have nerves of steel."

"Yeah, you do." He set down his thermal cup and leaned toward her, taking her hands. "I know I haven't been easy to be around."

"There were moments."

"You're too forgiving. I've been a cantankerous SOB. You, however, were remarkable. Raine never had to worry, and you kept me from losing it."

"You weren't bad. And even if you were, you had every right. I can't imagine what you and Raine have gone through."

"What do you think of this place?" He wouldn't waste a beautiful evening talking about his childhood.

"I've been to the park several times and rode the pedal boats once. It was during the day, so lots was happening. This is much better. It's amazing how this place is different at night. It's enchanting, serene—" She abruptly stopped.

"What?" he asked.

"I'm ruining the peacefulness with my endless chatter."

"It's nice hearing what's on your mind."

"No one has ever described my babbling as *nice*. The closest had been *amusing*."

"They're fools."

She loosened her hand and pulled away.

He hadn't intended the compliment to sound like a dumbass line. He meant it. He loved listening to Quinn. Her voice rose when she got excited, and her shoulders shook when she giggled. She was his new addictive pleasure.

"I'm guessing Gunnar has done this before for you?"

He smirked. "Are you asking—"

"No. No. It's not my business who you took here. I have a quirky habit of asking inappropriate questions when nervous."

He tilted forward, his eyes riveted to hers. “Today is the first time I asked Gunnar to arrange a moonlight sail.”

Her smile broadened.

He briefly shifted his gaze to the night sky. “As a kid, I’d come here, sit on the grass, and watch the lake ripple. I would stay for hours.” Being at the iconic park settled his rage and provided a break from his shitty life. “I called in a favor tonight. Two years back, Gunnar’s brother got into trouble. Nothing major, but the kid’s college scholarship was on the line. I used a bit of discretion, and Gunnar appreciated it. He told me if I ever wanted anything, to call. He’s a tattoo artist—a horrible one. When I rang him, he was ready to lay down ink. I would never tell him, but I’d chop off my arm before allowing him anywhere near my skin. This here is far more pleasurable.”

“Hanging out with me is better than a needle penetrating your body? Such flattery.”

He chuckled. “Okay, not the smoothest thing to say. Let me try again.”

She winked. “Go for it.”

He inched forward, his eyes dark and serious. “I want hanging out with you to be as permanent as a tattoo.”

“Much better.” She rose from her seat. The boat shifted.

“Hey, be careful,” he shouted.

Quinn lost her footing. She tumbled forward. A loud gasp escaped her mouth as she fell onto his lap. Her face was inches from his. Now would be the perfect time to kiss her. He leaned forward. A crack rippled through the air. He pulled back. One of the oarlocks had snapped from the rowboat. The oar set inside it splashed into the water. Quinn hauled herself off of him and leaned over the side. The tiny boat wobbled.

Eliot eased her from the edge. "I'll get it." Once the rocking slowed, he reached into the water to retrieve the metal oar. He was too late. It had already sunk. Noticing rust on the other oarlock, he dragged the remaining oar into the boat.

Quinn scrunched her shoulders. "I'm sorry."

"It's fine, Sprinkles. I can paddle with one oar."

"Should we head back before I do something klutzy again?"

"It was my fault for not checking the oarlocks, but if you want, we can leave."

She paused and looked around. "It's a beautiful night."

"Sure is."

"Let's stay." Quinn pointed to the sky. "There's the Seven Sisters."

"Impressive."

She listed several more constellations. "I went to astronomy camp when I was ten."

"You had a good upbringing, didn't you?"

"I did."

He imagined losing her mom was tough, but at least her childhood hadn't been stolen. They continued talking, discussing places they had both visited—hers on family vacations and his with work.

He smiled when she finished chatting about London. "I guess we should head back and let Gunnar lock up the place." He swung the remaining oar into the water. As he adjusted his grip, the shaft slipped from his hand.

"Dammit," he grunted. He dove his hands into the

lake. Again, he was too late.

"You've got to be kidding."

"Okay, that one was entirely my fault."

"Can we paddle by hand?"

"You can swim, right?"

She peered into the dark water. "You never took lessons as a kid?"

"Nope."

She reached behind her back, grappling her zipper.

"Um, what are you doing?"

"I'm not jumping in wearing a cocktail dress."

"I see," he said, biting back laughter. "And what will you do once you're in the water?"

"I'll push…or pull the boat. Whatever works."

"With me in it?"

"Do you have a better idea?" she snapped.

"Maybe."

"Don't tell me it's to sit here and hope Gunnar finds us."

"Perhaps."

"What if he heads home and forgets we're out here? You're prepared to stay here all night?"

"Hmm…It's not a bad idea."

She frowned.

"No, Sprinkles. We won't stay here. Even though I'm immensely entertaining, I'd hate for you to fall asleep on our first date. Terrible for the old ego."

"So what's your plan?" she asked.

"Turn around."

"Why?"

"Please, just do it."

Though she listened, he could tell by her strained voice her patience had grown thin. He hoped he wouldn't freak her out.

He gradually stood. The boat swayed. “Don’t look,” he warned. After more wobbling, the craft leveled out. “Lean over the side and hold on,” he yelled.

“Why?”

“Please, just do it.”

He waited until she gripped the boat, and then he moved. The boat tilted. A loud splash echoed, and the boat rocked some more.

“Eliot,” Quinn shrieked. She scanned the water’s surface. “Eliot,” she yelled again.

“Behind you,” he shouted.

Quinn stretched out her arm. “Take my hand.”

Eliot’s bare shoulders peered above the waterline. He grabbed a cleat near the boat’s bow and began to sway. For a man his size, he was rather graceful.

“What in the world are you doing? You can’t swim.”

“I said I never learned to swim as a child. I took lessons as an adult.”

“Not funny. You nearly gave me a heart attack.”

He ran his hand over his face, clearing the water droplets. “I’m sorry, Sprinkles. I didn’t mean to scare you.”

“Is the water cold?”

“Yeah,” he responded, hoping for sympathy.

“Jeez, Eliot. We should have waited for Gunnar.”

“I wasn’t about to have another dude rescue my date.”

“You’ll get pneumonia.”

“I’ve swum in far colder water than this. Hey, thanks for offering your hand. There’s no way you could pull me out, but I appreciate the gesture.”

He could easily backstroke to shore. But after the

stunt he pulled, he decided not to show off. Instead, he pushed the boat forward. Reaching the bank, he requested privacy. Grabbing a blanket, he dried himself and dressed, disappointed she didn't peek.

"Are you still mad?"

"I should be, but thanks for getting us back."

"Did you honestly believe I would sit idle while you plunged into the water?"

"Yes, if you couldn't swim."

He stroked her cheek. "I would never put you in harm's way."

****

His course fingers grazed her cheek, igniting a trail of fire on her skin. He held her gaze and she felt his warm breath. She leaned in, closing the distance, and waited for his mouth to claim hers.

He dropped his hand. "We better tell Gunnar we're done."

A surge of disappointment washed over her as she straightened her dress. She followed him up a hill. His warm fingers intertwined with hers. She longed for him to touch more than just her hand.

"What happened to you?" Gunnar asked Eliot when they entered the office.

"The damn oars fell into the water."

"You lost all four paddles?"

"There were two, and both are now at the bottom of the lake." Eliot pulled out his wallet.

"Put your money away. I've got plenty of paddles." Gunnar turned to Quinn. "You okay?"

"Yes. I stayed in the boat while Eliot pushed us to shore."

"The telescopic plastic oars work as well as metal

ones, and they float," Gunnar said.

"What telescopic oars?" Eliot asked.

"I might have shoved them too far back under the seat," Gunnar replied.

Quinn exploded with laughter. Although the moonlight rowboat excursion didn't unfold as anticipated, she got Eliot naked. Next time it wouldn't be by accident.

Chapter Seventeen

Eliot spent a lifetime taking risks, facing challenges, and saving others, but this time, someone else took a turn. And it wasn't a colleague but his warmhearted neighbor. Quinn was ready to dive into the lake and push him to shore. Although she didn't know it, she had rescued him months ago. Quinn motivated him to stay sober. Because of her, he was less of an asshole, and he was becoming the big brother his sister deserved.

Eliot opened the door and waited for Quinn to climb the stairs of their apartment building. He considered inviting her over, but feared they'd wind up watching sports highlights or some dumb movie like two platonic buddies. Ending the evening as is and hoping for another shot seemed right. Sure, he'd love to get into her pants, but for the first time in his life, getting into a woman's heart was as important—hell, it was more important.

He let go of her hand halfway down the hallway. "Sprinkles, thanks for tonight. I've wanted to take you out for a long time."

"Is that why you were at my apartment that night?"

"Huh?"

"Before Raine came to live with you, you knocked on my door. You were about to say something, and then your phone rang. Were you planning to ask me out?"

"That was the night Alisha called about Raine." He didn't dare reveal his true intention. "I rushed off to get her."

"Oh, you weren't there to ask me out?"

"Good thing I didn't," he replied, not answering her question. "You didn't like me."

"I didn't know you. And to set the record straight, you weren't keen on me either."

"Not true."

She let out a chuckle. "You treated me like an annoying mosquito."

"I had a lot of stuff going on, and you were huffy."

"Huffy?"

He smirked at her indignation. "You gave me the once over, but I've forgiven you."

"Mighty generous of you."

He laughed and then turned serious. "I'm glad we got to know each other."

"Me too," she responded.

He stuffed his hands in his pocket. Handling what came next was like racing across an ice arena in socks. He was incapable of being anything but clumsy.

****

Quinn decided to go for it. After all, what could go wrong? They were no longer on a rickety boat?

Standing on her toes, she placed her hands on Eliot's chest and puckered her lips. Without warning, her ankle wobbled off her shoe. Eliot reached for her wrist, but it was too late. She crashed to the floor like a medicine ball rolling off a balcony.

"Are you okay?" he asked.

"Argh," she muttered as she grappled Eliot's outstretched arm and pulled herself up. "How tall are you? Six-nine? Seven feet?"

"Six-five, but why does it matter?"

"Great," she huffed.

"You're annoyed with my height."

"I'm frustrated."

"You're not the one whose feet dangle off the bed. You could sleep on an armchair and fit."

"It's impossible to kiss you while you're standing. And these stupid shoes…" She glared at her scuffed stilettos. "I'm like a flamingo in a hurricane."

He let out a chuckle.

"I'm such a klutz," Quinn confessed.

"No, you're amazing." He leaned down and planted his lips on hers.

Her face scrunched, and she retreated.

"Hmm…not the response I was hoping for."

She pointed downward. "Ankle," she whimpered.

"Time to sweep you off your feet."

"No," she protested when he went to pick her up. "I'll hobble."

"Are you sure?"

"The way the night is going, you'll stumble and drop me."

His dimples retreated.

"I'm referencing the mishap with the oars."

"I'll be careful." He swooped her into his arms. "My place, okay?"

She gritted a smile. "Of course."

Inside his apartment, he placed her on the sofa. "I'll get ice." He hurried to the kitchen. "Can I get you anything else?" he shouted.

"Ibuprofen and some water."

Moments later, Eliot returned. He set a cloth-covered ice bag over her ankle. "Maybe I should give you a new nickname. How about Bouncing Babe?"

"I'm partial to Sprinkles. Its origin is a little less embarrassing." She took the pain reliever, downing it with water.

He lifted her foot onto the coffee table and settled beside her. Although she stopped herself from screaming, she couldn't help but wince.

"Urgent care is closed, but we could go to a hospital."

She patted his thigh. "I'll be okay once the pills kick in."

He leaned forward, examining her swollen ankle.

"It hurts, but I can move it. It's not broken. Besides, I hate hospitals."

"Because of your mom?"

Tears filled her eyes. "The nurses gave her excellent care, but she deteriorated quickly."

"I shouldn't have asked. I'm a lousy date."

"I'm okay talking about my mother. It may make me sad, but many good memories are mixed with sorrowful ones. I had a great time tonight, though tumbling in the hallway was not how I envisioned the evening ending."

He inched closer. "So, what would be a nice ending for our first date?"

"A kiss. One where I don't end up on the floor."

He lowered his face to hers, his lips brushing against her skin with a gentle warmth. He kissed her softly, tenderly.

Heat rose between her thighs. Eliot moved back. She yanked his shirt and tugged him forward. She parted her lips, welcoming his tongue. Whether it was the extra-strength ibuprofen or the warmth of his hand under her dress, her ankle pain lessened. Lost in the moment, she undid his shirt's center button.

He pulled away. "Sprinkles, we can't."

His refusal hurt more than her ankle.

"Why?"

He stared at the ceiling. Her mind raced, trying to decipher his body language.

Too forward?

Too fast?

Maybe not his type?

Please don't let it be the last one.

"We've known each other for months now," she said, her face flush as she explained her desire to remove his clothes.

He took her hand, interlocking his fingers with hers. "I love what you're doing. But we don't have to…It's okay if you rather—"

"What I want is to get you naked."

His jaw dropped.

Embarrassed, she glanced away. "If you're not ready, that's okay," she lied.

He let out a chuckle. "Hell no. The first time I knocked on your door, I was ready to go. But I know you now and don't want to rush you."

"My God, Eliot, we've known each other for months. I trust you."

"And I promise I'll never betray your trust."

"Then what is it?"

He heaved a sigh. "The lights are on and—"

"You're shy?"

"No," he growled as though she had suggested going vegan.

"I'm not understanding."

"I don't want to freak you out."

Her brows furrowed.

"The tattoos."

"You're worried I'll hate them?" An uncomfortable silence followed. "El," she said, rubbing his knee, "I've already seen several of them."

"When?"

"The day we first met. You know, the day I was all *huffy*. The wolf with the bloody fangs sinking into the skull was clearly visible, as was the guillotined horsemen."

"Weren't they covered?"

"You had on a black T-shirt that day. I noticed an entire arm full of ink." She also noticed his gorgeous eyes and how his biceps flexed when he carried her belongings to the door. "And the snake's head is obvious, even with a jacket collar up. You have more, don't you?"

"Seventy percent of my skin is inked."

"It's not a big deal. At least not now."

"What does that mean?"

"I'll be honest. The snake freaked me out when we first met, but so did that awful beard. But none of it bothers me anymore. Look, I'm an artist. I'm used to explicit works. I doubt I'll be startled by anything else. Unless, of course, there's a long list of women's names on your body." She caught the hurt in his eyes. "Sorry, bad joke."

He rubbed his thumb over her cheek. "Do you have any?"

"No."

"Promise me you won't get inked."

"Not that I'm planning on it, but why does it matter?" She gestured her hand over him. "You're fond of tattoos."

He tucked her hair behind her ear. "You're perfect the way you are. And in my case, the tatts were necessary."

"How?"

"I needed to cover my skin." A peculiar unsteadiness coated his voice.

"You tattooed your body as part of an undercover operation? But didn't you say you had them before you joined the NYPD?"

"I got most of them when I was seventeen and the remainder in my early twenties." He sucked in a deep breath and exhaled. "They camouflage my scars."

"Scars?"

"Burn marks," he clarified. "Most are on my chest and upper arms. The ink masks the scar tissue. With burns, you don't cover up with hearts or poetic words. I instructed the tattoo artist to replicate blood oozing out of flesh. It makes the sores blend as if they belong."

"Were you in a fire?" she asked.

"No." He rested his elbows on his knees. He stared at the carpet, clenching his hands, his knuckles whitening. "Carly went beyond neglecting me. She abused me."

She reached for his arm, but he shifted away.

"Let me finish," he said.

She nodded, unsure if she could keep it together while learning about the extent of Carly's cruelty. Quinn knew violence. She experienced its horrors herself. But what happened to her was different than Eliot's story. And knowing it was his mother who hurt him made Quinn livid.

"There were always men around when I was a kid. Most paid Carly for what they wanted and moved on, but a few stuck around for a while. Carly called them boyfriends, but they were drug dealers or pimps. One, in particular, was the cruelest son of a bitch I ever met, which says a lot considering my career path. I was fourteen at the time. I had enough of all the bullshit: the needles in the sofa cushions, the lowlifes hanging around, the dumpster diving when hungry. I tolerated a lot of crap, but this guy gave me the creeps. One day, I lipped off at Carly. He was within earshot. He didn't care about her, he said far worse to her than I did, but he wanted to teach me a lesson. So, he heated a metal spoon and placed it on my chest. It hurt like a bastard. I hollered every imaginable four-letter word at the sick son of a bitch. I charged after him, but he ducked, and I fell. He booted my head, yanked me from the floor, and tied me to a chair. Then he heated the spoon again. When Carly yelled at him to stop, he hauled her into the bedroom. While they were in the other room, I struggled to get loose, but it was impossible. I hoped Carly could reason with him and get me out of there, but instead of negotiating, she got high. They returned from the bedroom strung out, and without a word, without hesitation, Carly joined him." He rolled up his sleeves and pointed to a tattoo that resembled a razor blade slashing his flesh. "They both burned me. She wasn't afraid of him. She did it because she wanted to. Before they passed out, he untied me. I stole twelve dollars from his wallet and left for good."

"Oh my God, that's utterly barbaric. I can't imagine going through something so horrible."

"I didn't get through it, at least not in a healthy way. That's why I'm telling you this. My childhood messed me up. I was fortunate to have Ty and his parents. I probably would have landed in prison if I hadn't met them. Paula and Malcolm provided me with a roof over my head and food. I owe them so much. There was a lot of anger fueling me back then. I'd have fits of rage. I broke objects, pounded my fists into walls, and…I pulverized guys for disrespecting me. Paula and Malcolm knew I was out of control, so when Ty suggested enlisting in the Marine Corps, they didn't fight us. Being a Marine saved my life, but it ended Ty's. He came home in a body bag."

She shifted closer, but he extended his arm and kept her away.

"I get what you're doing, but don't. I didn't tell you about my mother for you to feel bad for me. I'm a grown-ass man. A hug won't make the past go away. I wish things could be so easy. I told you because you ought to know who I am. Having you around has been good for Raine…and me. I want what's happening between us to go further, but you might want to step back."

"Seriously? You think—"

"I'm not done. There's more."

She snatched a sofa cushion and hugged it to her abdomen. "Go on."

"The only fights I get into anymore are work-related, and I don't start them. I'm not angry at the world. I'll admit Carly's game-playing pisses me off, but I control the anger. It doesn't control me. It hasn't for years."

"That's good."

"Not entirely. I dropped the rage for something else."

"What do you mean?"

"There's a reason I don't drink or have booze

around. I tend to hit the bottle when life hits the shitter."

"How often and how much?"

"It's more than a few. I drink to excess when things are tanking and sometimes when life is good. Once I start, I keep going until I pass out."

"You're an alcoholic?"

"I haven't had a drink since Raine came to live with me."

"Okay, sobriety is new to you, but kudos for doing it."

"There's something else you should know. I swear I've given this up for good. Even if you walk away after I tell you, I'm still done with it."

She braced herself, afraid of his revelation. There was a limit to what she would tolerate.

"The other way I've been dealing is through women."

"No surprise there." She giggled and bit her lip. "I pictured you as a serial dater."

"I'm talking about a lot of women—too many to count. I've always taken precautions, and I've been tested. Fortunately, I've never caught anything other than a bad cold."

The phrase *too many to count* troubled her, but how he said it made her believe his shame. Besides, he swore he was finished chasing women. She swallowed the lump in her throat. "I'm not sure what to say."

"I'm sorry if this bothers you, but I want to be honest."

"You never had a long-term relationship?"

A strained laugh escaped his lips. "Sprinkles, I've been a *one-and-done* guy with the ladies. I justified my actions, thinking the women were also looking for casual sex. Perhaps most did, but it still didn't make it right. I should have known better, but I was a jerk until I started raising Raine. I used women for my own pleasure. I never called them back, made breakfast, or offered them coffee. I showed them the door as soon as I could."

Eliot had changed. Why else would he reveal his flaws on their first date? In her experience, guys concealed their misconduct. They would rationalize their behavior if caught red-handed in their failings, but not Eliot. He was honest and forthcoming with her. He attempted to protect her from his body's physical scars, which he assumed would repulse her. And when it didn't, he revealed the extent of his drinking and irresponsible behavior. She listened without judgment, for she understood pain. To her, Eliot was a survivor. A warrior. He was a flawed but good man committed to raising his sister, providing Raine with a childhood he never had.

She scooted toward him. Because he had moved to the couch's end earlier, he had nowhere to go unless he stood. She placed her hands across his chest and stared into his eyes. "Nothing, and I mean absolutely nothing, has changed my mind."

"I don't deserve you," he whispered.

"Yes, you do," she responded, "but I need something from you."

He stroked her cheek with his thumb. "I'll give you whatever I can."

"Leave the light on. I want to see every amazing part of you."

"I don't think that's a good idea."

"I won't ask, and you don't need to explain your tattoos and scars. Just know you never have to hide who you are."

He placed her hand on his dress shirt. She moved from button to button, sneaking kisses along his chest. When she finished, he took off his cufflinks and removed his shirt. She swallowed the lump in her throat. She had seen plenty of men without shirts at the gym, but none like this. He was in a special division—a division of rippling muscle and perfect abs. He made her weak in the knees. She diverted her gaze, reluctantly leaving the contours of his chest, and examined his tattoos. Within all that ink was a prevailing theme of torment. She took her time, studying the intertwining tattoos: the crazy-eyed beasts with blood dripping from fangs and devouring their vulnerable victims; the ink replicating stab wounds, bullet holes, and gorges of flesh; and the burn marks which were real. The tattoos didn't camouflage the branded skin. Instead, they exaggerated the wounds. The exaggeration was so real. They appeared like pulverized flesh created by a Hollywood special effects artist. But hidden within the turmoil was a small cross. She promised not to ask, so she traced her thumb over this tiny symbol of faith and forgiveness. Though the tatts were badass, they told a story. The battle, the rise from chaos, and the winding path to redemption were inked on his skin.

"Tell me the truth," he demanded.

"I'm undressing you, and you want to chat?"

He chuckled. "Trust me, I'm eager to use this mouth for something other than speaking, but I must know."

If it were anyone else, she would taper her response, but honesty had become their thing. She cleared her throat. "You're right not to show Raine."

His face tightened. "Go on."

"She's too young. Give it a few years, and then explain them to her. It won't be easy, so wait until she's older and less likely to be overwhelmed." She let out a broad smile. "Now, from an artist's perspective, it's a show-stopping work. Whoever did them is phenomenal at their craft."

"Most were done by an old acquaintance new to the business. He's well-known now, but that's irrelevant. How do *you* feel about them? I've considered getting a few removed, though the ones near the burn marks could end up worse."

"I'm no expert, but isn't removing them painful?"

"Nah. It's done with lasers."

"That doesn't sound good. You've endured enough pain. Besides, this work of art is you. Yes, it's intimidating, even a bit scary, but there's a remarkable story here. I know it's not pretty, but it's your life. And I hope there's room left on your sexy body, as I'm sure the best part is coming."

He smiled. "Are you feeding me lies to get into my pants?"

"No, but I could if you want."

He chuckled.

"Explaining your tattoos takes courage. Thanks for constantly persuading me to be part of your life."

"You make it sound like I hounded you. I invited you for ice cream."

"You begged me to come along." She grinned and stroked his chest. "It's okay. I like where it got us."

"You do?"

"Look, normally, I love chatting about feelings, but this painkiller has kicked in. There's a small window of opportunity here. Either we waste the next thirty minutes talking, or you drop your trousers."

"Did you just tell me to shut up and put out?"

Her face flushed. "I'm—"

He held his finger against her lips. "You can boss me all day long if it leads to seeing you naked."

****

Without hesitating, Eliot undressed Quinn. Leaving her clothes scattered across the living room floor, he carried her to his bed and eased himself over her ready body.

Though he fantasized about taking her against the wall, he'd be gentle—to avoid hurting her inflamed ankle and to experience something special. Pushing aside his own primal need, he peppered kisses along her neck. She tugged his belt. He reached his hand between them and undid it for her.

"Take your clothes off," she whispered. "If I'm naked, you're going to be too."

"Yes, ma'am." He kicked off his pants and whipped off his T-shirt.

She lifted her head and claimed him with her mouth. He teased her with his tongue. She was fine whiskey but without the guilt. She squeezed his ass. He deepened the kiss. Slow, gentle lovemaking would be more difficult than anticipated. She gripped him harder, her hands greedy and demanding.

He pulled back and grinned. Her eyes were serious, her lips swollen. He had never felt this wanted. "You're incredible," he said.

A shy smile flashed across her face.

He slid his lips against her ear and whispered, "We'll be in this bed for hours. You won't get much sleep, but you won't want any."

She ran her hands up his back. This time it was he who moaned. Her fingertips were magic. He hardened even more. This was how he had sex. Fast and hard. But he swore not tonight. He gasped and rolled onto his side.

"I love everything you're doing," he reassured, "but I want this to be…" He stopped himself from blurting *special*. Every moment spent with Quinn was special. "This should be less about me and more about you."

"Oh, El," she cooed, "This isn't about you or me. It's about *us*."

Choked with emotion, he buried his face into her neck and nodded. Though sex was clearly what his body craved, for the first time, his heart had needs. He ran his fingertips over her curves. He'd sample every inch of her body by morning. No matter where life took him, he would always have this memory.

She giggled, tickled by his slow and methodical touch. He grazed his hand between her thighs. She whimpered. He dipped his fingers into her folds. She moaned into his chest. "You like this," he whispered.

She spread her legs. He continued, increasing the pressure ever so slightly. Her eyes fluttered. Her body quivered. Giving her a moment to relax, he returned to pleasuring her.

"I want you," she growled.

He dug into the dresser drawer and grabbed the foil package.

She took it from his hand. "Let me."

Her bossiness was hot.

She trailed her fingers up his thighs. His shaft throbbed in anticipation. She unrolled the condom.

"Please," she begged.

He slipped into her, burying himself in her heat. She

wrapped her smooth legs around his buttocks, rocking him. Her raspy moans grew louder and louder with each of his thrusts.

"Yes, yes," she moaned.

He picked up momentum, pumping faster and harder.

"El," she screamed, her nails digging into his skin as her body quivered.

He gave one last jolt and filled her. Rolling off her, he pulled her into his arms. One date with Quinn, and he was now a snuggler.

Chapter Eighteen

Quinn pulled the quilt over her head, hoping Hudson would stop whining. *No such luck.* She sat up. Eliot tugged her back to the mattress. She snuggled into Eliot's chest, ignoring her impatient canine. After all the special treats she had given Hudson over the years, she deserved five more minutes. Her dog howled, sounding like a sea lion caught in a net.

"Argh," Quinn grumbled, detangling her feet from the covers.

Hudson's bark continued incessantly. His agitation was at a whole new level.

She nudged Eliot. "Someone's at the door."

"They'll go away," he mumbled, pulling her back toward him.

She freed herself from his grasp.

Eliot's eyes popped open. "What's wrong?"

"Raine's here." She scanned the room for her clothes.

"She's with Paula and Malcolm," he mumbled.

"And now they are all at the door. I can't stay."

"But I like you here," he replied, patting the mattress.

She spotted a blanket across an armchair and hurried over.

Eliot sat, resting his elbows on his knees. "You don't like my bed?"

"Don't be ridiculous," she chided, lifting the blanket. "But Raine shouldn't see us like this."

"I don't plan to open the door naked."

"I realize that, but Raine will need an explanation."

He climbed out of bed. "I certainly won't explain last night to a five-year-old."

Quinn gawked at Eliot's body. Hot and chiseled didn't do him justice.

"Did you hear me, Sprinkles?"

"You know that's not what I meant. Where are my clothes," she mumbled.

"Then what do you mean?"

She stood and stared at him. How could he be so clueless? "Before introducing me as your new bedmate, you must tell Raine we're dating. Let her get used to me as…as a woman. We are dating, aren't we?"

He walked to the door and opened it. Hudson barreled out.

"What are you doing?" she yelled.

He tossed her one of his flannel shirts. "I'm answering the door. And yeah, of course, we're dating."

"No, don't."

He walked towards her. "Relax, it's fine."

"Oh my God, what will Paula and Malcolm think?"

"Malcolm will high-five me, and Paula will call you a tart."

"What?" she croaked.

He chuckled. "I'm teasing. Paula says you're the best thing that has ever happened to me. She's right."

Eliot was now fully dressed. Meanwhile, she hobbled around the bedroom, searching for her clothes. She lowered onto all fours and glanced under the bed. "Argh," she mumbled, coming up empty. "Do they have a key?"

"Who?"

"Does Paula and Malcolm have an apartment key?"

"Yeah. I gave them—"

"Eliot," she shouted, remembering the details of last night. "My clothes are in the living room."

"Oh," he responded with an annoying smirk.

"Sputtering *oh* won't make my clothes magically appear. Go get them."

****

Laughing wouldn't earn any points with Quinn, but the situation was comical. Malcolm and Paula had come across far worse than women's clothing in his apartment, but he wouldn't tell Quinn that. She expected—no, she demanded—that he leap into action and retrieve her clothes. He snuck a kiss and sprinted to the living room. "There," he mumbled, seeing her lace bra and panties by the coffee table. He picked them up and tucked them under his arm. Hudson ceased whining and trotted over.

He patted Hudson's head. "Give me a minute, buddy."

Eliot skimmed the living room. Spotting a floral garment should be easy.

Keys jangled in the hallway.

Dammit. Soon, the Wilsons and Raine would barge through the door. He peeked under the sofa. He found the misplaced dress. His gaze switched from the bright-colored garment to the entrance. He felt like he was in a relay race. It didn't matter who had dropped the baton. It was his responsibility to retrieve it. He bent down and scooped Quinn's dress in one swift motion. All he had to do was sprint to the finish line. But before he could pivot, the door flew open.

He shoved Quinn's undergarments into the center of the dress and tightened his fingers around it. No amount of scrunching would make the garment invisible. "You're early," he muttered.

"It's ten," Paula responded, staring at the dog by her feet.

Raine's attention drew to the bright-colored cloth in her brother's hand. "What's that?"

"A dress," he replied.

"For me?"

"It belongs to Quinn."

"She weft her dress?" Although Raine made progress with her speech, she still occasionally mispronounced words.

Malcolm chuckled. "I don't reckon she left it."

Paula swiped her husband's arm and glanced at Eliot. "Why don't you run Quinn's dress into your bedroom."

The flat tone in her voice made Eliot nervous. Though she loved him like a son, she'd be as mad as a rat under a bucket if he disrespected Quinn.

Paula smiled half-heartedly. "Go on, get to your room. Don't keep the poor girl waiting."

"Yes, ma'am." He hurried away.

Stepping through the doorway, he received a whack to his arm.

"What's wrong with you," Quinn snarled.

He couldn't wipe the grin off his face. Sure, Raine's arrival meant no morning sex, but he still felt damn lucky. Quinn's flared nostrils indicated he should nix his elation, but he couldn't stop gawking at her legs. His flannel shirt never looked so great.

"Here," he said, handing over her clothes.

She lightly kissed his lips. "Thanks."

"No, thank you."

She removed the shirt, put on her undergarments, and yanked the dress over her tangled hair. "You know what this looks like?"

"Like we had an amazing evening?"

"I don't want them assuming I'm—"

"Incredible? Kind? Loving?" That was how any lucky bastard who had met her would see her.

"You don't understand. You're a guy. It's different for you."

"Come here." He pulled her into his chest. "Staying over is okay." His lips curled into a mischievous smile. "It was also fun."

"Yes, but—"

"We're adults. We have lives beyond plush toys and pastel-colored cereals. I won't apologize for last night, and neither should you."

"Raine will have questions."

"I doubt it, but if she does, I'll explain it so she understands."

"And Paula and Malcolm? How do you expect me to deal with them?"

"Don't worry. They adore you. They're chuckling out there, not because I got some last night, but because I'm happy. And I'm grinning because of both."

She shook her head. "What will I do with you?"

"Anything you want, Sprinkles."

She turned her back. "Zip me," she ordered.

He kissed her neck and pulled the zipper to the top.

"Let's get this over with." She opened the bedroom door. As soon as she hobbled into the living room, Raine hugged her. "Hi," Quinn muttered to Paula and Malcolm.

“What were you doing in Eliot’s bedroom?” Raine asked.

“I’ve got this,” Eliot whispered to Quinn. “I invited our neighbor for a sleepover,” he answered his sister.

Quinn sputtered a cough.

“Did you play games and eat pizza?” Raine asked.

“We didn’t have pizza, but Quinn insisted we play a game.”

Quinn’s eyes bore into him.

Hudson let out a bark. “I better go,” Quinn grumbled and limped to the door.

“Umm…maybe I should take Huds,” he volunteered. “You’re a little sore.”

He should have clarified she sprained her ankle, but he enjoyed making her blush. Though he had changed, old Eliot still existed.

****

Quinn reached for the pliers. “Argh.” The tool was inches away from her grasp. She swung her foot off the empty chair and stood. In one swift motion, she scooped the pliers into her hand. Her day was spent elevating her ankle and working. She loved creating one-of-a-kind pieces.

She drew inspiration from her emotions. Her loneliness and heartache gave birth to her most stunning artworks. She turned cheating Chad’s betrayal into a successful career. She was proud of her achievements but would have traded it all to avoid the pain.

She sighed, frustrated not by her work but because she chickened out again. Though her father would disagree, she wasn’t brave. At least not as courageous as Eliot. Last night, he bared his soul and revealed the brutal truth about his upbringing. She, however, didn’t reciprocate. The timing wasn't right, and besides, her past didn't haunt her…well, not like Eliot's. Yes, she was overly cautious, and irrational fear surfaced more times than she wished it would, but it wasn't her family that hurt her. Hearing about his past made her admire him even more.

The night she worked on the colored serpent piece became a turning point. Embarrassed for assuming the worst about Eliot, she pulled out the box of shard-like sprinkles. Initially, she designed a happy face to make him laugh, but inspiration hit her halfway through the night. She wanted to create something unique and personal for Eliot. Though she never told him, she titled the work, *Compassion.* Compassion and pity would be too intertwined for Eliot's liking. And though he could not see it, kindness and generosity were at Eliot's core. He readjusted his entire life for his sister and put himself in harm's way for strangers.

The serpent piece turned out better than she imagined. She would have sold it for three or four hundred dollars had Eliot not wanted it. But he called it beautiful. She had an inkling then how much he meant to her.

She placed the chandelier she was working on down. Its completion would have to wait until tomorrow. She promised Eliot she would show up for dinner and thus needed to change. She wasn't about to drag herself across the hallway wearing baggy jeans and a T-shirt. Tonight, she would make an unforgettable impression. After all, it was payback time.

Eliot's blatant insinuation about wearing her out last night mortified her, and doing so in front of Paula and Malcolm made it incredibly annoying. Sure, the sex was next-level amazing, but her pole-vaulting kiss was what led to her ankle injury.

Darn it. How could she stay mad? Those endearing dimples made festering impossible. However, if she didn't take control, his teasing would continue. He had offered to cook her dinner. He even texted her with smiley faces, but a cute emoji wasn't enough. She wouldn't settle for anything less than bringing Eliot to his knees.

She marched to the bedroom closet and thumbed through the hangers until she found the perfect outfit. Tonight, she would exact revenge.

Chapter Nineteen

The door flew open, and Eliot hurried off, cursing.

"What's wrong?" Quinn yelled.

"The potatoes are boiling over."

Raine came charging from her bedroom. She leaped into Quinn's outstretched arms. "Where's Hudson?"

"I left him at my place. Maybe Eliot can go get him later."

"Get who?" Eliot asked, returning to the living room.

"Hudson. I wasn't sure if I should bring him."

"Huds is always wel—" He stopped and stared. "You're wearing glasses."

"Yes," she responded to his ambiguous statement.

"They look good."

Good? What in the world does that mean?

He gave her a chaste kiss on the cheek. "Sorry about running off. I hate the stupid stove. It cooks everything too fast."

Eliot had pecked her like a timid chicken. Did she miss the mark? Maybe sexy librarian wasn't his thing. Or perhaps her eyeglasses reminded him of his grade school teacher.

"You smell good," he whispered. "Real good, Sprinkles."

Now you're talking.

Raine wormed between her brother and Quinn. "Can

we get Hudson?"

"Sure," Eliot responded. "Let's go get him."

"No," Quinn snapped.

Brother and sister stared at her.

She let out a giggle and pushed the bridge of her glasses. "Er…Eliot, you go. And Raine, you stay with me and…umm…show me your room." Her request was pitiful. She had seen Raine's room numerous times, almost every time she visited.

Raine reached for Quinn's hand. "Come see my stuffies."

****

Eliot stared as Quinn walked away. She seemed out of sorts. Maybe she popped one too many pain meds for her ankle. Would it be overbearing to ask what she took and how much? *Nah*. It wasn't as though she had to drive home or handle heavy machinery. Climbing on top of him wasn't what the drug company meant when they recommended no handling of dangerous equipment.

He keyed open her apartment door. Hudson bumped his nose against Eliot's leg, leaving a wet mark on his jeans.

"Hey, bud." He leaned down and scratched Hudson's ear. "Let's get your pillow."

Eliot looked up and burst into laughter. He had been lured here to receive a message. He picked up the sexy bra and panties strung across the hallway mirror. Quinn was in his home, wearing nothing under her cardigan and skirt.

"She doesn't play fair, Huds."

He returned and found Quinn and Raine watching cartoons. He grabbed the remote and turned up the volume. The blaring television would distract his sister while he mounted his counterattack. He let go of Hudson. As anticipated, Hudson jumped on the sofa, nudging his nose into Raine's face.

"In the kitchen, Quinn."

Smiling, Quinn rose and brushed past him. Her flouncy skirt swished as she shimmied her sweet ass to the other room. Had they been alone, he would have grabbed her smooth bare bottom and taken her against the wall.

He turned his head, ensuring Raine wasn't behind him. Reaching the kitchen, he stood as close to Quinn as he could without touching her. Round two would be his. Quinn's sensuous perfume drifted in the air. If the fragrance hadn't had a name, he would have suggested *Uncontrollable Urges*.

"What can I help you with, El?" She fell back against the counter, arching her body. Her chest heaved forward, and her head tilted up. The position was perfect for laying kisses along her neck. He restrained himself. Any contact would be too much of a teaser. Raine's bedtime was a good three hours away.

He stuck his palms on the laminate countertop. Tension filled the air. His lips hovered near her ear. "I could turn up the heat if it's chilly."

"And what makes you think I'm cold?" She undid her loose cardigan to the last button.

Her perky nipples and firm breasts were within reach.

He admired her bold move. "You might have forgotten some clothing at your place. It would be a shame if you caught a cold and were bedridden."

"I assure you I'm warm."

Warm? Not a chance. She was fricking hot.

She rose on her toes and pressed her breasts against his chest. “Later, after Raine goes to bed,” she whispered, “you can break my fever.”

He lifted his hands, freeing her to leave. Her fingers grazed him, tickling his arm hair.

“A suggestion,” she moaned, staring at the bulge in his jeans, “stay here until things settle down.”

Once she left, he stuck his head into the freezer. “Dammit,” he cursed. She had won another round. Going the distance would be impossible.

Quinn kept up the torture. He handled her flirtatious little winks, but her hip swaying undid him.

When seven thirty rolled around, and Raine wanted to watch a movie, he nearly lost his mind. It was a weekend, and he usually would cave, but not tonight.

He smiled at his sister. “Remember how I mentioned Quinn might stay for another sleepover?”

“Yup.”

“She can’t do that unless you go to bed.”

“Why?”

“Because she’s staying in my room.” What he said made no sense, but he was too frustrated to make a logical argument. “I promise Quinn will be here tomorrow morning. And if you go to sleep now, I’ll make all of us chocolate chip pancakes.”

“Read me a story, now?”

“Whatever it takes,” he mumbled.

He read faster than normal, but it still took twenty fricking minutes.

As soon as Raine fell asleep, he grabbed Quinn’s hand and hurried to his bedroom.

She giggled. “Slow down, big boy.”

“You won, Sprinkles. I promise I won’t embarrass

you again." He kissed her neck while his clumsy, impatient fingers struggled to undo her blouse's tiny buttons.

"Don't you get it, Eliot? When I win, you win too."

****

Quinn set the finished chandelier on her coffee table.

Gabby walked around it, inspecting the polished crystals. "Five hundred dollars is a deal. I bet you could get double."

"I think so too, but the company sets the price."

"Look at you. Such confidence. I'm glad you're yourself again."

"What are you talking about?"

"You're embracing life, not sitting alone in your apartment. You're back to being the girl who wears bright colors and dreams large. The Quinn I first met."

"I'm sorry for not being a good friend."

"Don't be silly. You're the best, but I am happy you're whistling bad show tunes again. Aren't you glad I pushed you to keep an open mind about your hot neighbor?"

"Eliot has been a godsend."

Gabby snatched her hand. "You know I like him," she said, softening her voice. "He's good for you, but remember, he's the lucky one."

Quinn pulled Gabby into a hug. "I'm fortunate to have you. You know that, don't you? I would have never gotten through…well, I don't know what I would have done without you."

"Okay, enough with the mushy stuff. Why don't the four of us hang out? We could go clubbing."

"Eliot doesn't drink."

"Then I guess he'll be on the dance floor shaking it."

Quinn sputtered a laugh. "I'll talk to Eliot about his schedule. We'll find something we all will enjoy."

Although finding a suitable activity would be challenging, she was thrilled Gabby suggested it. Gabby and her ex never liked each other. Chad had said her friend was flighty, and Gabby complained Chad was rigid. Both were right, though Quinn preferred Gabby's spontaneity to Chad's obstinacy. Though neither knew it, Eliot and Gabby had common ground. Both had horrible mothers.

Chapter Twenty

"How about a basketball game?" Quinn was on the phone, discussing tonight's double date with Gabby.

"Kiefer hates sports. He won't even watch the Olympics."

"Really?"

"Yup. He hates every single event."

Quinn scrunched her face. *How can anyone dislike the one-hundred-meter dash? It's over within seconds.*

"Don't worry," Gabby said. "I'm sure Eliot and Kiefer will find something in common. If it helps, Kiefer loves literature and poetry. Oh, he's also into hot yoga."

Quinn let out a belabored sigh. "Any other options?"

"No, but I'm sure you'll figure something out."

"Thanks," Quinn grumbled. Gabby would make a great executive. She wore a dazzling smile while others did the work.

"We'll drop by at six. Can I bring anything?"

A different boyfriend. "No, I've got it covered."

After she hung up, she continued to rack her brain. For a second, she considered a rant poetry event, but she doubted Eliot would appreciate the musings of an angsty teen. At a loss, she typed *what men like* into her laptop. Boobs and bacon prevailed.

In the end, her worry was for naught. Without any prompting, Kiefer and Eliot started talking about the blues. Their conversation lasted twenty minutes before they proclaimed Muddy Waters the greatest. Seeing Eliot engrossed, she caught up with Gabby. Her friend's latest audition was a bust. After giving her a pep talk, Quinn turned her attention to the guys.

"I love ducks and drakes. I could play for hours," Kiefer said to Eliot.

"Is it like Dungeons and Dragons?" Gabby asked.

Both men laughed. The kind of chortle reserved for when someone tells an inside joke.

Quinn pulled out her phone. "I'm sure I can find out."

"It's skipping stones across a pond," Eliot confessed.

"Oh…I've done that," Gabby said.

"Yeah, me too, at camp," Quinn added. "We chucked rocks when bored."

Kiefer laughed.

Gabby punched his arm. "What's so funny?"

"How many did you do?"

Gabby stared at Kiefer.

"When you threw the rock, how many times did it skip?" he clarified.

"I don't know," Gabby responded. "It was a long time ago. Maybe three or four."

"I did five…once," Quinn said in the spirit of competitiveness.

"Do you want to know how many I did?" Eliot said.

Quinn feigned a yawn. "Go on, impress me with your ducks and water."

"Ducks and drakes," Kiefer corrected.

Eliot kissed Quinn's cheek. "I did twenty."

"No way," Gabby yelled.

Kiefer glanced at Eliot. "I believe you, man. I did

twenty-five at a county fair."

Eliot gave Kiefer a fist bump.

Quinn smiled. Of all the things to have in common.

The guys spent another ten minutes blathering about technique. Speed, spin, and the right angle for hitting the water were critical.

Gabby stood. "I'm done hanging out at your apartment, Quinn. There's a new place—"

"How about a movie?" Quinn interjected. "That new rom-com received rave reviews."

"Or we could check out MoMA," Eliot suggested. "It's open late tonight."

Quinn lifted her brows. "You want to visit the Museum of Modern Art?"

"Yeah, why not? Unless no one else wants to go."

Kiefer tapped Eliot's arm. "Great idea, man. I've never gone."

Gabby glared at Kiefer. "You've lived in New York for four years. How could you have not gone?"

"I seldom get to Midtown."

"Don't worry," Eliot reassured his new buddy. "Us real New Yorkers avoid the tourist areas. So how about it, ladies?"

Gabby bounced on her heels. "Absolutely."

"And you don't need to ask me twice. I love being mesmerized by Rousseau, Gauguin, Matisse—"

Gabby pulled Quinn to her feet. "Please, no drooling at the van Gogh, my little art nerd."

Quinn left her apartment, accompanied by the actress, the musician, and the man who continually surprised her. Arriving at the museum, Gabby and Kiefer broke from the group, leaving Quinn with Eliot.

After spending a ridiculous amount of time admiring

Starry Night, Quinn glanced at Eliot. “Let me know if I’m going too slow.”

“Don’t worry about me. I’m exactly where I want.”

She smiled at his gorgeous dimples. “Thanks for doing this for me.”

“I’m glad you love this place, but I didn’t do it for you.”

“Oh. Well, it’s a generous gesture coming here for Gabby and Kiefer.”

“Can’t a guy be interested in art?”

“Yes, of course.”

He squeezed her shoulder and kissed her. “Ever since I met you, I wanted to try different things. This is one of them.” He turned, taking in the various paintings and sculptures. “This place is amazing.”

“And so are you,” she muttered under her breath.

****

Quinn stuffed her last fry into her mouth. “Thanks for suggesting this place, Eliot. The food is delicious.”

“The trick to Midtown eating is hitting the back alleys and escaping the overpriced tourist traps. There’s another great place…” His phone buzzed. He snatched the device from his jacket and glanced at the screen. “Work,” he mumbled to Gabby and Kiefer.

Without prompting, Quinn slid from the booth. Eliot kissed her cheek and hurried out of the restaurant. After listening to Gabby moan about how all the good parts went to famous actors or their talentless children, Quinn glanced out the window. She caught sight of Eliot. He stomped the pavement with his phone against his ear, waving his hands frantically. Thankfully, neither Gabby nor Kiefer could see him.

“Eliot’s been gone for a while,” her friend

commented.

"Yeah. I'm sure it's nothing to worry about."

"What does he do?" Kiefer asked.

"He's a teacher," Gabby replied. "Adult education, right?"

Quinn twirled her unused spoon. "He deals mainly with adults." She hated deceiving Gabby, but Eliot asked her not to tell anyone. Though she trusted Gabby, she worried that her friend might pillow talk to Kiefer, and who knew who he would tell? People sucked at keeping secrets, and Kiefer would be no different.

"Does he teach high school equivalency classes?" Gabby asked.

"It's more life skills-based learning." Quinn wasn't lying, for Eliot delivered life lessons to bad guys.

She stole another glance out the window. Eliot continued pacing. At least his troubles weren't about Raine…unless… Quinn's pulse quickened. She rose from her seat. "I'm going to check on Eliot." She feigned a smile and hurried off.

The crisp night air sent a chill down her back. She crossed her arms and walked toward Eliot's gruff voice.

"How the hell did that happen?" he yelled into his phone.

"That's not about Raine, is it?" Her voice quivered with emotion.

He glanced at her and raised his hand. "Call me when you find out," he told the caller.

Quinn grabbed Eliot's arm. "What's wrong?"

"Carly's back on the street."

"But how?"

"She's a sex worker, not a violent criminal. There's insufficient evidence linking her to drug trafficking, so she was set free."

"That's ridiculous."

"It's how it works," he grumbled. "I'm sure Carly's more interested in scoring drugs, but I'll collect Raine…just in case."

"Give me a second. I'll let Gabby and Kiefer know we're leaving."

"No, it's okay. I'll get Raine." He pulled out his wallet. "Here, this is for dinner. Tell your friends I enjoyed hanging out with them."

She swatted away his hand, refusing his money. "Don't you dare ditch me. I'm coming with you. I care what happens to Raine."

"Fine. But I'm paying the damn restaurant bill."

Quinn plopped beside Raine on the living room sofa and increased the television's volume. They were at the Wilsons' home and the adults were in the other room discussing Carly.

Why couldn't the vile woman disappear?

Carly had inflicted enough pain on Eliot to last a lifetime. And now she was targeting his vulnerable little sister. She hated Carly for what she had done to her offspring. Yes, Eliot was fearless regarding his job, but he crumbled every time Carly dropped into his life.

Raine poked Quinn's arm. "Why the face?"

"What face, sweetie?"

"You're crinkly in the head."

Quinn laughed. Raine was right. She had been scowling with her forehead. She scrunched her nose. "How about this?"

Raine giggled. They continued making silly faces until the adults entered the room.

"Ready to go?" Eliot asked Raine.

His sister pulled her cheeks down with her hands. "Not until you make this face."

He tilted his head sideways, bulging his eyes.

"You're funny," his little sister said.

He grabbed Raine's coat from the closet. "Go thank Paula and Malcolm for taking you to the movies."

On the ride home, Raine fell asleep.

"Want me to wake her?" Quinn asked Eliot when the cab stopped at their building.

"Nah." He lifted his sister into his arms. "Sorry, Sprinkles, for ruining our date."

"There's no need to apologize." She glanced at Raine's long lashes snuggled into her brother's massive shoulder. "You do know Raine's welcome to stay at my place."

"Carly won't show up tonight. She'll head to the nearest drug house. By now, she's passed out."

Quinn's face crumbled under the weight of sorrow. She wanted to hug him, but restrained herself. He detested pity like a poison. "See you tomorrow, El."

"Hey, Quinn?"

She pivoted, her shoes squeaking against the floor.

"It has been a long day but can…." His voice quivered. "Will you stay, Sprinkles?"

"Of course."

"I'm sorry about being a dick earlier. I didn't want you canceling your evening because of my problems."

"I care about Raine."

"I know."

"I care about you too."

He leaned down and kissed Quinn. "Let's get little Sleepyhead to bed."

****

Quinn awoke to Eliot staring at her. She tugged the covers and retreated under the blankets.

"What are you doing?"

She patted her frizzy hair. "I look like a startled alpaca caught in an electric fence."

He removed the bedsheet from her face. "You're beautiful."

She scootched into his chest. He brushed her lips with his. There was no flinching at her stale breath. A tinge of blue emerged from his eyes' outer rims. Yesterday's fear and panic had vanished from his face.

"Thanks for staying, Sprinkles."

"Thanks for inviting me."

His hands slid to her bottom. "Perhaps I should express my gratitude."

"I appreciate politeness in a man."

"What I have in mind is far from polite."

An intrusive buzzing spoiled her excitement.

"Stupid phone," he muttered.

Knowing Carly was still out there, Quinn leaned across the nightstand and handed Eliot the phone.

Chapter Twenty-One

Eliot scowled and climbed out of bed. “This can’t be good.”

“Perhaps it’s nothing to worry about,” Quinn said.

He yanked his jeans over his hips, scowling at her perpetual optimism. “Omeir insists on coming over.” In Eliot’s experience, people delivered bad news in person. “I won’t let Carly take her.”

Quinn squeezed his hand. “Don’t assume the worst. We’ll figure it out, I promise.”

He kept his gaze down, hiding his watery eyes. Crying in front of others made him feel weak. He hadn’t publicly shed a tear since he was a boy.

Quinn kissed his cheek. “I’ll check on Raine and make coffee.”

Once she was gone, Eliot pounded his fist into a pillow. He’d give anything to rid Carly from his life.

****

Eliot had yet to drink the coffee Quinn had placed in his hands ten minutes ago, but he had splattered half of it on the wooden floors while pacing.

“What’s taking Omeir so long?” he grumbled, taking a reprieve from spilling coffee.

Quinn glanced up from the sofa. “He’s probably caught in traffic.”

“Or at Fazaris having lunch.”

Hearing a knock, Eliot jolted. “About time,” he

grumbled, marching to the entranceway. He flung the door open. About to erupt, Eliot noticed Safia. He stepped aside and gave Omeir a heated glare.

Raine bounded into the room. "Are you here for pancakes?"

"No, kiddo, not today," Omeir replied.

Safia crouched down. "Hey, Raine, why don't you show me your room? I hear Eliot painted it."

As soon as Safia and Raine left, Omeir addressed Quinn. "Can we talk at your place?"

Eliot stormed into the hallway before Quinn replied. He waited until they were inside her apartment before he spoke. "So, where the hell is Carly?"

"Buddy, you should sit for this," Omeir said.

Eliot remained standing. "What's she planning?"

"Nothing," Omeir replied.

"Right," Eliot grunted and started pacing. "You can't be that naïve."

Quinn stepped in front of him. "Give Omeir a chance to speak."

Eliot dodged around her, increasing his stride until he was trapped again, this time by Omeir. "Move," Eliot ordered.

Omeir didn't budge. "Carly won't be bothering you."

"Yeah, right. She'll get out of jail and try this shit again. She'll get a lenient judge to hear her sob story about how she's a victim, how—"

"She's dead."

Eliot stood motionless. Not a single body muscle twitched.

Quinn hurried to his side. He raised his hand, warning her not to invade his sacred space. After several silent seconds, he sat.

"What happened?" Quinn asked Omeir.

"They found her at a flophouse in Queens. They're waiting for the toxicology reports, but it appears she OD'd on opioids, likely heroin."

Eliot dropped his gaze, fixating on a snag in the carpet. "Are you sure it's Carly?"

"An outreach worker ID'd her." Omeir softened his voice for a moment. "I'll take you to the morgue if you want."

"Seen plenty of corpses with needles stuck in them. No need to see another."

Quinn's hand pressed his shoulder. "I'm sorry."

He rose from the sofa, distancing himself from everyone. "It was bound to happen. I'm surprised it took so long."

Quinn marched over and touched his arm. He shook loose like an injured animal recoiling from an open wound. "I'm fine," Eliot grumbled. He turned away, hiding the tears that threatened to spill.

****

Quinn entered Eliot's apartment and cleared her throat. "Maybe we should talk about Carly's death." Two weeks had passed since Omeir had dropped the bombshell.

"It's bad taste to rejoice, and I sure the hell ain't gonna mourn the woman."

Eliot's reply was cold and candid, just as Quinn expected but not as she hoped. She had comforted him when his mother was still alive, and he was terrified. But now, he had shut her out, becoming avoidant and despondent.

He still gave Raine his time. He sat on the floor

mimicking play, but his face held no expression. Quinn knew about growing numb. Because of Michael, she had pushed people away and refused to talk. But her parents and Gabby persisted. Eventually, she stopped hating herself.

"Will you turn off the TV?" Quinn asked. Eliot despised two sports—golf and tennis—and he had watched both today.

"What for?"

"So we can get to Lights Outs on time. Remember, you promised you'd spar." The kids loved when Eliot entered the ring. While Walt doled out the encouragement, Eliot supplied them with technique.

"What about Raine?"

The Wilsons had picked up Raine an hour ago. They had a full day of fun planned for her.

"Paula won't be dropping her off until dinner."

"Fine," he grumbled and rose to his feet.

Arriving at the gym, Quinn hurried through the office paperwork and then hung around to watch Eliot spar. "Liven up," she muttered, seeing Eliot's half-ass effort in the ring.

He was with Jordie, a sixteen-year-old boy who tended to move slowly. His punches were solid, but he lacked speed. Jordie habitually lost his balance and tumbled to the mat when his opponents ducked.

The teen had taken several jabs, which Eliot blocked. They had another two minutes left when Eliot dropped his guard, and Jordie landed a solid hit to Eliot's chest. The kid connected hard—not enough for Eliot to fall, but he wobbled.

Jordie froze. A few younger kids had landed shots on Eliot before, but only because he allowed them to.

"Hit me again," Eliot demanded.

Confusion flashed over the teenager's face.

"Keep going," Eliot barked. "Come on, give it all you got."

Jordie glanced at Quinn. She mouthed *don't*, but he didn't see as Eliot had diverted Jordie's attention by striking the teen's shoulder.

"Take a hard punch," Eliot yelled.

And Jordie did, landing a heavy blow to Eliot's chin. This time Eliot's head snapped back. Within a nanosecond, he straightened, bouncing from toe to toe.

Fear flashed across the kid's face, like a hiker encountering a hungry grizzly.

"Now that's how to land one." Eliot stepped out of the ring with a satisfied smirk.

Quinn's shoulders sank. Dragging Jordie into Eliot's mess was uncalled for. She glared at Eliot. A wry grin lit his face. Whether he enjoyed the pain or felt the need to be punished was unclear. The situation was, however, disturbing. And though pissed at him, she was far more worried. Eliot, who had fought hard his entire life, had ceased battling.

Chapter Twenty-Two

Since the incident early in the week, Eliot hadn't returned to the gym, and Quinn didn't urge him to. His foul attitude had no place around the kids. Thankfully, Walter hadn't been around, and Jordie didn't understand what Eliot had done. In all likelihood, the teen's so-called clobbering of the big guy would make him a legend with his peers.

She had confronted Eliot about letting Jordie hit him. "Life is rough. He needs to toughen up to survive," he had said and then avoided her for several days. So today, when he called and asked her to take Raine overnight, she was surprised.

"I have to work," he explained, "An all-nighter. I'd get Paula and Malcolm, but I gotta go now."

"Sure," she responded. Getting away from Eliot would do Raine some good. He was never ill-tempered with his sister, but he wasn't as engrossed in her activities as he should be.

After an evening doing crafts, Quinn made up the futon in her studio room and tucked Raine into bed. She fell asleep within minutes. At least one Traversini was easy to deal with.

She hadn't expected Eliot until morning, but a knock sounded at her door around two a.m. At first, she ignored it, figuring someone had mistakenly called on the wrong apartment. But when Hudson barked, she got up and checked.

Peeking through the peephole, she recognized Omeir. Confused, she opened the door. "What are you…" She stopped and glared at the arm hanging around Omeir's neck. An overwhelming stench of alcohol permeated the air.

Eliot lifted his head. "Hey, Quinnie, how ya doin'?"

"Better than you," she sniped.

Eliot's chin dropped. He appeared to pass out.

"Where do you want him?" Omeir grunted.

"Not here." She motioned across the hallway.

"Great," Omeir grumbled.

"Hold on." She dug into her purse for the key Eliot had given her.

"You're heavy," Omeir mumbled, dragging his friend's dead weight.

"Nope. I'm drunk and chw…chwisseled," Eliot slurred and then laughed.

Quinn unlocked the door and shoved it open.

"Sofa or bed?" Omeir asked.

"Sofa." Eliot deserved to be uncomfortable, though he could probably lie across barbed wire and feel nothing.

Omeir maneuvered around the coffee table and unloaded his friend onto the leather couch. He swung Eliot's tree trunk legs over the end and heaved a sigh. "Should I tilt him on his side?"

Quinn nodded because shaking the stupidity out of Eliot wasn't an option. She leaned to remove Eliot's boots. Eliot's large hand touched her shoulder. He pulled her close, mumbling incoherently. She whacked his hand away. A second later, he delivered a clamoring snorechestra.

Grunting, Omeir placed Eliot in a position commonly used to prevent overindulgent college students from asphyxiating on vomit. “That should do,” Omeir said, leaning over and stretching.

“What happened?” Quinn whispered.

“I hauled a brick house on my shoulders. I’m trying to get sensation back in my body.”

“No, not you,” she snapped. “What happened to him?” Concealing her annoyance proved futile.

“He drank too much.”

“I can see that. What I meant…” She stopped mid-sentence. Omeir wouldn’t have the answer she wanted. Only the lump on her sofa could answer why he had chosen drunken stupidity over discussing his feelings.

“I found him this way.”

She bit down on her lip. Omeir wasn’t to blame. He didn’t drink. This was all Eliot’s doing. “Where did you find him?”

“At a sports bar in Queens. He called me around ten, asking me to meet him. He sounded sober, so I didn’t think anything of it. I was having coffee with…” He glanced at his feet. “I was with a friend. I told Scorp I would drop by in an hour or so. I assumed you were with him.”

“I wasn’t.”

“Yes, I realized that when I got there.”

She grew suspicious. Omeir wasn’t telling her something. She leaned forward as if interfering with Omeir’s personal space would rattle the truth from him. “Was someone with Eliot?”

“No.”

“Sure,” she grumbled. *Men. They always covered for each other.*

"I'm not lying. Ask Safia if you don't believe me."

"Safia?"

Omeir stuck his hands in his pockets. "I was with her. We were having coffee when Scorp called. She accompanied me to the bar and helped me reason with him."

Though the detective was guilty of concealing a coffee date, he seemed to be telling the truth.

"He didn't want to leave?"

"He's drunk. Nothing he says makes sense. I worried he'd pass out at the bar. We got him to his feet and paid his tab. I still can't believe he drank that much."

"Did he say why he got drunk?"

"His speech was all slurry. Anything I did understand, I wouldn't repeat to a lady. After loading him in my car, we brought him here. I tried getting his apartment keys, but he was combative when I dug into his pockets. She figured you might have a spare."

"She?"

"I already told you. I was with Safia discussing a case."

She ignored the trailing cloud of desperation in his explanation. He could have told her they had tequila shots in a strip club, and she wouldn't have cared. She was, however, curious about Safia's take on Eliot. "Where's Safia?"

"She's downstairs. She thought it best…er…I mean, I told her I could handle Scorp by myself. I better get going."

As he turned to leave, Quinn grabbed his arm. "I'm sorry about snapping. I'm not mad at you. I'm…" She stopped, unsure of what to tell Omeir. Eliot's behavior stung. Why had Eliot not come to her? Did he believe she wasn't strong enough to handle his grief, or was she insignificant to him? After Carly's death, he iced her out. She stayed patient, giving him ample time to come around. Instead, he turned to the bottle. Though Eliot falling off the wagon was troubling, there was something bigger gnawing at Quinn.

"I haven't known Scorp for a long time," Omeir said, "but he's a good guy."

She huffed. The so-called good guy was acting like a tool.

"He's been sober for quite some time until tonight. He's trying, Quinn. He really is. It's why he called me. He knows I wouldn't get drunk with him. He knew I would deliver him to you."

"Did he mention he wanted to see me?" A moment ago, Omeir had said Eliot's speech was incoherent.

"Um, not exactly in those words."

She forced a smile. "I appreciate you bringing him home. Tell Safia thanks."

"No problem, but as far as you're concerned, Safia wasn't involved."

"Sure," she muttered, gazing at Eliot. He had drifted to sleep. Had he irrevocably drifted from her too?

Chapter Twenty-Three

Hudson's bark alerted Quinn to someone at the door. She anticipated Eliot's visit, though she suspected he'd arrive much later. When she checked on him earlier, he was sleeping like a clobbered caveman. She made periodic visits throughout the night to ensure he was still breathing. Although he was a drunken numbskull, he was all the family Raine had.

Quinn wiped her hands on the dish towel. "Finish your breakfast," she said to Raine and followed Hudson from the kitchen. She opened the door to Eliot's ashen face. A roadmap of red lines engulfed his once-piercing mischievous eyes. He stepped forward. She jabbed her finger into his chest. He retreated. She joined him in the hallway, shutting the door behind her.

"Go shower. You smell like a rodent caught in a beer vat." She wanted him gone before Raine finished eating her Honey Sparkles.

"Yeah, I will. I just came to tell you I'm sorry." He smiled as though cute dimples would excuse his behavior.

"Save your apology for Omeir."

"What did I do to him?"

"For starters, he covered your bar tab. You owe him a couple hundred."

"I drank two hundred dollars' worth of booze?"

"No, but he'll need the extra for chiropractic

treatments. He practically carried you home."

His gaze dropped to the carpet. "I'll call him later."

"Go," she ordered. "Raine's eating breakfast. I'll send her over in an hour. I hope you're completely sober by then."

"I'm truly sorry."

"So I heard." She stepped back and then stopped. "Raine doesn't need this. She's gone through enough. You, of all people, should know that. I'll cover for you this time, but you better not put her or me in this position again."

"Thanks," he mumbled, shuffling across the hallway. "Hey," he said, turning around. "What did you tell Raine?"

"I told her you made it home but were too sick to care for her."

"What?"

"Did you want me to tell her you got plastered and passed out?"

"You told her I'm sick."

"What's with the tone? I did you a favor."

He raked his fingers through his hair. "You should never have said…" he gasped. "Carly," he stammered.

"What about her?"

"When Raine asked why her mother yelled and hit her, I said she was sick."

She shrugged. She hadn't the foggiest what he was rambling about. Perhaps he was still drunk.

The pained expression on his face intensified. For a moment, Quinn worried he might vomit.

"Raine will presume I'm like Carly. That I'm a sick bastard who will hurt her."

"Oh my God, what have I done?"

"It's my fault. I'm the one who screwed up. You didn't know."

"We have to fix this."

He rubbed the back of his neck. "Yeah, I know. Let me think."

His brainstorming seemed to last forever.

"I'll be back in a minute," he hollered, breaking the silence. "Go get Raine."

She didn't move.

"Please, Quinn…for Raine." he pleaded.

****

Eliot rummaged underneath the kitchen sink. His headache had gone from throbbing to exploding. "How could I be so foolish?" he muttered.

His sister's thought processes weren't like an adult's. Raine wasn't even an average kid. She was an abused and neglected five-year-old. And because of his stupidity and weakness, she had been re-traumatized.

He barreled back through Quinn's door with an empty liquor bottle. He had kept the container as a reminder of his promise to do and be better. He was strong the day he poured the booze down the sink. Now with the bottle in hand, doubt flooded him. Would this work, or would it make things worse? With no other sensible idea, he kneeled. He wanted his sister to see his face and not his kneecaps.

Raine edged toward Quinn, gazing at the floor.

"I promised I would never lie to you, and I meant it," Eliot said, terrified he had lost his place as his sister's protector.

Raine was so close to Quinn that she was practically on top of her.

He swallowed his breath. "When Quinn said I was

sick, she wasn't referring to a Carly kind of sick."

Quinn crouched and took Raine's hand. "It's true. Eliot's nothing like Carly was."

His sister gazed at him. Though unsure, he sensed trust in her eyes. How could he have been so careless? Regret flowed through his body. He glanced at Quinn, aching to hold her and his sister. "What happened to me last night is what Quinn feels when she eats ice cream." He felt the sting from Quinn's heated glare. Panic had made him compare lactose intolerance to a drunken stupor.

Raine's bottom lip protruded. "You had ice cream without me?"

"No, I drank what was in this bottle and became sick. But it's a different kind of sickness. It's more like a tummy ache. It's not a sickness that causes me to hurt others. It's not like Carly's illness. I'll never hurt you…or Quinn."

His shoulders sank. He had hurt Quinn. He had let her down.

"I would never hit you," he corrected. He lifted the bottle. "This stuff is bad for me. Real bad. I can't tolerate it. Some people can, but not me. It's like…It's like ice cream." *Shit, back to the lactose.* He shot Quinn an apologetic grin and went back to Raine. "You and I can eat ice cream, but Quinn can't. And I can't *ever* drink this."

Raine pointed at the bottle. "Lemme see."

"Sure, but there's nothing left." He reached out his hand. Raine ran to him. Although the tiny fingers wrapped around his hand didn't lessen his guilt, he realized he was a lucky bastard to have her in his life. With his free hand, he twisted off the whiskey bottle's cap.

Raine stuck her nose over it. “Eww. It’s stinky.”

“So I’ve been told,” he said and hugged Raine.

A tear trickled down Quinn’s cheek. He reached for her. She shook her head. Women had rejected him before, but this was the first time it hurt.

Chapter Twenty-Four

Raine forgave him, but Quinn still wasn't there. Perhaps forgiveness was easier for his kid sister, who didn't grasp the extent of his problems or how complex they were. Though he had gone on far worse benders, this one felt different. He wasn't just messing up his life. He was affecting others. After several weeks of mulling over what happened, he hauled his stupid ass to Dr. Momani, the NYPD shrink.

Eliot didn't tell a soul about the counseling sessions—not the Wilsons, not his colleagues, and certainly not Quinn. There was no need to worry them or further their disappointment if he failed.

At the psychiatrist's suggestion, he went to AA meetings. He chose a group specific to first responders. The majority of the attendees came from law enforcement. He dreaded those meetings. Even after the fifth one, he still felt a knot of discomfort and shame in his stomach. But his life was never about comfort. It was about survival. And to survive, he needed both Raine and Quinn. So he sucked it up, ignored his ego, and continued attending. He spent years kidding himself that his drinking was under control, but when he risked everything, including Raine and Quinn, the truth became apparent. He was an addict.

Through therapy, he recognized the connection between his destructive behaviors and the past. He spent a lifetime wishing his mother would cease to exist, and then it happened. Logically, he knew he bore no responsibility for her passing. He couldn't use mind powers to find Raine's lost coloring book, so thinking malicious thoughts had killed his mother was stupid. Besides, the toxicology reports confirmed a heroin overdose. But Carly's death messed with his head. He should have told Quinn, but he was terrified his vulnerability would lead to exposing one last secret—the one which would forever ruin his relationship with Quinn. But he screwed up anyways, and now he spent today's session talking about the consequences of telling Quinn everything.

"It's a big decision," Dr. Useless said. "Write down your worst and best possible scenarios."

The psychiatrist, who others described as top-notch, never provided answers. He hardly ever spoke other than to ask vague questions. Unsure how this therapy crap worked, Eliot revealed events he had blocked out long ago. He was powerless about his violent upbringing, and now, a lifetime later, he felt the same crushing helplessness.

Near the end of the session, Eliot stopped mid-sentence and cursed, though it was not in anger. "That's it," he muttered.

"Elaborate," the man said in his calm, therapeutic voice that could make a caffeinated toddler sleep.

"I know what you're doing."

"I'm doing something?"

"Yeah. Week after week, I come here, seeking answers. I always leave confused and frustrated. You never tell me what to do. You spin around what I say and ask how I feel about this or that. The same old routine."

"Not how I would phrase these sessions, but go on."

"You want me to resolve my own issues."

The man smirked. "As you repeatedly reminded me, it is your life."

"That's the point, isn't it? You want me to be…what's the word?"

"If you cannot recall the word, describe the feeling."

"Hmph," Eliot grumbled. *Here we go with feelings.* "You want me to figure things out for myself. I'm right, aren't I?"

"Yes. And why might I do that?"

Eliot let out a breath. "Because I have choices."

"Yes. Not as many as you want or easy ones, but you have options."

Dr. Momani glanced at the wall clock. "See you next week."

Eliot shuffled out of the therapist's office, muttering, "Shouldn't I get a refund for providing my own damn answers?" Stepping into the building's empty elevator, he called Quinn. "Hey," he said when she answered. "Raine's at Paula and Malcolm's on Thursday, and I thought maybe you could come over for dinner. I'll order pizza from that place you like."

"I can't."

"How about Friday? I can see if Paula can switch days."

"It's not the day that's the problem."

"Then what is?"

"I need some time."

"For what?"

"To decide what I want."

"Quinn," he begged, "give me a chance to—"

"Give Raine a hug for me," she said, ending the call.

He stared at his screen. “Choices,” he said, trying to convince himself. There were alternatives to drinking away his sorrows. He thumbed through his phone, placed a call, and headed out the door.

He arrived at Fazaris a little after six. The tiny Middle-Eastern eatery had the best beef kebabs, but he had no appetite today.

“What’s with you?” Omeir asked when Eliot sank into the booth.

“Nothing,” he grumbled.

“You look like you’ve lost your best friend, but that can’t be because I’m here.”

Eliot scowled. He was in no mood for Omeir’s joking.

“Sorry, Scorp. I gather Quinn’s still upset.”

“She talks to me when Raine is around. Otherwise, she avoids me.”

“I’m no relationship expert, but shouldn’t you take her to dinner instead of me? Not that I mind a free meal.”

“She refuses to spend time alone with me.”

“That’s rough. Quinn was livid the night I dropped you off, but I thought she’d relax once she realized you weren’t with another woman.”

Eliot jolted. “She thought I was with someone else?”

Omeir nodded.

“But why?”

“An assumption, I guess. You do have a pretty bad track record. But don’t worry. I made sure we told Quinn we found you alone.”

“We?” he asked.

“English is my second language. Sometimes I mix my pronouns. Anyways, Quinn knows you weren’t with a woman.”

Eliot pounded his fist on the table. “That’s it.”

Coffee overflowed and spilled on Omeir’s hand.

“Sorry,” Eliot said, wiping the spilled beverage with his napkin. “I figured out what’s really bugging Quinn. Because I went back to drinking, she’s afraid I’ll be *that guy* again.”

“What guy?”

“The Scorp you first met.”

“Oh, that schmuck,” Omeir said, snickering. “If it weren’t for Zak, I would have punched you out.”

He let the comment go and pulled a stack of bills from his wallet. “Here’s for the other night. And don’t tell me it’s too much. I know what an A-hole I was.” He leaned in and whispered, “And sorry about interrupting your date.”

Omeir glanced at him.

“I wasn’t passed out the entire time,” Eliot said.

“We met for coffee, that’s all.”

Eliot smirked and pulled the menu from Omeir. His appetite had returned.

****

Eliot had made his decision. He would tell Quinn the truth as soon as his shift was over. She would know more about his life than even Omeir could hack into. Omeir was incredible at his job, but sometimes he missed a few details. For instance, he did miss the woman who had visited his table that night at the bar. But that was irrelevant, for Eliot had sent her away. Even when drunk and miserable, his heart belonged to Quinn. Eliot had been done with one-night stands months ago. His skirt-chasing days ended the night he brought Raine home. He had no intention of staying celibate forever, but he was done picking up random women. Abstinence was never the goal, but neither was a long-term relationship. But somewhere between watching baseball and shopping for kids' clothes, he fell for Quinn. And now he couldn't imagine his life without the sexy ginger. He cared about Quinn, really cared. And it was past time he told her.

Okay, maybe he'd give Quinn a condensed version of his drunken night and leave out what Lieutenant Pratt called the extraneous details. Talking about the woman who offered to ease his sorrows served no purpose. What was important was that the only woman he wanted that night, and for all future moments, was Quinn Merrick. Hell, he'd go all out with the truth. Quinn would hear about his counseling sessions and the AA meetings. Though he preferred not to, he'd tell her about his father. Eliot kept his promise. He never lied to Raine or Quinn. He merely omitted information. But a relationship deserving of Quinn meant divulging the truth—all of it. So, after work, he'd find out how much the past mattered.

Chapter Twenty-Five

Quinn's body went cold. "A work incident? What do you mean?"

"Scorp went to Queens to question a witness," Safia said. "It was a routine follow-up on a case, nothing which would require backup. When he got there, a guy jumped him. Information received indicates the perp was high. Not sure what he had ingested. My guess is meth. Ironically, the guy wasn't connected to an official case."

"How's Eliot?"

"Why don't you sit?"

"Tell me." she snapped.

"He was roughed up, but nothing major."

She despised the female detective's calm voice. Eliot had been assaulted, not bumped by a toddler with a grocery store cart. "Where is he? I need to see him."

"He's in the hospital."

"Hospital? You said what happened wasn't anything major."

Safia patted her shoulder. "It's not. He needs to remain overnight because of the concussion."

"Concussion? I have to see him."

"He doesn't want you or Raine visiting him, but you should go to him, and so should Raine."

"It's bad, isn't it?" She panted. "He might not make it?"

"I'm sorry, Quinn—"

"Oh no," she screamed.

Safia shook Quinn's shoulders. "Calm down. He's not dying, nor is he in ICU. He's bruised and has a few broken ribs, but he's healthy enough to grouch at Omeir and me. Essentially, he doesn't want you or Raine visiting because he doesn't want you guys worrying, but he's miserable. He's been like that for a while now. Seeing you and Raine might make him a little less ornery, or at least I hope so."

"He's okay?"

Safia let out an exasperated breath. "Yes. I'm sorry I didn't convey it better. My lieutenant tells me I should work on my people skills. He might have a point."

"Are Eliot's bruises bad?"

"I haven't spoken to the doctor, but I assume he's not permanently disfigured if that concerns you."

"Geez, Safia, I'm not concerned about how he looks, but maybe we should hold off taking Raine. Seeing Eliot in the hospital might be too much for her."

"I'm not an expert on children, but I think it's important she sees that her brother is okay. You might not know this, but my father is with the force. My parents tried to shield me when he got hurt the first time. I was around Raine's age. They meant well, but not visiting him made me imagine the worst. Raine's a smart kid. She'll know something's wrong when her brother doesn't come home after work. Sure, you can lie, but kids are perceptive. Look at how unglued you were. I doubt you could fool her for long."

Quinn sniffled. "He's really all right?"

"You'll see how healthy he is when he yells at me for ignoring his wishes."

****

Quinn sat in the backseat of Safia's vehicle, preparing Raine for what she would experience.

"You know how Eliot keeps bad guys from harming people?"

"Um-hum."

"Well, a bad guy punched Eliot today, but your brother is strong, and his owies will heal."

Raine crossed her arms and pouted. "I don't like bad guys."

Quinn pushed back the soft curls from Raine's face. Her eyes were the same beautiful color as Eliot's. "We're going to visit your brother in the hospital. He has cuts and bruises, so he'll look different. You understand?"

"Josh in my class got owies. He fell and cut his knee. The blood was gross."

"It's kind of what happened to Eliot, but it's his face, not his knee. Seeing him might scare you, and if it does, please tell me. It'll take time for the marks on his face to fade, but he's okay."

"If he looks gross, can I tell him?"

Quinn nodded. Having dealt with terrorists, Eliot could handle his sister's candid comment.

"Eliot says we should always tell the truth."

Quinn flushed, embarrassed she hid her secrets. At first, staying quiet was the right thing to do. Eliot's issues with Carly took priority. Then later, Quinn lost her nerve, fearing the fallout from speaking the truth.

Entering the hospital, she spotted Omeir in the corridor. Her heartbeat quickened, returning to a normal rhythm when Omeir smiled.

"The nurses booted me out of Eliot's room to change his bandages," he said. "They'll let us know when they're done. I'm headed to the cafeteria. You want anything?"

"Can I have ice cream?" Raine asked.

"Absolutely, kiddo," Omeir replied. "Want to come with me to get it?"

Raine glanced at Quinn.

"Go ahead, sweetie, but get a small cone. We'll be eating dinner later."

Raine took Omeir's hand and hurried off.

Quinn leaned against the wall next to Safia. A moment of silence passed. Safia glanced at Quinn and then stared at the nurse's station. She repeated this a couple more times, all without uttering a word. Unsure what was bothering Safia, Quinn checked her phone for messages.

"Ahem…" Safia said, clearing her throat. "I've already meddled in Scorp's life today, so why not continue?"

Quinn lifted her gaze.

"I don't get why you're fighting with him."

"I'm not." Safia's knowledge of her personal life irritated her. Eliot, who avoided discussing his feelings, had no problem babbling to his attractive work colleague.

"There's considerable tension between you two. Yes, Scorp messed up getting drunk, but he hasn't done so since…not since Raine came into his life. If you're unwilling to give him a second chance, be honest and tell him it's over."

"I never said I was done with him."

"That's the impression you're giving."

Quinn stepped forward and glanced down the hallway. "You think the nurses are done changing Eliot's bandages?"

"You lack patience," Safia said.

And you, lady, lack tact.

"Getting back to our discussion. I'm not a warm huggy person, so I don't have a lot of friends, but I protect the ones I do have."

"So, I'm the problem, and Eliot is some innocent bystander?"

"I didn't say that. Just hear me out. He wants what we all want—someone who loves us despite our imperfections. To Scorp, you were that person. I was happy for him. I truly was, but then you abandoned him when he desperately needed your support."

"Excuse me? Eliot's the one who—"

"Yes. I know. He got drunk. I'm not dismissing his behavior."

"Sounds like you are."

"I just don't get how you think a man who suffered so much trauma won't stumble along the way."

"It's not so simple."

"You're the one making it complicated." Safia's voice rumbled with harshness. She was intimidating. Gabby could be blunt, but Quinn had known Gabby forever and understood the vulnerability behind her tough exterior. She doubted this woman had any weaknesses.

"Safia, I need to ask you something, but I don't want you mad at Omeir."

"Why would I be mad at him?"

"Because it's about the night you and Omeir collected Eliot from the bar."

"What's wrong with that man? He can't zip his lips about anything."

"That's not what this is about. Besides, I forced the

story from Omeir." She hadn't, but she'd hate for Safia to go ballistic on the guy.

Safia sighed. "Go ahead."

"Was Eliot…was there…"

"What?" Safia barked.

Now, who's the impatient one? "Were any women around him? I don't mean, were any women inside the bar. I mean, was he flirting?"

"I know what you're asking," Safia snapped.

Quinn rubbed her temple. "I didn't mean any offense."

"I know what Scorp's like. He's charming. He's wickedly smart in a way different from the college grads I work with. He's… Let's say he's intriguing. But I've seen how he operates. The bad boy image is so cliché. Ever since I met him, I wondered if he realized the ridiculousness of jumping from one woman to another. Obviously not, as he continued to be a player."

Safia's words boiled like water, evaporating Quinn's faith in Eliot.

"Omeir sees the good in others, but I'm a cynic," Safia continued. "People always say they can change, but few do. When Omeir told me Scorp wasn't the same guy he once was, I didn't buy it."

Quinn opened her mouth, but Safia continued speaking.

"I was surprised Scorp had a kid sister and shocked to learn he wanted to raise her. From what I can see, he's doing a great job. Though he's good for Raine, she's also been good for him. But she's not the only one who makes him happy. When I first met you, Eliot was having an awful day. I've witnessed a few of them. He does a good poker face, but this time he didn't. He let his guard down.

He doesn't do vulnerable. But he did with you. He trusts you."

"And I want to trust him."

"Scorp's like an annoying big brother in a close-knit family. I can be fond of him and still hold him to account."

"What does that mean?"

"I don't owe you any loyalty, but I hate seeing any woman being strung along. It's different when they know the score."

Quinn swallowed the slab of anxiety in her throat. "Go on," she squeaked.

"When we arrived at the bar, Omeir rushed to the restroom. He's incapable of handling more than one coffee. I've done stakeouts with him. It's like being with a toddler. He either babbles incessantly or runs to the lavatory."

Yadda, Yadda. Get to the point, lady.

"Omeir told me to wait. He was worried I'd make a scene. How ridiculous is that? Scorp was the drunk one, and Omeir was concerned I'd be loud and argumentative."

"And you listened?"

"I used his suggestion to my advantage. Scorp hadn't seen us walk in, so I observed him."

Safia's recounting of events, was the equivalent of at-home dentistry—slow and excruciatingly painful. "Scorp was drunk. I could tell by the way his head swayed. He seemed to be minding his own business until this woman intruded. She was young, pretty, and as easy as grade school math."

Math had always been difficult for Quinn, but she gathered Safia had excelled.

"She brought him a shot of clear liquor. I assume it was tequila, but it could have been vodka or gin. He didn't touch the drink. I suppose he had had enough. I wasn't expecting Scorp to go home with the woman. She approached him. Only a stupid detective would allow a stranger to seduce them when drunk. Normally Scorp would flirt, perhaps get a phone number for later. But he didn't. In fact, her salacious offer seemed to have ticked him off. He waved her away and stood when she persisted. He was too drunk and dropped to his seat. His display of disinterest worked. The lady left."

Though relieved Eliot hadn't been with another woman, Quinn's stomach remained knotted.

"You don't look happy," Safia said.

"I'm worried he'll cave to temptation one day?"

"Scorp's not interested in other women. You're the one he wants. It has been that way since he met you."

"But what if—"

"If you're looking for perfection, Scorp is not your man. He's a work in progress. But I do know this, you can trust him. He's not a cheat. Disappointing you or Raine is what he fears the most. He's incredibly tough on himself. Can you imagine being raised to believe you're not good enough? Stop looking for guarantees in life. No one, not even Allah, promises a stress-free life. So if a man comes your way and promises a life without any rough patches, walk away, for he's either stupid or a liar."

Quinn's mouth curved into a smile. She couldn't argue with logic. "One more question, and then I'll swear I won't ask anymore."

"As long as it's not about Omeir."

Although she was curious about why Safia was

adamant about keeping her coffee rendezvous a secret, it wasn't what she planned to ask. "Did Eliot say anything that night…uh…um…about me?"

"No."

Quinn frowned. Safia's curt response had disappointed her.

"It was all slurred ramblings, gibberish, non-stop chatter from a normally quiet man. All we learned was Eliot has a sweet tooth. I might have been amused if I wasn't so irritated with him."

"He likes that awful black licorice."

"No, this was more along the lines of cupcakes."

"Cupcakes?"

"Or donuts. He kept going on about sprinkles and how he loves sprinkles. He repeated it so many times, Omeir was going to stop at a bakery. I told him no. We needed to get Scorp home, not feed him cake. Thankfully, he passed out and shut up about sweets."

Quinn rushed forward and gave Safia an exuberant hug. The woman stiffened like laundry pinned to a clothesline during a cold snap.

"We're back," Omeir shouted, rounding a corner with Raine. The man had more drips of ice cream running down his mouth than the five-year-old.

A nurse darted across the hall.

"Excuse me," Quinn said, hurrying toward the woman. "I'm waiting to see Eliot Traversini."

"Are you a co-worker?" the nurse asked.

"No. I'm…"

"She's family," Safia interjected. Can she go see Traversini?"

"Yes," The nurse replied.

"Come on, Raine, let's go visit your brother." Quinn

glanced around. “Raine?”

“Where is she?” Safia snapped at Omeir.

He glanced up from his phone. “Isn’t she with you?”

Panic flooded Quinn. She had lost Raine.

****

Three frantic adults running into a hospital room was not a good sign. But when the group collectively sighed, Eliot realized they had no idea his sister had snuck into his room.

“Hey,” he said, elevated in the bed with Raine tucked under his side. The cotton blanket had slid, exposing his sleeveless hospital gown. His right eye was swollen shut, and his cheek and lip abrasions had scarred over. He was quite the sight. But instead of staring at his mangled face, his sister focused on his tattoos—the ink he had spent months hiding.

“You’re like a coloring book,” Raine said.

Eliot smirked with relief. “Don’t go getting any markers.”

While everyone chatted, Quinn remained quiet. After thirty minutes of uncomfortable silence from her, he looked up at Safia and Omeir. “There’s a cafe across the street. Can you guys take Raine and get me a decent coffee?”

“Sure,” Omeir replied. He glanced at Quinn. “You want to join us?”

Safia leaned toward Omeir and whispered, “He wants to be alone with her.”

Omeir’s face reddened. “Oh, sorry, buddy.” He held his hand to Raine, “Come on, kiddo, let’s see if they have any cookies.”

Safia let out a sigh and followed Omeir and Raine into the hallway. Quinn closed the door behind them.

"You didn't have to come." Eliot was unsure whether Quinn truly wanted to be here or this was simply an obligated visit.

She proceeded toward him. He scooted his body, providing inadequate space, and patted the mattress. She accepted his invitation and sat.

"You comfortable?" If she wasn't, there was nothing he could do. If he moved any farther, a large thud would sound, and a team of nurses would rush in.

Quinn nuzzled against his chest. His ribcage throbbed, but the tension in his body faded. She began sobbing.

Shit, this isn't good. Normally, when a woman began crying, she would curse, slam the door, and shout, "You asshole."

He tightened his arm around her quivering body. "Sprinkles, what's wrong?" Were her tears slow-building anger, a preamble to a final goodbye, or was she shaken about his hospitalization? Although he hated her fretting, he could at least manage her concern. What he couldn't handle was her leaving. His kid sister would miss her immensely…and he would be devastated.

Before he fell off the wagon, he realized how much Quinn meant to him. Caring about her terrified him, but he became less freaked out over time. He wasn't ready to say *I love you*—there are no taking back those words—but he was prepared to give her closet space.

He eased her off his chest, wiping her tears with the scratchy hospital blanket. "It's okay. Speak what's on your mind."

"I was…" she stuttered. Her choked sobs prevented further words from departing her lips. She tried again, but the words were jumbled, combining *I's* and *you's* without a coherent thought.

"Take your time."

"I'm okay," she gasped.

"No, you're not." He rubbed her wrist with his thumb. He wasn't sure what was wrong. He just knew he was to blame.

She took a few more deep breaths. "I was so scared when Safia told me you got hurt. I thought…" She began crying.

"I'm fine. Some bruising, but nothing serious."

"You're…You're all banged up," she sobbed.

"I'm not my usual pretty boy self, but I'll live." He stroked her cheek. "Honestly, I don't need to be here. A simple bandage would have worked, but my colleagues called an ambulance."

"I'm sorry…" she sputtered.

A lump formed in his throat. A girl crying coupled with an apology spelled disaster.

His gaze settled on the blanket's thick stitching. He waited. Quinn remained silent. His heart pounded.

A laugh escaped her lips. Eliot feared she had snapped from all the stress. She continued laughing. Thankfully, the giggle was sweet and not unhinged.

"You really are okay?" she asked.

"Yup. Just waiting for the doctor to sign the discharge papers. I was hoping she would do it soon. This hospital gown is ridiculous. It's no bigger than a thong. I feel like a coed on spring break."

Quinn playfully tugged the cotton garment. "Let me see."

"Not happening, Sprinkles. Hey, you know what *can* happen?"

"What?"

"You can come home with me. I missed you."

Her mouth grazed against his lips. He winced.

She pulled back. "That hurts, doesn't it?"

"Not as much as thinking you might never kiss me again."

****

"The doctor instructed me to rest, not lie in bed like a pampered princess," Eliot argued after Quinn ordered him to stay in bed.

A mountain of pillows, including two pink ruffled ones, kept his legs elevated. His lower limbs weren't the problem. The problem was that he wasn't using them. He was reprimanded any time he left his bed other than to take a whiz. Even his five-year-old sister took to scolding him.

He threw back the covers and eased himself up. Pain radiated from his ribcage. He winced. "I'm getting bedsores."

Quinn glared. "Seriously?"

"No, but it could happen. When the doc said to relax, I doubt she meant doing nothing. Besides, I'm hungry."

"Just ask, and I'll make you something."

"Yeah, woman, get me a sandwich." He gave a mocking Neanderthal grunt and shuffled to the kitchen. "I need to move around." He grabbed a carton of orange juice from the fridge.

Quinn took the carton out of his hand. "All right," she said, pouring the beverage and handing him the glass. "I'll arrange some cushions on the sofa."

He drank the orange juice in one gulp. "So much for escaping the evil kingdom of frilly pillows," he muttered, setting the cup in the sink.

She leaned forward and kissed his lips. He gritted

his teeth and gave her a tight smile. He refused pain meds, instead choosing a natural anti-inflammatory. He tucked her hair behind her ear. “Sorry for being difficult. I appreciate everything you’re doing—everything you’ve done. I’ve just never had someone take care of me.”

“I know,” she said, softening her voice, “but get used to it. I’m not going anywhere.”

“I don’t deserve you.”

“I wish you wouldn’t say that. We should talk once Raine goes to bed tonight.”

“Yeah, we will.”

****

He flicked the lights off in Raine’s bedroom, followed Quinn to the living room, and plopped down on the sofa. “How come she wants a quick bedtime story when I’m not busy, but when I need alone time with you, she brings me several books?”

Quinn snuggled against him. “Decoding child logic is impossible for us adults,”

“All kidding aside, I hope she always loves reading.”

“She’s amazing.”

“And so are you, Sprinkles.” He kissed her cheek. “I’ve said sorry a zillion times, and I hate that I keep saying it. Not because I don’t mean it, but because I mean it so much. I betrayed your trust.”

“It hurt that you didn’t confide in me, and seeing you drunk made me angry.” She scratched her nails. “I was scared, Eliot.”

“I regret letting you down. I’m lucky the social worker didn’t do an unannounced visit and see me passed out on the sofa. I don’t know what Alisha would have done, but Raine might have been apprehended."

"But she wasn't."

"I get why you're angry and disappointed, but I don't understand why you're scared. I've never been a violent drunk, and I swear I'd never—"

"I know." She dropped her head. "I thought you might go off with another woman and forget about me."

"I'm an idiot, but my womanizing days are long gone." He let out a labored breath. "I'm aware of my reputation. I can't expect you to believe me, but give me a chance, and I'll show you how much I've changed." He dipped his face, coaxing her to meet his gaze. When she did, he continued. "I'm sorry I made you feel that way, but don't ever think you're forgettable."

"I've always been a wallflower. I'm not the girl who ends up with the cute guy."

"I'd be devastated if you wound up with the cute guy. You should be with *me*." He dropped the smirk. "You are so many things. Funny. Smart. Sexy. But you are not forgettable. I've been in utter agony the last few days. Being patient and giving you time has been hard. I physically ache from not seeing you. Trust me, Sprinkles, you are not forgettable. Drinking was stupid. I should have talked to you. Carly's death brought up a lot of old feelings."

"Like what?"

He took a breath of courage. "I accepted not having a relationship with my mother. Even if a miracle occurred and she got clean, I wouldn't have forgiven her. She damaged my childhood. She damaged me. The drugs messed her up, but it wasn't just the opioids. She despised me."

"Why do you say that?"

"Because she repeatedly told me. Not once in twenty-nine damn years did Carly feel anything but utter hatred for me." Though he agreed to talk, he wasn't ready to disclose the reason behind his mother's raging contempt. "Even the most flawed human beings have mothers who love them. It stings knowing I was loved less than a serial killer. Regardless, I acted like a jerk. I fueled my pity party with booze. As soon as I felt a buzz, I regretted it."

"So why didn't you call? I would have dropped everything and got you."

"I was ashamed to be so damn weak. It's a shitty excuse, but it's the truth."

"But you reached out to Omeir and Safia."

"I called Omeir, not Safia. The guy's seen me drunk before. I'm sure he thinks I'm an idiot, but he hasn't stopped being my friend."

"And you think I would."

"If I keep messing up, you should."

"You'd have to do something pretty bad for me to walk away. And as far as Carly hating you, it isn't because you're not worthy of love. A lot of people love you. Paula and Malcolm. Your work friends. And Raine is over the moon about you. And I—"

"Don't. Not like this. I'm an addict. I know what it's like to live with someone who uses. No one should go through that."

"Are you saying—"

"I need to get my act together. I started counseling and AA meetings. I'm trying. I really am, but recovery is a process. Give me a chance to get there. I want things to be right with us."

"They are right."

He shook his head. “They’re better. But I need to earn your trust back. I’m asking you to give me time, not because I’m unsure, but because I want you so damn much.”

She slid closer.

His body ached from his injuries but also from desire. There were times when Quinn knew what she was doing, like when she teased him with a chest-heaving stretch. And then there were times, like now, when she had no idea how her sensual curves affected him.

“Dammit,” he grumbled. Getting ambushed sucked.

“What are you cursing about?”

“I hate being sidelined. It’s impossible to have makeup sex without causing an emergency room visit.”

She giggled. “We could cuddle and talk about feelings or sit through a chick flick marathon.” Her sweet, sassy tone made him even harder.

He let out an agonized groan. “How about I silently hold you while I work on being a good man?”

“You’re a wonderful guy.”

“I can do better.”

Chapter Twenty-Six

As Quinn discovered, Eliot wasn't mourning Carly herself. She had never been a true mother. Instead, Eliot lamented a missed opportunity. His hope died with Carly, not the hope of reconciling with his mother but of redeeming his unworthiness. Through her words and deeds, Carly had convinced her son he was unlovable. Quinn was ready to rectify this, but Eliot stopped her. The wall around him would eventually come down, but Eliot needed to control the when and how.

In a way, not declaring *I love you* was a relief. Not because the words weren't true but because they were. Before Eliot's life ran amok, Quinn was ready to reveal her past dealings with men. But the more she thought about it, the more afraid she became. Rehashing Michael was always difficult, and discussing Chad wasn't easy. Chad had cheated on her. She was more than justified in kicking him to the curb. But explaining why her ex took up with his co-worker was the hard part.

She poured Gabby another cup of steeped tea. "I haven't told Eliot."

"Discussing Michael is your choice, but if you're serious about Eliot, you better tell him the rest. Stalling will make the situation worse."

"What do you think he'll do?"

"You said he was in love with you, so maybe it won't be an issue."

"He didn't exactly tell me he loves me."

"Either he said it, or he didn't. You're as confusing as canned sausages at a seafood buffet."

"He told Safia in a drunken stupor," Quinn replied, regretting the entire discussion.

"Okay, but I'm sure he meant it."

"It doesn't matter what Eliot meant because he's not ready to say it now."

"And what makes you say that?"

"Woman's intuition," she replied, hoping Gabby would back off.

"The man spends practically all his free time with you, and he's always finding ways to touch you. He kissed your cheek before going to the restroom during our double date. Men in real life don't do that. They just send you unsolicited pictures of their anatomy and expect you to be impressed."

"You're right," Quinn acknowledged. "I need to tell him. But when I do, I may destroy any future we have."

****

Eliot lay under Quinn's kitchen sink, fixing a leak. "How do you feel about weddings?" he asked, handing her back the wrench.

The metal tool slipped from her fingers and clanged to the floor. Two weeks ago, Eliot stopped her from declaring her love, and now he was asking her views on matrimony.

He slid from underneath the cabinet and stood. "I've got a wedding next month, and I thought maybe you'd come with Raine and me."

"Oh," she mumbled.

"Is that a yes?"

"Isn't that what I said?" She knew it wasn't.

"Right," he responded. "My buddy Zak is getting married. The wedding is in Baxley, which is not far from Chicago. We could drive out on Thursday, spend time with your dad, and then head to Baxley late the next day."

"You want to meet my dad?"

She had repeatedly mentioned Raine to her father but downplayed her relationship with Eliot.

"I'll wear long sleeves."

"To the wedding?"

"When I meet your dad. Hell, I'll wear a tie if you want."

"Why would I care what you're wearing?"

"The tattoos. I don't want your father to worry you're slumming."

"Stop it." She was more annoyed than angry. "You don't understand my dad."

"Hey, it's okay. I'm aware I don't fit in and…"

"Hush. Let me finish. What you wear is up to you. Throw on a gorilla suit if you want. As far as my dad's concerned, he'll care about how you treat me, not your shirt."

"Really?" His voice flooded with skepticism.

"I get people make assumptions about you. I did when we met, but my father won't. He doesn't judge people by their appearances. He'll ask one thing of you."

"And what's that?"

"That you make my happiness a priority."

"And how am I doing so far?"

"I'll show you exactly how happy I am." She puckered her lips and jumped.

He caught her waist, swirled her in the air, and kissed her.

Chapter Twenty-Seven

Eliot's twelve-hour drive to Chicago had now exceeded fourteen. He stopped seven times already, five of which were for restroom breaks. He swore his shirt buttons were larger than Raine's bladder. Despite all the road stops, traveling by car was better than flying as Omeir and Safia had planned. For Eliot, boarding a plane was like running into a lion. He didn't care about a bruised foot. He cared about what came next.

Eliot drove past the harvested fields along the interstate with the radio playing a repetitive bubblegum pop song. Earlier, when an equally obnoxious melody blasted, he snuck his hand on the dial, but Raine and Quinn protested.

He gazed at Quinn. She leaned against the side window, her eyelids heavy and her hand on his thigh. He glanced in the rearview mirror and saw Raine napping. A calmness fell over him. Boy, was he lucky to have these two in his life.

Quinn opened her eyes and let out a yawn. "How long was I out?"

"An hour."

She wiggled in her seat.

"Want me to pull over?" he asked. "It's no problem. There's a gas station up ahead."

"Why?" she replied.

"You're fidgeting. I'm guessing you have to pee."

"No, I'm good."

A few seconds later, she was biting her thumbnail.

"Are you nervous about taking your boyfriend home to meet your father?"

"Boyfriend?"

"Your amazing lover might be too descriptive of an introduction."

"Very funny. I wasn't sure where you stood with labels."

"Just because I've never been in a relationship doesn't mean I'm unfamiliar with the term. I've seen those romantic comedies."

Her brows lifted.

"Okay, I've only watched part of one, but it's because my hot girlfriend prefers hockey over *My Heart Aches for You*."

"What are you talking about?"

"There's gotta be a chick flick with that name."

She patted his thigh. "When we get back, we'll binge-watch rom-coms, so you don't publicly embarrass yourself with ridiculous movie titles."

"Will do, with one condition."

"What's that?"

He glanced, ensuring his sister was still sleeping. "We make out during the credits."

****

Eliot entered the code Quinn gave him. A large metal door rose, and Eliot drove into the building's parking garage. His gaze drew upward. The place had more security cameras than his precinct.

"What did you tell your father about me?' he asked as he wheeled a small suitcase into the elevator. He preferred not to be surprised or needled with personal questions.

Quinn punched a series of numbers, and the doors closed. “I told him you’re a police officer, but I didn’t elaborate.”

“And what else?”

“I mentioned you’re raising your kid sister and doing a terrific job.”

The elevator glided past the twenty-fifth floor, showing no signs of slowing down.

He glanced at Raine. She was examining the artwork on the wall. “Did he ask why?” he mouthed to Quinn.

“No, and I didn’t explain.”

The elevator continued without stopping. “Will he offer me a scotch?”

“I told him you don’t drink.”

“And let me guess, he didn’t ask why, and you didn’t elaborate.”

“Stop fretting. Dad will like you.”

“I’m not trying to hide my flaws, but I don’t want you spending the evening justifying why you are with me when you could be dating a lawyer.”

“After the last lawyer, my dad will be relieved you’re not one.”

“What does that mean?”

The elevator beeped. The door opened into a large living room. A man stepped forward.

Quinn dropped her handbag and hugged him. After a moment, her father stepped back.

“Dad, this is Eliot and his sister Raine.”

Eliot extended his arm. “Nice to meet you, sir.”

Mr. Merrick shook his hand and smiled at Raine. “Call me Tom.”

When Quinn said her father lived downtown, Eliot

pictured a small apartment, not a penthouse suite four times the size of his Brooklyn apartment. And this wasn't her father's primary home. There was also a house in the suburbs, though Quinn said her father seldom lived there. Last year, while undercover, Eliot stayed at an exquisite New York hotel. The exclusive suite reserved for A-listers and diplomats was fancy, but he wasn't there long. Mr. Merrick lived like a celebrity every single day.

It never crossed his mind that Quinn came from money. She lived in the same New York apartment building as him. The place was decent enough, but evidently, her father had the resources to set her up in Chelsea, Greenwich Village, or some other affluent artsy area.

Eliot had met his share of girls with rich fathers, women whose lives centered around spa appointments, designer labels, and extravagant trips. But Quinn wasn't a spoiled socialite. She opted to be self-sufficient. There couldn't be a better role model for his sister than her.

Tom Merrick didn't pry into his personal life and only inquired about his work. Eliot answered the best he could. "I work with a specialized unit of the NYPD." He omitted the counterterrorism details, and Tom didn't ask.

When Tom commented on how difficult policing must be, Eliot downplayed his job for Quinn's sake. "More people die in car accidents than policing," he said. In hindsight, it was a horrible analogy, as he had coerced the man's daughter into an eight-hundred-mile road trip instead of a two-hour flight.

Eliot accepted the hazards his career presented, and although he hadn't had a death wish since the night his mother burned his flesh, he never shied from danger. Taking risks was second nature, but now he had Raine and Quinn to consider. His sister was a permanent fixture in his life, and he was edging toward Quinn being so too. Thinking he might not make it home one day troubled him. The Wilsons would care for Raine, but he didn't want to miss seeing her grow up, and he couldn't bear the thought of leaving Sprinkles. But policing was what he did, who he was. He could never be a paper pusher. He respected Lieutenant Pratt, who spearheaded covert operations and sat through meetings with politicians, but Eliot couldn't imagine a desk job.

Tom Merrick checked his watch. The timepiece likely exceeded Eliot's monthly salary. "It's late. Sorry for talking so much, but I enjoyed catching up with my daughter and getting to know you and your sister."

"Likewise," Eliot replied. He glanced over at Raine. She had dozed off.

"I'll get her ready for bed," Eliot told Quinn. He lifted his kid sister and carried her down the hall. He glanced inside the first door and noticed a home office. He continued until he heard Tom Merrick's voice.

"Head back to the room on your right," Quinn's father said. "I set the den up for Raine. You and Quinn have the room at the end of the hall."

****

Quinn smiled at her father. Like Eliot, she had expected separate sleeping arrangements.

"Honey," her father said, interrupting her thoughts. "Your mom would be better at dealing with this, but seeing that you brought him to meet me, I figured you were—"

"Thanks," she interjected, sparing him the embarrassment of discussing her sex life.

She and her father talked for another twenty

minutes, discussing their jobs, her collection's new pieces, and his thoughts on a Super Bowl ad for a multinational apparel company.

"Let me know if you need anything," her father said, kissing her forehead.

She grabbed his arm. "Thanks, Dad."

"What for?"

"Everything."

"Care to elaborate?"

She chuckled, thinking about her earlier conversation with Eliot. "I appreciate the book you bought for Raine, for being kind to Eliot and always being there for me."

"I considered getting her a video game, but my assistant dissuaded me."

"I'm glad she did. There's plenty of time for that when she gets older."

"Eliot's special to you, isn't he?"

"He is."

"I could tell by how you spoke about him during our calls. Though I must admit, he's not what I expected."

A grin stretched across her face. "He's not what I expected either."

"Mentioning the man makes you smile. I was like that with your mom."

"I remember. I miss her too."

"She'd be pleased knowing you found someone who makes you happy."

"Even though he isn't anything like Chad?"

"Had she lived, she would have felt differently about the man."

"Yes, I suppose so."

"Your mom wanted someone there for you. She

knew the cancer would take her long before you and I were ready to admit it. She worried I wouldn't be strong enough to deal with my grief, let alone yours." He glanced away. "She was right."

"You and Mom were together for thirty-two years. Grief is normal."

"Let me finish," he said. "Your mom liked Chad because she figured you could lean on him. But as you and I discovered, that wasn't true." He twirled the wedding band on his finger. "You don't know a person's true nature until you journey with them through their worst moments. Good people have a strength of character that won't allow them to destroy others. Even though they're going through a rough patch, they still care for the ones they love. Chad never shielded you from his pain. Instead, he threw you into the middle of his inferno. But something tells me your Eliot is a protector. He's raising a polite, happy girl who adores him. He may not be perfect—none of us are—but he seems to do right when it matters. Making my daughter happy is all I'll ever demand of him."

Chapter Twenty-Eight

"See," Eliot said, patting Quinn's leg, "there was nothing to be worried about."

"You were the nervous one. And what was up with the silly grin last night?

He signaled and turned off the highway toward the town of Baxley. "Can't a guy be happy?"

"You acted like a hormonal teenager."

"Only because your father announced we'd be sleeping together."

"He didn't announce…" She shook her head. "Never mind. Just realize you'll be in the same boat when Raine grows up."

"La la la, I can't hear you. La la la."

"And she's your kid sister. Imagine what it's like when it's your daughter."

"Nope, not happening."

"You don't plan to have kids one day?"

He swung around to her, jerking the steering wheel. The car swerved. He straightened the tires, steadying the vehicle. "I'm pulling over." He glanced in the rearview mirror. His sister continued to snooze. Kids in cars were the equivalent of dogs basking in the sun. His gaze darted, searching for a freeway exit. They had passed several rest stops along the way, but now there wasn't a single one.

"Eliot, what's—"

"Give me a moment."

A sign appeared. To the east was a secondary road. He eased off the gas pedal and signaled.

"Where are we going?"

He veered off the highway. "Somewhere where we can talk."

"About what?"

"Having kids."

"That's not—"

"There," he shouted, pointing to a harvested field. He slowed the car, unbuckled his seat belt, and rammed the vehicle into park with his palm. "C'mon," he said, opening the door. His boots hit the gravel, and he started pacing.

"Eliot, I wasn't pressuring you about the future. I was trying to steer the conversation toward…" Quinn's voice quivered as though she was close to tears.

"Please don't cry," he begged. "I do think of the future. Since I met you, I have thought about it a lot. But the kid thing?" He walked toward her. Seeing her disappointment would crush him, but he had to look her in the eye. She mattered. Quinn meant the world to him. "I don't want kids."

"You don't?"

"Being a big brother is great, and I wouldn't change having Raine in my life, but…but babies are a whole different ballgame. They're tiny. They're needy. They leak. I'm terrified to hold one." He took a deep breath. "But if it's important to you, Sprinkles, I'll figure something out."

"Stop," she shouted. "I can't have children. I broke up with Chad when he fathered a child with a woman who could."

Though she was loud and clear, he repeated, "You can't have kids?"

"I should have told you sooner, but I love what we have. I thought…I don't know what I was thinking other than being selfish." She turned away and sniveled. "What a horrible time to tell you this—on our way to your friend's wedding. I'm…I'm so sorry. I'm such an idiot." She wiped her tears with her sleeve.

He grabbed her hand. "Aww, Sprinkles, your ex didn't cheat because you weren't producing button-down yuppie clones. He cheated because he's a jerk. Being unfaithful to an amazing woman he claimed to love was nothing more than a dick move." He took her hand and pressed it against his chest. "As far as you, me, and a bunch of rug rats, I had a vasectomy when I was twenty. Do you know how difficult getting snipped is when you're young and have never had kids? I saw five different specialists before a doc agreed to do it. They assumed I would change my mind. With such a messed-up childhood, I thought it was best for everyone if I didn't father any kids. But listen, if there ever is a way for you to have kids, and you truly want them, then I would get the stupid thing reversed. And if that's not possible, we could adopt. I'll do anything to make you happy."

"And you have. You make me smile all the time. Thanks to you, I have the laugh lines of an eighty-year-old woman." She glanced at her nails and then at him. "But what is it that you want?"

"This life with you. Sure, Raine needs to be around other kids, but that doesn't mean we should have babies. We're all the family she needs. And you are all that I want. I love you, Sprinkles, because of who you are, not what you can give me."

Quinn laid her head against his chest. "I love you too."

"Where are we?" a tiny voice shouted.

Somewhere between calling her ex a jerk and jabbering about his vasectomy, his boisterous voice woke Raine.

His little sister huddled near the car and looked around. "Why is Quinn crying?"

He marched toward Raine, concerned about her standing near the road. He lifted her and pointed at Quinn. "This remarkable woman loves me."

Quinn rushed to him. He tucked her under his open arm. Her love wouldn't make his demons vanish, but it dimmed their presence.

****

Quinn stared out the vehicle's window at the towering trees shedding leaves. A bouquet of yellow and orange hues flooded the autumn landscape. Mesmerized by the rich foliage, Quinn didn't notice the cabin until it was a few yards away.

"Zak moved in with Lexie some time ago," Eliot said. "His place is ours while we're here."

"An entire house to ourselves. I like your friends already."

Eliot laughed and turned off the ignition. "I'll get Raine if you grab the cooler."

Quinn emerged from the vehicle and climbed the painted porch steps.

Eliot unbuckled Raine and met Quinn at the door. "The home's been on the market for months. Few people move to the area, and those that do, prefer the lake communities further north."

"Does Lexie live in town?"

"No, she's a few minutes away. You'd love her place. It's big and old."

She redid her ponytail, which had loosened during the drive. She hoped *big and old* meant historical and not haunted.

His phone buzzed. He checked the device's screen. "It's Zak. He's running late, but he'll be here soon. He left a key under the mat in case we arrived early."

"That's an obvious place," she said, reaching down and handing Eliot the key.

"There are cameras in the trees, but he assured me there's none inside."

Eliot opened the door. Raine brushed past him.

"Bathroom is on the right," he hollered.

Eliot kissed Quinn's cheek. "I'll go get the rest of our bags."

"I'll give you a hand," she said and followed outside.

"You'll like Zak and Lexie." He popped the trunk and lifted out their bags. "They're like Omeir and Safia without the bickering."

She snatched Raine's stuffed unicorn from his hand. "Were Omeir and Safia ever a couple?"

"Only in Omeir's mind."

"Well, I think he would be good for Safia."

"A word of advice, don't mention it to her. She's not exactly receptive to—"

"Don't worry. I'd never interfere." Though Safia had softened toward her, Quinn wouldn't push her luck.

"I'm glad we sorted our relationship, even though we did so before a herd of eavesdropping cows. Do you think they were mocking me?"

She let out a lighthearted laugh. "I'm sure I scared them. I was quite the sight with mascara smeared across my cheeks."

He put the suitcases on the ground. "Sprinkles, you're always beautiful." He engulfed her in his arms. "Thanks for loving me."

"You make it easy," she replied, wishing he would believe it.

****

Eliot eyed Quinn. "Damn," he muttered.

Quinn lowered the mug in her hand. "What are you cursing about?"

"I should be the only one who gives you pleasure."

"You are."

"That's what I thought, but you moaned when you sipped that coffee."

"Don't worry, El. I still prefer you keep me up all night. Now getting back to our conversation. I'm okay hanging out with Raine."

The salacious grin slipped from his face. "Lexie will be disappointed if you don't go."

"I'm sure she'll understand."

"What about Safia?"

"What about her?"

"She's counting on having someone she knows there tonight."

"She knows Lexie."

"Yes, but Lexie's friends will be there, and Safia will feel… I don't know how she'll feel, but she's a disaster when left in the company of women."

"You're asking me to babysit her?"

"Except for Lexie, you're the only other woman I've seen her befriend. She would be hurt if you bailed."

Though she questioned whether Safia would consider her a friend, she wouldn't mind going out. "What about Raine? You can't take a child to a bachelor party."

"There's no bachelor party. We're having a pool tournament at the fire station. The guys won't mind Raine tagging along. And if they do, too bad. You deserve a girls' night out."

"You sure?"

"Yeah. Besides, it's to my advantage."

"And how's that?"

"Zak told me you ladies are going to some honky-tonk saloon. Bald cowboys in Stetsons with jeans strangling their manhood will make you appreciate this fine, chiseled specimen even more."

"You're pretty confident, city slicker."

"After my awesome declaration of love today, I reckon you're still swooning."

"Reckon? Who's the cowboy now?"

He let out a deep chortle before his dimples retracted. "I'm sorry about earlier."

"What exactly are you regretting?"

"I should have done things right, done something special when I told you for the first time. Shouting I love you near a field reeking of cow shit is not a romantic gesture, even I know that."

"Extravagant displays of affection aren't important. It's your sincerity that matters." She wrapped her hands around his waist. "You, my love, scored major points today."

The front door squeaked. Someone had entered the house.

"Detective Scorp Traversini," a voice bellowed.

"We're in the kitchen," Eliot shouted.

Zak Ahmadi walked into the room with his fiancée Dr. Lexie Draden beside him. Eliot extended his hand, but Zak pulled him into a hug. After nearly losing his friend last year, Eliot accepted the embrace.

Eliot kissed Lexie on the cheek. "So you've made up your mind to tie the knot with Zak, huh? Are you sure you can handle him for the rest of your life?"

She wrapped her arm around her fiancé's waist. "Absolutely."

Eliot laughed. "Yeah, I figured. I guess you could do worse."

"Thanks for coming, Scorp," Zak said. "It means a lot to us."

"Wouldn't miss it, bro." He turned and smiled at Quinn. "This is my girlfriend."

Zak reached out and shook her hand. "It's Quinn, right?"

"Yes," she replied.

"It's nice to meet you. I'm a gentleman, so I'll bite my lip about this big lug." He winked at Quinn and whispered, "He's one of the good guys. I wouldn't be here if it weren't for him."

"It's true," Lexie said. She slid in front of her fiancé and welcomed Quinn with a hug. "Eliot saved Zak's life."

Lexie was one of the few people who didn't call him Scorp. Last year, when he called to check on Zak, Lexie answered. He introduced himself as Scorp, but due to poor phone reception, Lexie couldn't hear. After two more attempts, he finally said, "The name's Eliot."

"You're coming out with us girls tonight?" Lexie asked Quinn.

“She’ll be there,” Eliot answered. “Zak, you don’t mind if I bring Raine to the pool hall.” No way would he let Quinn sacrifice a night out for his sake.

“Hanging out with you guys will scar Raine for life,” Lexie teased. “My friend’s teenage daughter is fantastic with kids. She’s babysitting my bridesmaid’s twins. They’re the same age as Raine. I’m sure she won’t mind one more child.”

Eliot rubbed his chin. “Thanks for the offer, but Raine’s not ready to be left with strangers.”

“It’s up to you, Scorp,” Zak interjected. “Your sister is welcome to join us.”

“How about this?” Lexie said. “We’ll visit my friend’s daughter and the twins. If Raine’s not comfortable staying, bring her to the fire station.”

Eliot glanced at Quinn. She nodded her approval.

“Okay,” he answered Zak. “I promise I won’t stay long if I bring Raine.”

His friend patted him on the shoulder. “Stay as long as you want…unless you’re worried she’s a better pool player than you? Seriously, I’m happy you found your sister.”

Eliot wrapped his hand around Quinn’s shoulder. “The year’s been full of wonderful surprises.”

****

Quinn crouched down by Raine’s side. “Want to stay and play with your new friends?”

Raine smiled and nodded. Though Sarah and Samuel Sanford were a handful, Raine took to the boisterous twins.

Quinn gave the babysitter her phone number.

Eliot ruffled his sister’s hair. “See you in a few hours.”

“We’re doing the right thing, aren’t we?” Eliot said to Quinn as they walked outside.

“Yes,” she assured. She, too, was nervous about leaving Raine with a teenage babysitter they had just met, but both Zak and Lexie had vouched for the girl.

After turning up her phone’s volume, Quinn kissed Eliot and jumped into Lexie’s waiting vehicle.

Thirty minutes later, they pulled into a parking lot.

“Here we are,” Lexie announced to Safia and Quinn.

Safia entered the bar like a cat with a vet appointment. Quinn didn’t mind the place’s ambiance. The Stompin Loft reminded her of a bar she had seen on a Nashville website. It was your typical country honkytonk saloon with scuffed wood floors and a large rectangular bar in the middle. And true to its name was a loft overlooking the main floor. Though Quinn couldn’t wait to crawl into bed with Eliot, she welcomed socializing with the women.

An older woman named Willow wedged herself between Safia and Quinn. “Hi, you must be Lexie’s city friends. I’m the chairperson of Baxley’s Bird Watching Society,” the woman boasted. Sipping a beer, Willow described the vast array of local birds. She was a fluttering encyclopedia. The band began playing. Willow slid her chair next to Quinn. “Your man Scorp is like the bald eagle.”

“Pardon?”

“The eagle’s incredibly powerful and fearless,” Willow shouted, keeping pace with the loud booming music. “This mighty bird faces difficulties head-on and never gives up. They encourage others and nurture the younger ones.” She raised her drink, and this time, she gulped a generous amount of ale. “The bald eagle may be overwhelming to some, but they're good to latch on to. Totally monogamous."

Unsure how to respond, Quinn nodded.

"This is Scorp's girlfriend," Willow shouted to three women who had stopped to talk.

"Interesting," one of the women hollered before leaving with the other two.

Lexie made her way to Quinn. "Pay no attention to them."

"They just stared at me as if—"

"You were a peacock without feathers," Willow interjected.

"Um, yes, I guess," Quinn replied.

"Just so you know," Lexie shouted over the pounding music, "it's not you. They're shocked by Eliot. He was a different guy last time he was here."

"What do you mean?" Quinn hollered back.

Lexie patted her arm. "Let's go upstairs. It's not so noisy."

Quinn trailed Lexie up the wide staircase into the open loft area. The music was loud but a smidgen lower than the ear-bleeding decibels downstairs.

Lexie gritted her teeth. "As a doctor, I'm appalled by this ruckus. This level of noise can lead to permanent hearing loss. Quality speakers should be the focus, not how quickly you can blast an eardrum." A cocktail waitress approached them, and Lexie waved away the young woman. "Getting back to our earlier discussion, when Eliot came to our engagement party last year, he drew considerable attention from the womenfolk. As you know, he's not the kind of guy whose presence goes unnoticed. As Willow would say, the chicks flocked to him like an overturned truck of sunflower seeds."

"Are you saying those women resent me?"

"No. However, some may be disappointed he's off the market. But the rest of us are happy for Eliot. He seemed so lost last year."

"Lost?"

"It was as if he was searching."

"You're right. He was trying to find his sister."

"Granted, that was part of it, but there was something else missing in his life besides Raine. And now he's no longer searching. He has what he needs. He has you."

"Thanks, but those ladies down there weren't the only ones shocked to learn I'm Eliot's girlfriend."

"The plight of small town living. City women also act ridiculous around good-looking men, but it's more noticeable here. They did the same with Zak. The single women, and a few married ones, were intrigued by my soon-to-be husband's mysterious past, which, believe me, is more horrific than fascinating. With Eliot, it's his bad-boy vibe. Some women like the idea of taming a man. But you came along, and Eliot became a new man within a few months. Yes, I know he didn't magically transform. Deep down, he's the same guy. What has changed is he's no longer afraid of love." Lexie let out a soft chuckle. "Sorry for getting analytical and sappy, but I sense you understand him better than he understands himself. Raine has made an enormous difference in his life, and so have you. You've both given him a sense of belonging. I know those women below us. They aren't being catty."

Quinn's brow shot up.

"Ok, some are, but only because they envy you."

"They're not envious of me. They're envious I'm

with Eliot."

"You're wrong. For Eliot to want to be with you, which no doubt he does, you must be mighty special."

"Thanks."

"Hey, it's the truth."

****

There were over two hundred people, yet Zak and Lexie's wedding felt intimate to Quinn. The quaint inn, which housed the reception, was almost as breathtaking as the flocked trees and shrubs surrounding Lexie and Zak as they pledged their vows. A wedding in mid-autumn seemed wrong. The big day should be on a warm July evening, but this chilly October afternoon was perfect.

Eliot handed her a glass of sparkling water. "Sorry, I'm stuck at the head table. I'll come and sit with you after the speeches."

"No worries." She had fretted about being alone among strangers, like a sad first grader without a friend. Her worry was for naught. She was introduced to more folks than she could remember. She sipped the water and glanced around. "There's a lot of people here."

"The townsfolk were there for Zak during some dark times," Eliot explained. "They wanted to ensure everyone was included. Hey, I never got a chance to ask how your night at the cowboy bar went."

"Yes, we were both tired. Getting Raine to sleep was a chore, but seeing her excited about making friends was nice."

"I take it you had a good time last night?"

"The music was great. A live band played country rock and a few sweet ballads. You know, the kind which is great for slow dancing."

A brooding scowl washed over his face. "You slow danced?"

"No. We didn't have time. The cowboys showed up to entertain us. Do you know the best way to remove tight jeans is to use Velcro? One quick swoosh, and the pants are off."

A vein protruded from his forehead.

She let out a giggle. "We sat around, listened to the band, and talked. Lexie's wonderful. She ensured Safia and I met all her friends." She traced her fingers over his bare chest easing the anxiety she created.

"I'm glad you had a nice evening."

"Thanks for insisting I go. How about you? What was your *wild* night like?"

"If you're asking if I enjoyed hanging out with the guys, then yes. But as far as a wild night goes, I hope that will happen when we crawl into bed tonight." He kissed her cheek. "I best go. Omeir is trying to get my attention, or he's hit the candy bar one too many times and is twitching from a sugar high."

Her gaze drew to Eliot's friend. "He's probably had a jar of jelly beans, but he's headed to the mic. I'll catch up with you later."

After the speeches, Quinn tried to make her way to the restroom. A sea of friendly guests, eager to introduce themselves, ensured it took forty minutes. Walking back, she stopped and waved at Raine, pleased to see her playing with the other kids.

"Hey, beautiful," a voice whispered in her ear.

She turned and smiled at Eliot, admiring his fitted dark suit and wicked grin. He was so ablaze with male sexuality. His warm hand stroked her back. She smiled as his rough fingertips slipped underneath the fabric of her low-back dress to her skin.

"Are you having a good time?"

"I am," she answered.

"Oh." Disappointment shot from his voice.

"You don't want me to?"

"I'm a selfish man. I want you to miss me."

She straightened his tie. "I do, but I don't want to interfere with your official groomsmen's duties."

"Zak has three groomsmen, so my shift is over. I'm free to tackle my official boyfriend duties."

"And what might those entail? Or must I wait until later to find out?"

He glanced over his shoulder. "Hmm…there is a coat room."

"Too small, and the kids keep running in there."

He let out a deep laugh. A few nearby guests briefly looked their way.

"I guess my main duty will have to wait," he whispered with a devilish grin. "But I have a few other matters to address."

"Like?"

He tilted his head, motioning toward a dozen young men drinking beer. "See those guys?"

"Yes."

"I'm going to give them a death stare."

"Why?"

"So they stop checking out my girlfriend."

"They're not even looking this way."

"Not now, but they've been scouting you out all evening. And if you didn't have such an intimidating man, I would ogle you too. But that Scorp guy scares me. How did you describe him? That's right. A hot and chiseled gladiator."

"And don't forget boastful."

"The word is fun-loving."

"Silly," she countered.

He leaned down and kissed her. "You turned me into a lovesick fool."

"That makes two of us. We should start our own club."

Quinn enjoyed teasing Eliot, especially since she started the trip all nervous. She worried about the interaction between her father and Eliot, whether Zak and Lexie would like her, Raine's reaction to unfamiliar people, and then her biggest fear—Eliot's response to her infertility. But miraculously, everything worked out. Eliot wanted her. He didn't care about the absence of little Traversinis in his future. In fact, he preferred it. For the first time, she was enough.

Chapter Twenty-Nine

Eliot unclipped Hudson from his leash. He had taken the pooch for a walk after cooking breakfast.

"You sure you don't want to go to Chicago for Christmas?" he asked Quinn as he entered the kitchen.

"No," she replied, scrubbing the stovetop.

He grabbed a bottle of cleaner from under the sink and sprayed the appliance. He had ignored Quinn's advice and cooked the bacon in a pan rather than in the microwave. The bacon was crisp and tasty, but the grease had flown everywhere. "If you're concerned about road conditions, I'll book us a flight." He meant it. He would board a plane and spare her another long road trip.

"But you hate flying."

"Don't worry about me. You deserve the best Christmas ever."

She dropped the scouring pad on the counter. "I have you. I have Raine. Dad's coming to New York, and Paula and Malcolm are joining us for dinner. There's nothing else I need."

"I want the holidays to be perfect for you and Raine."

"And it will be. Let's pick out a tree today. Perhaps a Douglas fir or an Arizona cypress. They last longer than pine. And maybe later, I'll bake cookies. Tomorrow we can build a gingerbread house."

"You go all out."

“I hope you don’t mind.”

“No. Whatever you want is good with me.” She could bring a reindeer into his apartment, and he wouldn’t object.

“I hope Raine will like what I have planned.”

He picked up the scouring pad and scraped the grease from the stove. “She’s in a real home, surrounded by love. That’s all a kid needs. Well, that and a dozen or so wrapped gifts.”

“Have you invited Omeir and Safia? I know they don’t do Christmas, so if they’re not comfortable coming for dinner, then—”

He burst into laughter.

“I’m babbling again, aren’t I?”

“Yup, and it’s adorable.” He gave her a soft kiss on the lips. “And I’ve talked to Safia. She’ll be happy to join us. I haven’t yet asked Omeir but count him in. Once I tell him Safia’s coming, he’ll accept. What about Gabby? Do you want to invite her and Kiefer?”

“They’re going to his folks.”

He wrapped his arms around her neck. “I’m excited too.” Since returning stateside, he spent Christmas day at the Wilsons’ home. He never felt entirely comfortable knowing how hard the holidays were for them without Ty. He also attended various holiday parties of well-intentioned colleagues. He used those gatherings to hook up with single ladies. There was plenty of loneliness around the holidays, so getting laid was easy. But this year, there would be no cozying up with a random stranger near the mistletoe. The only woman he intended to kiss was right here in his home. Seeing her go all out for his sister confirmed he was a damn lucky man. What he wouldn’t give to be worthy of Quinn’s love.

****

Christmas came at last. Eliot marveled at how Quinn had managed to tick off every single item on her ambitious to-do-list. He had tried talking Raine out of the crooked shaped fir tree, but she batted those lovely lashes, a trick she had learned from Quinn. Thankfully, his sexy artist girlfriend created handcrafted ornaments. The sad tree was now an array of beautiful colors. Raine never noticed flaws, not in the bare tree or him. She adored them both. Quinn wasn't oblivious to his imperfections, but she loved him, nonetheless. He circled the tree and smiled. Perhaps finding an ugly tree would become a new Traversini tradition.

The Christmas dinner guests filtered in, filling his home with love and savory foods. Paula brought her special baked yam dish, and Safia brought baklava from Fazaris. Omeir prepared a tabbouleh salad, and Tom Merrick flew in with enough smoked salmon for two meals. Quinn stuffed and roasted the turkey, and Eliot did whatever was needed. They used Quinn's kitchen to cook. She called his oven antiquated, whatever that meant.

"Paula," he shouted, catching her by the door. "Where are you going?"

"It's not right for Quinn to do all the work."

"You've done enough holiday cooking over the years. I'll go help." He stuffed an envelope in his pocket and wandered across the hall.

"Hey," he yelled, entering Quinn's apartment and scowling about the unlocked door. Criminals didn't take holidays.

"In the kitchen," she bellowed back, her cheerful voice erasing his frown.

She stood at the counter, wearing an apron with printed yellow ducks. She lifted her head from chopping vegetables and smiled. He stepped closer and ran his lips against her neck.

"If you keep nibbling my ear, I'll ruin dinner."

"Can't help it."

"Can't or won't?"

"Both," he said with a grin. "Do you need any help?"

"I got everything under control."

"Good, then you can open your Christmas present."

"So, where's your bow?" she teased. "Or do I unwrap this?" She tugged his belt buckle.

He let out a breathy groan and removed her hands from his pants. "I'm here to give a gift, not receive one." He reached into his pocket and handed her an envelope. "This, my naughty elf, is for you."

"But you already gave me a gift."

This morning, he gave her a silver cuff bracelet. He had *Life is better with Sprinkles* engraved in the metal.

"Consider this a stocking stuffer."

She opened the envelope and removed the single piece of paper—an itinerary of a flight to Chicago departing next week.

"New Year's in Chicago? You hate flying."

"I'm hoping a gorgeous woman will sit beside me and hold my hand."

"I don't know what to say."

"We'll be gone for four days. We'll visit your dad and spend the rest of the time with Lexie and Zak."

"In Baxley?"

Great, she hates the idea. What was I thinking? Why would any sane woman enjoy Hicksville on New Year's

Eve, let alone any other time? "I'm sensing you're not crazy about going."

"There are only two tickets. What about Raine?"

"She's headed to Paula and Malcolm's. And don't worry. They agreed to take Hudson too."

"You're okay with leaving her?"

"She'll be in good hands. I figured we could have alone time. Zak offered his old house, so we'll have privacy."

She wrapped her arms around him, snuggling into his chest.

"Is that a yes?"

"I love the idea."

****

Quinn set the baklava between the chocolate yule log and the gingerbread trifle.

Omeir slid his plate to the desserts. "Everything looks so good."

"Try one of each," Quinn said. She had enjoyed numerous calorie-laden treats leading up to the holidays. Any leftovers would be going home with her guests.

Just as Omeir dumped cake onto his plate, a phone went off.

"Sorry, that's mine," Omeir said, digging into his jacket pocket.

"I told you to turn it off," Safia chided him.

"It's Pratt." Omeir tapped the screen and accepted the call.

A surge of nausea ran through Quinn's gut. No way was this a social call.

"I'm here with him," Omeir said. "Yeah, I'll tell him." Omeir glanced at Safia. She scowled and shook her head. "No, Lieutenant," Omeir said, "I don't know where Detective El-Moudawi is." He ended the call and muttered to Safia, "Turn your phone on." His jovial mood was now gone.

"What's happening?" Eliot asked.

Omeir wrapped several pieces of baklava in a napkin. "I'll explain in the car."

"Sorry, we have to go, Quinn. Dinner was great." He playfully tugged Raine's curls. "Merry Christmas, kiddo."

"Go ahead. I'll meet you downstairs," Eliot said to Omeir.

A loud beep shot into the already tense air. "Hello, sir," Safia said into her phone.

Omeir grabbed his coat and stormed past her.

Eliot leaned down and kissed his sister's head. Quinn forced a smile and rose from the table. "I'll be right back," she said, addressing her remaining guests. She accompanied Eliot down their apartment building's stairs.

"Sorry for bailing," Eliot whispered.

She straightened his collar and kissed him. "Be careful."

"I'll be fine," he reassured her.

"Call as soon as you can."

He stroked her cheek with his thumb. "I will," he promised and barreled out the door.

"Where's Paula?" Quinn asked, returning to Eliot's apartment.

"Across the hall, tidying up," Malcolm replied.

"I'll go help her."

Stepping into her kitchen, Quinn cleared her throat. "Thanks, Paula, but the dishes could have waited."

"It's the least I could do for the wonderful meal you

made."

Paula grabbed a sponge and began scrubbing the already clean oven. Quinn kept quiet. As far as she was concerned, Paula could retile her kitchen floor if it would keep her from clenching her teeth. The holidays were hard on Paula, and Eliot running off didn't help matters.

An hour later, the kitchen was spotless. "Let's head back to Eliot's," Quinn said when Paula eyed the dust in the air vents. They locked up her apartment and went across the hall. The bicycle her father had given Raine was now assembled and leaning against the entranceway. She smiled at Malcolm, whom she assumed did the work. Her father might be an advertising guru, but he struggled to assemble a stool.

"Solid as a rock," Malcolm said, tapping the bike and assuring Quinn it was safe for Raine.

"I don't know who is more excited about this. Raine for learning to ride, or Eliot for teaching her. Did you have any problem getting her to bed?"

"Nope, she went on her own," Malcolm replied.

"Did she seem worried about Eliot?" she asked.

"No," her father said. "She was exhausted from all the excitement."

Quinn excused herself and checked on Raine. The child's chest rose and fell with shallow breaths. She envied her peaceful slumber. Though beat, Quinn was too on edge to sleep. She returned to the living room and found Paula and Malcolm gathering their coats.

"You'll call me as soon as you hear from Eliot," Paula demanded. "I don't care what time it is."

"Of course." She hugged the couple.

"You okay, honey?" her dad asked once the Wilsons had left.

"Yes," she lied. "I know it's early by Los Angeles time, but why don't you go next door and relax? I'm headed to bed soon."

"If you need anything, come get me."

"I will." She walked him to the door. "How does breakfast at eight sound?"

"Perfect." He kissed her cheek and left.

Quinn went to Eliot's bedroom and removed her clothes. She donned Eliot's old T-shirt. The cotton fibers were infused with his drugstore deodorant. Unable to sleep, she rearranged his sock drawer. Aware there was no right way to fold socks, she paired them in various ways—none to her satisfaction. She tackled the next drawer, doing the same. After folding everything in sight, she sorted his closet from light to dark-colored clothing.

Her phone rang. She glanced at the screen and stiffened. It was 3:22, and Safia was calling.

"What happened?" she shouted. "Please, Safia, tell me he's okay."

"Relax, Sprinkles. I'm fine. We're in the office, wrapping up the paperwork."

"Why aren't you calling from your phone?" she snapped at Eliot, relieved yet irritated by his voice.

"I left it in the vehicle. Didn't you tell me to call as soon as possible?"

Tears flowed down her cheeks, and a sob escaped her mouth.

"Are you crying?"

"When Safia's number came up, I thought something horrible—"

"Shit. I'm so sorry, Sprinkles."

A thump sounded in the background. Either he

pounded his hands against his desk or bashed his big head.

She wiped her face with the T-shirt's hem. "El?"

"Yeah?"

"If I'm asleep when you get in, wake me."

"You sure? I might be a while."

"I didn't properly thank you for my Christmas presents."

"I love how you show gratitude. I'll be home as soon as possible."

She hated her overreaction. Being nervous wasn't fair to Eliot. If she broke down every time he went to work, she'd worsen the situation for them both. Dealing with criminals and terrorists was difficult enough. He didn't need the added stress of a jittery girlfriend. She'd do better, even if it meant hiding her fears.

Chapter Thirty

Quinn pumped her fist. Slowly circulation returned to her fingers. Eliot wasn't kidding. He was terrified of flying.

"Did I hurt you?" he asked, staring at the hand he had squeezed.

"Next time, I'll wear steel gloves so my nails don't pop off."

He gently massaged her fingers. "I'm sorry, Sprinkles."

"I'm teasing." She was only half joking.

"Thanks for putting up with me today. I hate flying."

She laughed. "I didn't notice."

"I'll be better on the flight home."

Not for a second did she believe him. "In exchange for crushing my hand, you'll have to kill all spiders…and anything else I deem icky."

"Deal. I'm sorry your dad's in Los Angeles."

"Me too, but I'll see him when he visits New York next month."

He arched his back and yawned. "Let's get the rental vehicle. I'm eager to relax in a spacious SUV. Those airline seats are brutal."

Try a middle seat between a snoring, flatulent stranger and a human tank.

The drive from Chicago seemed to have settled Eliot. By the time they reached Zak's cabin, Eliot's dimples had overtaken his scowl. The ground was covered in snow, and icicles hung from the for sale sign, but otherwise, the place was just as Lexie remembered.

The porch door swung open. Zak and Lexie came out of the house.

Zak kissed Quinn's cheek. "Great to see you." He climbed down the stairs to Eliot and gave him a pat on the back. "I'll help you unload the car."

Lexie greeted Quinn with a hug. "How was the flight? I know Eliot hates flying."

"He was a nervous wreck the whole time. He repeatedly checked the weather forecast before we boarded, and when the pilot announced we were taking off, I thought he would pass out."

"Maybe he'll get used to it eventually."

"The important thing is he did it."

"I guess we all have something we're afraid of."

"True."

The guys returned. Zak tossed his wife a set of keys. "Take the vehicle, Lex, and I'll go with Scorp."

"Is it that time already?" Eliot asked.

"Will be by the time we get there," Zak replied.

Eliot gave Quinn a quick kiss on the cheek. "I'll see you in a couple of hours."

Lexie watched as Eliot and Zak drove away. "Where are they going?" she asked Lexie.

"He didn't tell you?"

"No."

"They're headed to the sheriff's office. You remember Sheriff Emmett McQuay."

"Wasn't he one of Zak's groomsmen?"

"Yes. Emmett has a problem which Zak believes Eliot can help with."

"Is that code for shooting pool at the firehall?"

Lexie chuckled. "It didn't take you long to figure them out. Come on, let's head into town."

Lexie drove to the town's administration office and picked up the sheriff's wife, Kristina. After browsing a local antique shop, Quinn and the women went to Colton's diner.

"The guys will meet us here later," Lexie said as the ladies entered the café.

Quinn glanced at the mismatched tables and chairs. She loved when people spruced up old furniture instead of buying new. "This place is adorable."

"Wait until you taste the baked goods."

Quinn followed the women to the refrigerated display case.

"Let's order something decadent while we wait for the guys to join us," Kristina suggested.

Lexie pulled out her phone. "I'm supposed to go into the clinic this afternoon. I'm going to check if there were any cancellations." She handed Kristina two twenty-dollar bills. "It's on me. I'll have a blueberry scone and a nonfat latte."

Kristina went to hand back the money, but Lexie edged away.

"She's far too generous," Kristina commented to Quinn. "Do you and Eliot have anything planned for the next few days?"

"Not really. We're okay with kicking back and relaxing."

"You've come to the right place then. Nothing happens around here."

"I'm looking forward to hanging out with Eliot's friends."

"And we look forward to getting to know you better."

"Thanks. I appreciate your kindness. So, what do folks do to celebrate the new year?"

Kristina let out a hearty laugh. "The older folks get together for a dart tournament, the young ones go into the city, and us married folks have game night. A year ago, I would have whined about how humdrum Baxley is, but small-town living has its charms. We better order before they run out of scones."

Lexie rejoined them at a booth near the back.

"What did I miss?" Lexie asked as she sat down.

"You know Baxley, not much is happening," Kristina answered.

Lexie turned from Kristina. "You okay, Quinn?"

"The lady behind the counter gave me a funny look."

"Like a scowl?" Lexie asked.

"Yes, how did you know?"

"I wouldn't worry about it," Lexie said.

"She seemed upset when Kristina told her I was Eliot's girlfriend. Please tell me she didn't want to date him too." Since Lexie and Zak's wedding, Quinn accepted getting the stink eye from Baxley's younger women, but this woman was at least twenty years older than Eliot.

Lexie giggled. "Oh, I'm sure that's not it."

"Then why was that woman annoyed?"

"That woman," Kristina said, tilting her head toward the counter, "is my mother-in-law."

"Oh…I'm sorry. I didn't mean…" Quinn stuttered, kicking herself for insinuating Kristina's mother-in-law was hot for Eliot.

"No offense taken. And she's not annoyed with you. She's upset with Emmett and me. She has issues with change and—"

"Don't worry about it," Lexie interjected, "Once Cicily gets to know you, she'll love you like we do."

"Exactly." Kristina reached across the table and squeezed Lexie's hand. "Thanks for the perspective." She turned to Quinn. "So, tell me about you. Were you a college girl like our doctor?"

"I attended an art and design school but dropped out before graduating." After all these years, it still stung not to have the degree she had worked so hard to earn. "But I have a great job in New York. I design light fixtures and home décor."

"Oh, you love what you do."

Kristina sounded disappointed. Perhaps she hated her own job.

"I work from home most days. The flexibility allows me to pitch in with Raine."

"That's fantastic," Kristina said. Her broad frown contradicted her words.

"Hey." Lexie said, "Do you have pictures of your work? I hear you take vintage pieces and transform them. What a great concept."

"I have some on my phone. Here, I'll show you."

The two women huddled close, thumbing through photos.

"My goodness. They're amazing," Kristina exclaimed.

"You're so talented," Lexie added.

Quinn swelled with pride as she discussed her earlier works and the pieces from her Resilience collection.

"I told you to keep those pictures of your hot man to yourself," a voice bellowed.

She giggled and turned. Eliot stood behind her, along with Zak and Emmett.

"I'm showing Kristina and Lexie how it's possible to take old junk and fix it up," she teased.

"Old junk?" He kissed her cheek and glanced at her hands. "Thanks to your wonderful touch, you transformed that heap into something presentable."

"Presentable?" she said, feigning offense. "It's incredible. And let's be clear. It's not scrap metal or worn lumber. It's a timeless piece that just needed polishing for its chiseled features to shine."

Emmett coughed. "You guys are worse than Zak and Lexie in the cheese department."

Kristina grabbed her husband's hand. "Honey, it's sweet. They're adorable together,"

Emmett pulled away. "Oh shit," he grumbled.

Kristina slapped Emmett's arm. "Why are you cursing?"

"Mother's coming."

"Go," Kristina shouted.

"Excuse me," Emmett said, leaving his friends and dashing across the diner.

"Family issues," Kristina muttered. "He'll join us after he receives his tongue-lashing."

****

Eliot snatched the vehicle keys off the bedroom dresser. "Let's go for a drive."

"And get caught in rush hour?" Quinn replied.

He chuckled at her joking remark. "Traffic congestion here consists of three cars at the drive-thru ATM. But let's be safe and head to the countryside."

"Drive around without a destination?"

"They call it sightseeing. Besides, it'll keep us busy until we head to Kristina and Emmett's for dinner."

She patted the bed. "If you're bored, we could give this comfy mattress a try."

"Can we wait until later?" he asked, curtailing his libido and silently cursing his words. Tangling the sheets with Quinn was a great idea, but leaving the bed would be hard, and they needed to be at Emmett's house by five.

Quinn hurried to his side. "Is it your fractured ribs? Should I call Lexie?"

Though it had been months since his hospitalization, Quinn still fretted. "Nah, I'm fine. There's no need to bother the good doctor."

"Don't lie to me, Eliot?"

He let out a sigh. "I'm not, Sprinkles."

"But it's not like you to…well, you never…"

"I never say no to sex?"

"I wasn't going to say that."

He lifted his brow. "Really?"

"Okay, I was."

He laughed. "You can strip me of my pants later, but let's go for a ride first."

"Are you sure you don't want to rest?"

He glanced at the mattress and gritted his teeth. No way would he get into bed and not have her underneath him. He grabbed his jacket. "Let's go."

Fifteen minutes later, he found the turnoff Zak had mentioned. He veered onto the quiet road.

"Wow," Quinn remarked, squeezing his hand, "it's beautiful out here."

A satisfied smirk darted across his face. He had worried Quinn might not appreciate the countryside. She was born and raised in Chicago and lived in New York. She spoke of family vacations to Miami, Los Angeles, and Atlanta. The city was in her blood.

He eased off the accelerator and glanced outside. Sunlight shimmered between the tree branches, and hoar frost had crystallized the thin needles. "It's peaceful here," he remarked. "I bet it's great for seeing stars at night?"

"And fireworks too."

He steered the vehicle into a vacant field and parked. "According to Emmett, the town's budget can only afford fireworks once a year. You'd have to attend the August Corn Fritter Festival to see the sky light up."

"You're kidding me?"

"Nope. Folks take their corn fritters seriously."

Quinn's forehead creased. She was either disappointed about the fireworks or confused about a town devoting an event to battered corn snacks.

"I can check and see if Lands Crossing has fireworks. Zak won't go. His PTSD is under control, but loud bangs are a trigger."

"You served in Iraq."

"Yeah, I'm not crazy about fireworks, but if you want to go, we will. Seeing that I handled flying out here, what's a few sparklers and Roman candles?"

She undid her seatbelt. "I am expecting fireworks." She settled her hand on his thigh. "But not the kind that shoots into the sky."

His dimples exploded. He fumbled for the seat lever. Locating it, he pushed his seat back and reclined.

She straddled him and paused. "Are you sure?"

He slid his hands and cupped her ass.

“I’ll be careful,” she murmured.

“Don’t be.”

Chapter Thirty-One

Quinn wiggled into her jeans and glanced at the vehicle's digital clock. "Sorry about making us late."

Eliot zipped his pants and eased his seat back into position. A wide smirk engulfed his face. He leaned over and kissed her. "Never apologize for seducing me."

She snorted a laugh. "Getting you naked is as easy as breathing."

"I said no to you earlier."

"Because you had this in mind."

"Sprinkles, when it comes to you, I always have *this* in mind."

She giggled and fastened her seatbelt. "If anyone asks why we're late, tell them I couldn't decide what to wear."

He shifted gears and steered onto the road. "What's wrong with the truth."

She whacked his arm. "Don't you dare."

"I'll say we went driving and got lost. I'll omit how I got lost in your beautiful eyes and wicked body."

She squeezed his hand. "I'm glad you brought me here."

"Sorry we haven't had much time alone, but as soon as I told Zak I was coming, things spiraled into all these obligations. I guess we could have skipped dinner at Emmett and Kristina's but—"

"It's okay. Zak and Lexie will be there. And Emmett

seems like a decent guy. And don't get me wrong, Kristina has been nice, but…" She stalled, unsure how to convey her thoughts while being fair to the woman. "When Kristina talks to me, she's distracted. Something is off with her."

"I'm sure it's nothing. Remember the elderly lady from the wedding?"

"Willow? The lady who compares people to different bird species?"

"Yeah, her. Many folks around here are peculiar, but they don't mean offense. I'm sure that's the case with Kristina."

"You're probably right."

Fifteen minutes later, he pulled into a driveway. A buzzing noise came from inside the car.

She opened her purse. "Oh," she said, realizing the sound was from his jacket.

He rushed to the vehicle's passenger side and helped her out the door.

The buzzing continued.

"Aren't you going to answer?" she asked, worried Paula and Malcolm might be calling about Raine.

He pulled out his phone. "It's a text from Emmett. They're stuck at his mother's house and won't be here for another hour. He says to wait inside."

Since Baxley residents hid their keys in conspicuous places, Quinn crouched down and lifted the welcome mat. "There's nothing here," she said, rising back up. "What the…" she stammered, seeing the front door open. "How'd you do that?" She assumed he picked the lock.

"I turned the knob, and then… Are you ready for this? I pushed the door open."

"The sheriff leaves his door unlocked?"

"Emmett has a smart lock that unlocks from his phone." He grabbed her hand. "C'mon, let's look around."

She stayed in the wide hallway like an immovable boulder after a landslide. "We can't snoop around."

"Why not?"

"It's wrong."

"Sounds like you're afraid of getting caught."

"No… Well, maybe."

He wrapped an arm around her shoulder and eased her into the unoccupied home.

She peeked around the corner. "Wow," she shrieked and beelined to the kitchen. Seeing the gourmet kitchen with custom cabinets and a sparkling quartz countertop had her forget about dinner guest etiquette. "Isn't this gorgeous?"

He leaned against the farmer's sink, shrugging his shoulders.

She chuckled. He would probably glimpse the Mona Lisa and say, *Yeah, it's a painting*. She slid her hand against the cabinets, admiring the workmanship.

"Hey, Sprinkles, come here."

She left the dream kitchen and found Eliot peering through the French doors to the outside.

He flicked the nearby light switch, illuminating the backyard.

A loud gasp escaped her lips. "They have all this space?" She squinted, glimpsing the southwest corner of the yard. "Is that a hot tub under a gazebo?"

"Sure is. Wouldn't jumping into that baby on a cold winter night be great?"

She wrapped her arms around his waist. "This place is something else."

He loosened from her grip and tugged her hand. "Let's check out the rest."

Enthralled by the beautiful home, she followed him to the living room.

She gawked at the wood beam ceilings. "This place is unbelievable. How much does a sheriff make?"

"Less than me."

"And what does Kristina do?"

"She's an administrative assistant for the town."

"And they're able to afford this home?"

"This place probably costs what a New York studio costs."

"Small-town living has its advantages."

"Let's check upstairs."

"Eliot, we can't."

"What's the harm?"

"Don't you know curiosity killed the cat?"

"Starvation kills a cat." He tickled her ribs. "C'mon, Sprinkles, let's go upstairs and feed the kitty."

She laughed and pushed his hands away. "Fine, but let's be quick."

She ran up the stairs. Taking two steps for each of hers, he rushed past and flung open the double doors.

"Insane," she stammered. "This bedroom is massive." She marveled at the bedroom's enormity while Eliot wandered away. "Even with a king-size bed, there's plenty of room," she muttered.

"You've got to see this," Eliot shouted.

She hurried to the ensuite. "Wow, a soaker tub and a walk-in shower."

He pulled her against him. "You do know what comes to mind?"

She met his lips and kissed him. The innocent peck

turned passionate when his lips parted. Feeling his ever-growing desire against her stomach, she stopped. “We can’t do this in their bathroom.”

“You’re right. The bedroom is better.” He ran his hands through her hair and took her mouth.

A slice of sanity jolted her. “Downstairs, now.” Her sharp tone betrayed her body’s desire.

“Fine,” he grumbled, “but let’s peek and see how many bedrooms they have.”

She nodded. Eliot was incorrigible, but at least Emmett and Kristina wouldn’t discover their guests naked in the shower. After checking the two spare bedrooms, she coaxed him down the stairs. “Stay,” she ordered when he sank into the sofa.

She started toward the kitchen for another glimpse, but he grabbed her.

Seated on his lap, she nuzzled into his chest. “You are mighty frisky today—not that I’m complaining.”

“I gather you like this place?”

She glanced up. “I love it. Your friends have a beautiful home. It has this classic ambiance, with all the wood and stone, yet there are these great modern conveniences. And the yard? It’s spectacular. I hope we get invited back during the summer.”

“Yeah, I love the place too. But you know what would make it even better?”

“Maybe different furniture, like a sectional, and a larger painting above the fireplace. The current one is overwhelmed by the massive stonework. Oh,” she said, thinking about the flooring, “a jewel-tone area rug would add warmth to this enormous space.” She took a breath. “Please stop me from jabbering. If Kristina came into my apartment, I’m sure she would point out numerous flaws, including how small and cramped the kitchen is."

He let out a quick chuckle.

"You're laughing at me." She wasn't offended. His hearty carefree laugh was sexy.

"There's one major thing that would make this place perfect, Sprinkles?"

"What?"

"You. This home needs you. You make everything in my life better. I'd love to live in this house with you. Raine could have a yard to play in. We could shower together in the large ensuite or soak in the hot tub while you name all those constellations. And imagine the mind-blowing sex by the cozy fireplace, night after night."

"Yeah. One day I'd love to live in a house too. It probably won't be as big or beautiful as this one, but that's okay."

"Quinn, I'm not here to celebrate New Year's. I came for a job interview."

She scooted off his lap. "I don't understand."

"When I ended up in the hospital, I realized how scared you were. I've always taken risks, but no child has ever counted on me, and I never had a woman I loved. Being scared isn't how you should live. So when Zak said Emmett was resigning—"

"Resigning?"

"Yeah, and I get it. Born and raised in Baxley, Emmett wanted to see the world. And a few years back, he did. He enlisted in the Army and left this sleepy little town. He only returned because his brother died and his mom needed help. Emmett never intended to stay more than a year; but like many folks, he got stuck. But now, he's ready for another adventure. He applied to the

Chicago Police Department and was accepted. I came here to interview for the sheriff's position. The interview went extremely well."

"You got the job?"

"There has to be an election, but no one's running, so it's a shoo-in if I want it."

"And do you?"

He stood, reached into his pocket, and withdrew a purple velvet box. He kneeled beside her. Taking her hand, he swooshed out a breath. "I've traveled alone for a long time. So long that I figured it would always be that way. But then I ran into you, or rather I ran you over—a red-haired beauty who thawed my heart with her weird sprinkles. Now I can't fathom a life without you. I want you with Raine and with me. My sister needs a strong, loving woman in her corner. And so do I. I promise I'll do right by you. I won't let you down. I love you, Quinn Merrick. Today and forever. Please allow me the honor of being your husband. Marry me."

Her mouth dropped. She was wrapping her mind around him interviewing for the sheriff's job, when he suddenly proposed. He asked to be her *husband.* He didn't say *be my wife.* The distinction, though subtle, mattered. He was declaring he belonged to her. His phrasing was selfless and beautiful for a man who usually fumbled with words. She stared at him, replaying his heartfelt words, captivated by his beautiful soul and vulnerability.

"It's too much," he said, his voice crackling. "Moving, marriage, a different life."

Overwhelmed with emotion, Quinn didn't answer.

"Sprinkles, please say something."

"Y-yes," she stammered.

He cupped her cheek. “Yes, you’ll marry me?”

She swallowed. Tears trickled down her cheeks. “Of course, I’ll marry you.” She wrapped her hands around his neck. “I love you, Eliot.”

His hands quivered as he slid a sparkling diamond over her finger. “I love you so much.” He rose and swung her into the air.

****

Busy kissing his fiancée, Eliot ignored his phone wobbling on the coffee table.

“Maybe you should get that,” Quinn gasped.

“Fine,” Eliot grumbled and scrolled through a series of text messages from Zak. His buddy had given him a glowing reference for the sheriff’s job, and thus he deserved a response.

—*Yes*— he typed with three exclamation marks. He forewent sending an emoji. No emoji could convey his level of happiness. Besides, he didn’t know how to find anything other than a smiley face. *Do you download an app or hit a button?*

He dropped the phone and slid his mouth over Quinn’s ear. The humming returned.

Quinn handed him the phone.

He scanned the message. This time it wasn’t from Zak. “Emmett’s asking if he should bring over the real estate papers for us to sign?”

“Can we afford it?”

“The mortgage payments are what I’m currently paying in rent. But if it’s not what you want, we’ll look at—”

She pulled the phone from his hand and texted —*SOLD*— “I would relocate to Antarctica to be with you.”

“It’s a big change. Leaving New York and moving

here. If you need time."

"Listen, Eliot, living in this gorgeous home, with a fantastic husband no longer tasked with dangerous assignments, is a no-brainer. The big yard is perfect for Raine. Moving here is an enormous win for all of us."

"What about your job?"

"I already work from home. I'll just be in a different state. We'll convert the garage into a studio."

"Don't you think it would make a better man cave?"

She wiggled onto his lap. Her lips grazed his ear. "Remember you have this enticing fireplace, the shower, and the hot tub."

His grin grew wide. "A studio it is."

Chapter Thirty-Two

Growing up, Eliot battled hard. Life was like climbing a mountain in a blizzard. He would reach a certain point and then turn back, but not so this time. He had finally reached the summit, and he couldn't be happier. Even the social worker supported Raine moving to Baxley. Telling Pratt he was resigning from the NYPD wasn't easy, but he did it. After tearing him a new one, ranting about being blindsided, and blaming Zak Ahmadi, Pratt settled down.

"Getting engaged and raising your sister are the best decisions you've ever made with your sorry ass."

A goofy grin spread across Eliot's face. "Thanks, sir."

"After all the grief you put me through, I want a wedding invitation."

"Consider it done."

"I imagine Ahmadi will be there.

"That better not be a problem for you." Eliot would not allow the rift between Pratt and Zak to ruin Quinn's special day.

"The missus will ensure I behave, but you tell Ahmadi there's no more poaching my people."

Zak Ahmadi was an NYPD legend. His departure left a big hole in the Counterterrorism Bureau. There was even a rumor that Pratt was grooming his protege to take over, but Zak pulled the plug on a policing career. He earned decent money working from home doing foreign language translations.

Eliot, however, preferred law enforcement. He loved being a cop. What he no longer enjoyed were the never-ending uncertainties of undercover assignments. Infiltrating terrorist cells and not knowing when he would get home weighed heavily on him. He had a sister who counted on him and a woman he loved more than life itself.

Risks still existed with what he would be doing in Baxley, and he swore he'd never become complacent, but statistically, the odds were better. Becoming a small-town sheriff wasn't done in haste. Taking Raine away from Paula and Malcolm had bothered Eliot so much that he almost withdrew his application, but Paula wouldn't stand for it. She made a big fuss, refusing to speak to him until he conceded. He didn't understand until Malcolm took him aside.

"She'd tar my ass for saying this," the older man had said.

"Saying what?"

"She doesn't sleep when you're on assignment. She never has. She lost one son. We both did. So don't screw this up, Eliot. You go and get this job. Crazy stuff happens in small towns, but it's not a tenth of what happens in New York. My wife deserves to sleep through the night."

Causing Paula so much stress pained Eliot, but he appreciated Malcolm's honesty.

"I'll go," he had told Malcolm, "but if I get the job and move, promise you won't argue when I spring for you guys to visit us."

The Wilsons opened their home and their hearts.

They showed him a life that wouldn't have been possible had he stayed with Carly. It was high time he showed his appreciation. He would fly them out every two months, and in between, he'd visit New York. Quinn would enjoy catching up with Gabby, and he'd call up Omeir. Someone had to ensure Omeir didn't make a fool of himself with Safia.

Quinn had planned to work for Beloved Re-Creations from Baxley, but she announced branching out on her own last week. She smugly claimed the garage as hers. Once her work took off, he'd inquire about leasing a commercial site for her—a building with ample room for both a studio and a retail store. Then he'd remove the floral curtains in the garage and get a billiard table.

Chapter Thirty-Three

A peppy song hummed inside Eliot's head as he strode through the precinct doors. He had initially heard the tune when he stopped into Quinn's apartment this morning. She had gotten up early to pack. The move to Baxley was still a few weeks away, but between both their places, there was a lot to do.

The more he tried to push away the upbeat tempo, the more it stuck. He snickered and rode the elevator to the sixth floor. Of all the problems he faced, this wasn't a bad one to have. The doors opened, and he withdrew his silly grin. The only smiling detectives were rookies or those near retirement. He reached the coffee room when his phone rang. He pulled the device from his pocket, ready to answer yet another question from Quinn. She was in the process of what she called *minimizing their moving costs.* She explained this involved donating duplicate household items and packing only essential goods. Eliot wasn't fooled. There wouldn't be any savings as his fiancée would buy new stuff. On her last call, she asked if he owned a garlic press.

"No," he responded, confused about pressing a clove. They weren't wrinkly.

The caller ID flashed across the screen. Eliot froze. He prayed the call was a mistake.

"Aren't you going to answer that?" Safia asked,

passing through the hallway. She rounded the corner and disappeared.

The phone continued ringing. Again, Eliot glanced at the screen. The call came from Cragburg in upstate New York. Although unfamiliar with the community, he knew its correctional facility housed the country's most violent and vile criminals. It was a place his biological father had called home for thirty years. The only thing that linked Eliot and Runnick Harris was their DNA. Eliot had never been to the maximum-security prison that held him, nor had he ever met Runnick.

Although Carly never spoke about it, Eliot suspected she had initially injected heroin to silence her screams, a way of dealing with the evil that befell her. And Carly might have been worthy of redemption if she had stopped there. Instead, she gave birth and transferred all her self-loathing and hate to her son. But the true source, which created and fueled Carly's anger, was Runnick Harris. His mother was a tyrant who trapped her children in dark closets, but his father was far more dangerous than the devil himself.

"Hello," he answered, hoping the monster hadn't secured his private number.

The caller was polite in his request. The man understood if his invitation was declined.

"Depending on traffic, I can be there in six hours," Eliot replied. Years ago, when he learned about Runnick, Eliot signed up to receive this call. At the time, he figured the authorities would never dial. Surely, the bastard would die in prison.

How a man, who had done what Runnick had done, could ever get a parole hearing baffled Eliot, but a lot about the criminal justice system bewildered him. He wasn't opposed to second chances—even third ones—but a man like Runnick didn't deserve to live.

Eliot returned to the elevator and pushed the button. A hand popped into sight, and the door stayed open.

"Where are you running off to?"

Eliot glanced at Safia. How did she reappear so fast?

"You're not leaving us yet, are you?" his buddy, Omeir, asked.

Eliot had no time for either friend. Besides, what would he say? *Off to check in on Pops. The courts were too gutless to give the son of a bitch a life sentence, so I have to ensure he rots in prison.*

The statement wouldn't end with a quick goodbye wave.

"Raine's teacher called," Eliot replied. "She wants to discuss Raine's progress."

He was a good liar. As undercover officers, they all lied, but their friend Zak had made them promise not to deceive each other. The former detective demanded they share their struggles and support each other. For the most part, they heeded his advice. Eliot was now the poster child for disclosing his screwed-up childhood, and Omeir was always easy to read. Though fellow officers preferred Safia conceal her thoughts, she was brutally honest—well, except for her feelings toward Omeir. But overall, the detectives remained candid with each other.

But not a soul knew about his father, not even the Wilsons. Hell, for most of his life, he hadn't known about Runnick either. He first heard about the bastard when he ran away from Carly and her psychotic boyfriend. An ugly confrontation had occurred. Carly had been so strung out she didn't recall burning his flesh the week before. When he unwrapped his sores, showing her handy work, she didn't blink. Instead, she spewed her vicious venom telling him to man up, like it was his fault for blistering.

Vowing never to hit a woman, he tried to walk away. However, she dug her nails into his arm and said his gouges were nothing compared to what she endured from Runnick. Eliot didn't believe her. He figured Carly invented the story to mess with him. *Forget it*, he told himself. And he did, thanks to alcohol and women. But after graduating from the police academy, he accessed the archived file. He read the victim's report signed by Carly. And if the official documents weren't enough to convince him, he came across Runnick's mug shot. He immediately spotted the physical similarities—the strong jawline, thick wavy hair…and cheek pits. Women, including Sprinkles, loved his dimples. He had, too, as they softened his rugged features. But when he came across Runnick's photo, that changed. Those big old facial dents were an unwanted link to that piece-of-shit rapist. He spent months scowling to avoid people commenting on his dimples. And when that didn't work, he grew a beard. But the itchiness drove him to shave when New York's summer humidity arrived.

Eliot drove six excruciating hours. He stopped once to fuel up and purchased a tasteless breakfast sandwich with a coffee. He chucked the food after one bite, his stomach too unsettled to absorb the grease. When he arrived at the prison, the deputy superintendent greeted him. The man apologized for not contacting him earlier, blaming the last-minute notification on a clerical error. *Typical bureaucrat faulting a subordinate staff member.*

Although Eliot hadn't visited this prison, his work took him to others. The stench of frightened men was all too familiar—predators and prey forced to live alongside each other, never knowing when violence would erupt. The clanging metal barriers closed with a thud, preventing even dreams from interfering in a dreary, hopeless world.

He marched along the prison's corridor, ill-prepared for what came next. Driving for hours, he concentrated on the freeway, not what he would say to the parole board.

The deputy superintendent pointed to a door. "They started earlier but adjourned when they learned you were coming. I've got a budget meeting, but I'll be in my office later if you need anything."

The man walked away, leaving Eliot outside the room. With sweaty palms, he turned the door handle and entered.

A woman, who he presumed was in charge of the parole hearing, halted mid-sentence and stared at him. The others soon followed. For the first time, he hoped his tattoos overwhelmed them, not his resemblance to Runnick Harris.

A uniformed officer whispered something to the woman and her colleagues.

"Afternoon, Detective Traversini," the woman said. "Do you need a moment before we bring Mr. Harris back?"

"No. I'm ready to go."

Concern overtook the woman's face as she glanced at her colleagues.

"I'm prepared to read my statement," Eliot clarified.

"Yes, of course," the woman said.

A portly balding man cut through the room and opened a side door. A uniformed officer stepped inside.

He headed to the board members but stopped when he noticed Eliot. Eliot opened his mouth and then shut it. The parole authorities could deal with the agitated correctional officer. The bald man handed the burly officer a note.

The officer glanced at Eliot, seemingly satisfied. "You can send Harris in," he said into the radio mic clipped to his vest.

The same door Eliot had entered moments ago creaked open, and a prisoner emerged. His metal leg irons clanged as he shuffled forward. Two correctional officers followed the incarcerated man. Though the officers were average-sized men, they appeared dwarfed by the enormity of the inmate.

One of the officers pointed to a chair. "Over there," he grunted to the prisoner.

"I'd rather stand."

"Not an option," the officer replied.

The shackled man conceded and sat with his back to Eliot. Eliot had no idea if the guy had seen him or not.

The woman in charge adjusted her eyeglasses. "Afternoon, Mr. Harris. Are you ready to continue?"

"Yeah," he grumbled.

"We have a guest attending today's hearing," the woman said. "Detective Traversini, would you like to say a few words?"

To Eliot's surprise, Runnick didn't turn around. Either the bastard forgot the last name of the fifteen-year-old girl he raped and impregnated, or he didn't care.

Though a storm brewed inside Eliot, he showed no emotion when speaking. He kept his voice calm and monotone, concealing the hatred and the unsurmountable disgust for the man before him. He focused on the task. The task of ensuring Runnick Harris would never see beyond the prison's walls. The words slid off Eliot's tongue with ease. Talking disparagingly about the man didn't bother him. He enjoyed conveying what a monster the guy was.

When Eliot finished his spiel, Runnick spun around and smirked. "Hello, son."

"Mr. Harris," the woman in charge said. "Let me remind you, speaking to the visitor is not permitted. You may only address the board."

Runnick looked at the woman and laughed. "It's rather amusing him showing up to contest my release. Never once did he visit his dear old pops. But don't worry. I won't hold that against him. I'm a changed man. It's sad I never got to be part of his life, but there's still time." He gritted a smile. "Obviously, I'll have to wait until I get released. But I guarantee I'll pay my boy a proper visit as soon as the prison gates open. It's past time he gets to know his daddy. After all, we have the same genes. He's essentially a younger version of me."

"That's enough," the woman said. "I'll give you one last chance to address why you are here and what you have done to deserve consideration for release."

After fifteen minutes of listening to Runnick's lies, Eliot had enough. He tapped his wrist even though he wasn't wearing a watch. "I have to go," Eliot mouthed to the parole board members. He rose quietly, his face as stone cold as when he arrived. There was no need to wait for a decision. The reports from the prison authorities were damning. Not a single favorable word could be said about the man. The hearing was just a bullshit mandatory requirement because of the amount of time Runnick had completed. The deputy superintendent had said as much.

Eliot's presence wouldn't sway the board, as Runnick suggested. There was no way in hell anyone would sign a release. So why did Eliot travel six hours to see Runnick? It sure the heck wasn't curiosity. Rather it was obligation. He came because the others were too terrified and because Carly couldn't. Though Carly's actions were inexcusable, she had been someone's child. And if Runnick hadn't ruined her, her life might have been different. He also came because Runnick was ultimately responsible for his stolen childhood, and the bastard would learn that no one messes with Eliot Traversini. But his poorly executed plan failed. For now, Eliot was more broken than if he had kept his ass home.

He drove to a nearby town. On the outskirts was a rundown bar, a place of cheap whiskey and lost souls. He parked in a secluded area within staggering distance. His phone rang before he could climb from the vehicle. He ignored the blasted call but not the screensaver. A lump formed in his throat. He dropped his head. The photo of Quinn, Raine, and the ugly Christmas tree became drenched with tears.

****

"Hi, Safia. Sorry to call, but I'm trying to locate Eliot," Quinn said. She had left several messages with Eliot, none of which he returned.

"Hold on. I'll ask Omeir if he's back."

Seconds later, Safia came back on the phone. "He's probably still at his sister's school."

Quinn's chest tightened. "Did something happen to Raine?"

"No, but the teacher requested a meeting. Something to do with an update on Raine's progress."

"Okay, I'll try him later," Quinn said, ending the

call.

She and Eliot met with the teacher a few days ago. Although there were areas she lagged in, Raine had done well in kindergarten. The teacher was confident she could finish the year in Baxley. Indeed, if anything were new, Eliot would have asked her to join him. *So where did he go, and why had he lied to Safia?*

Chapter Thirty-Four

Near midnight, Quinn heard Eliot speaking in the hallway. He appeared to be on the phone.

"Yeah, Paula," he said, "I realize the time."

Paula must have been upset as Eliot muttered, "I'm sorry. I didn't mean to worry you."

Quinn heard a faint click and assumed he had unlocked his door.

"I'll explain when I pick up Raine in the morning." Though he spoke coherently, his speech seemed strained.

A creak sounded, and the hallway became silent. Eliot had gone inside.

"Wait here," she whispered to Hudson, who tried escaping out the door. She snuck across the hall and turned the knob. "Darn." Eliot had already engaged the deadbolt. She tapped her knuckles on the door, apprehensive about what she would discover.

No response.

She raised her hand to knock again. She stopped midair, hearing heavy boots stomping toward the door—a slow and uneven walk, like a soldier contemplating crossing a minefield.

The door drew open. Quinn stepped inside Eliot's apartment. Neither the stench of alcohol nor the fragrance of a women's perfume permeated the air, but Eliot's eyes were puffy.

"I tried calling you," she said.

"I know."

She waited for him to elaborate, hoping he had lost his phone or the battery had died.

A pained expression formed across his face. "We need to talk."

"Safia said you went to Raine's school."

He ran his hands through his hair. "I lied."

"What?" Eliot was freaking her out.

"Sit, and I'll tell you where I've been."

She plopped down. Her heart plummeted when he stayed standing. Thoughts of him with another woman ran through her head. "What's going on?" she demanded, suppressing the urge to knead the large knot stuck in her chest.

He averted her gaze. "I had a hell of a day."

"Work?" she asked, hoping he'd say yes.

"I visited the man responsible for the other half of my DNA."

"Your father? Didn't you tell me you had never met him?" She was glad he hadn't been with another woman, but his dull, lifeless eyes worried her. He seemed broken, making her wonder what had shattered him.

"I know his name and more details than I wished I did, but I swear, until today, we've never crossed paths."

"It's okay," she said, confused why Eliot seemed more fragile than glass.

"It's not okay, Quinn. It's never been okay, and it won't be."

"Why don't you tell me about…" she paused. Saying *your father* didn't sound right. "Tell me what happened?"

"Runnick Harris is my father."

Eliot said the name as though it should mean

something to her—as if his father was an actor or a well-known sports figure. "He lives in New York?"

"He's in upstate New York…in a prison." His jaw twitched, and his face reddened. The air grew cold. "The man's a frigging rapist."

She stared in shocked silence.

"I went to his parole hearing," he said.

Dread twisted in her gut. "Tell me he didn't get released."

"I have no doubt he will die in prison. He raped two young girls and…and Carly."

"When?" she asked, desperate that her assumption was wrong.

"I was born because of that rape. My existence is because of a violent crime. That's why Carly hated me. I'm a living reminder of the horror that Runnick Harris inflicted on her." His eyes darkened. "I can't do this to you."

"Do what?"

"I know what happened." Eliot's voice rose. "I know how Chad hurt you. Beyond the cheating."

"What are you talking about?"

"How he forced himself on you."

"Why in the world would you think that?"

"Because I recognized the paralyzing terror in your eyes the day we met. It's different than a fear of spiders or flying. Perhaps I should have asked you about your ex, but talking about the past is painful. Reliving trauma sucks. And I was also terrified… I'm not good with…let's just say I'm not nice when somebody hurts someone I love."

"Eliot, Chad never…."

"I'm not a paranoid cop. I know the signs. When I

told you about Runnick, you froze. I'm not mistaken, am I?"

"It wasn't Chad. His name was Michael," she sputtered. "We were in college. I was at a party. I had a few drinks. I wasn't drunk, but I was tipsy. He offered to walk me to my dorm. I knew and trusted Michael, so I said sure. When we reached my room, he pushed me inside. I thought he was protecting me from the dorm hall director. I was underage and not supposed to be drinking. But then he grabbed my wrists and shoved me onto the bed. He ripped the buttons from my shirt, but I…I got away before he could do anything else. Michael's why I left college, why I don't drink, and why hearing about…"

He marched over. "Quinn, I'm so sorry."

"Don't be. Michael is the one who should be sorry, not you. You're a good man."

"But I have the same blood running through my veins as Runnick. And no matter what you see in me, you'll eventually see a monster. I won't subject you to continuous painful memories. There's no future with me."

"No." Her voice quivered. "You can't…Eliot, you can't—"

"I have to."

"You're walking away from us because of your father?"

"I don't want to," his voice shook, "but I have to."

"And what about your sister? Are you going to abandon her too?"

"It's different with Raine. She doesn't know my origins, nor will she ever. But I couldn't keep the truth from you. I thought I could, but when Runnick called me son today, I realized you need to know who I really am."

"I know who you are," she shouted. "You're the man I love. The guy I'm going to spend my life with."

"I'm also a man created out of Runnick Harris's depravity. I wish I could escape being his son, but I can't. It took everything within me not to beat him to a pulp today. My hatred for the man is as deeply rooted as my mother's hatred for me. Trust me. You don't want to be around such anger."

"Are you saying I should be scared of you?"

"I would never lay a hand on you or Raine. But hatred consumes me. I hate who I am. Do you have any idea what it's like to have that level of contempt for yourself? I look in the mirror, and I despise everything I see."

"But I love everything about you."

"I know, but no amount of love can make my self-loathing go away. Pretending otherwise is selfish. Staying with you means destroying you. You deserve better than a bitter, angry man."

Although he had physically escaped his circumstances, his consciousness never did. Quinn ached to set him free, but her verbal reassurances were failing. She took her sleeve and wiped her tears. Crying about the past was futile; although she could spend the next hour weeping for him, tears wouldn't help.

Gripping his hand, she cleared her throat, hoping to get the words out before getting overwhelmed. "I can't change how you view yourself, but I can tell you how I see you. You're this terrific guy who places yourself in harm's way for strangers. You've undoubtedly had a horrible life, but you take responsibility for your mistakes. Yes, you're not perfect. None of us are.

You've got flaws, but you're always striving to do better. And you have. You're a great friend to your work colleagues. The Wilsons adore you like a beloved son. You're an incredible big brother to Raine. But most of all, you're the greatest love I will ever know. Eliot, you're so incredible to so many people. Don't let Runnick or Carly ruin who you are."

"Sprinkles, you grew up in a loving home with amazing parents. It's impossible for you to grasp having a father like Runnick Harris. But trust me. You're better off without me."

Heat burned in her cheeks. "I'm not a feeble woman who needs rescuing. And especially not from you. You're beyond ridiculous. Stop treating me like I'm too stupid to decide for myself. I can easily separate you from your dysfunctional family. You're not your parents. You, of all people, must know that." Her entire body vibrated. "You don't view Raine the way you viewed Carly. So why do you think I'm incapable of seeing you for who you truly are? Why do you believe some criminal? Runnick Harris is a monster. You know who he is and what he has done. But he doesn't know anything about you, yet you allow him into your head. Whether your father is a rapist or a church pastor, it doesn't change how I feel about you."

She waited. Hoping the truth would sink into Eliot's stubborn noggin. Moments passed. Neither uttered a word.

Tears flowed down her face. Frustration and sorrow flooded her heart. "I thought you were different," she shouted. She yanked her engagement ring. The ring was stuck. Her hands were as swollen as her eyes. She marched to the door. Fumbling with the handle, she threw the door open.

"Hudson," she yelled. Her dog didn't budge from Eliot. "Now," she screamed. When he continued to disobey, she stormed out alone.

Chapter Thirty-Five

He was an idiot to think he wouldn't shatter Quinn's heart. He was no better than her ex Chad. Eliot had blindsided her too. And she wasn't the only one caught off guard. Going into work this morning, he had expected to be writing stupid reports, interrupting Omeir to ask how to spell *sectoral*. But instead, he ended up at the Cragburg Correctional Facility. Meeting face-to-face with Runnick Harris was comparable to having a grenade thrown at you. He couldn't get out of the way, and he couldn't deactivate it. The blast knocked him down, and the steel fragments severed his relationship. He would never stop loving Quinn, but he couldn't shield her from his storm. He was a flawed man and not in a trivial way like smoking cigarettes or leaving the toilet seat up. His faults were unsurmountable and carved deep into his soul.

He would do his best to care for Raine. He would provide her with opportunities he never had, give her stability, and protect her. But even if he raised a happy, well-adjusted child, he still didn't deserve Quinn's love. And he couldn't take the easy road and fake being worthy. She ought to be with someone whole, not fractured like him. He'd have lifelong regrets about what he said tonight, but she wasn't getting it. She had no clue how damaged he was. A woman so kind and pure could never comprehend his life and his emptiness. He was a nobody, a man who never inherited an ounce of goodness.

He committed what others labeled as heroic acts and good deeds. He received medals which validated this. He saved lives. He loved Raine from the moment he took her home, and his love for Quinn would never waver. But no selfless action would ever be enough to rid the volcano of self-hatred in his veins. He spent his entire life despised by his own mother. He could understand her failings—her addiction, her instability—but why the vengeance to destroy him? Unless the same evil that lurked inside Runnick also lurked inside him.

****

Eliot hauled his miserable ass over to Paula and Malcolm's, arriving an hour early. He had been awake for twenty-four hours, not the least surprised by his inability to sleep. The hurt imprinted on Quinn's face haunted him when he closed his eyes. He remembered the tears rolling down her cheeks—the tears he had caused. And combined with Runnick Harris's gravelly voice calling him son, it was too unbearable to withstand. So at three a.m., he climbed out of bed and stormed around his apartment, restless and confused. Two hours later, he walked Hudson and then headed to the Wilsons. He figured he'd take Raine out for waffles before school started. What kid wouldn't love a breakfast smothered in strawberries and whipped cream? A kid who stayed up late last night and now wanted to sleep, that was who. Therefore, he planted himself at Paula's kitchen table, having more coffee and conversation than he wanted.

"Why are you so early?" Paula asked. "Not that I mind."

"Couldn't sleep. Raine is normally awake by now,

so I thought I would take her for breakfast. I didn't know you'd allow her to stay up late. Not that I mind," he grumbled.

For a second, it appeared she would challenge his surly mood. Instead, she shrugged, returning to her early morning ritual of reading the news.

Malcolm poked his head into the kitchen and interrupted the silence. "Hi," he muttered and headed to the bathroom.

Paula poured Eliot his third coffee. "Rough case? Wanna talk about it?"

"I can't." He had wrapped up a complex case a few days earlier, making the lie less troublesome.

"I'll miss you like crazy when you go to Baxley, but I'll be happy you won't have those undercover assignments. I'm sure Quinn will be too."

He forced a smile and glanced at his phone, checking the time. He wasn't sure what was worse, sitting here dodging Paula or stewing in misery. At least Paula was used to his moods. Clamming up around his chatty little sister would be near impossible. After downing a cup of coffee, he planned to let Paula know there wouldn't be a wedding. But now, three cups in, he held off. He figured he should seek Dr. Momani's advice. The department's shrink might have tips on how to deliver bad news. Eliot came close to banging on Quinn's door this morning. He wanted to apologize, tell her he would fix it, fix himself, but giving her false hope would multiply the cruelty he had already inflicted upon her.

When Raine finally strolled into the kitchen, it was too late to go for waffles, so he didn't mention it. She jumped into his arms.

He kissed her forehead and scooted her away. "Go get ready," he urged, knowing he'd end up in tears if he held her.

When his sister returned, he was halfway through his fourth coffee. She sat in front of a cereal bowl. She smiled as if he was some superhero. Clamoring guilt punched his gut. Raine picked at her breakfast for an excruciating amount of time before she was ready to leave. Like him, she was more tired than hungry this morning. He considered reminding Paula about sticking to Raine's set bedtime, but a simple statement, coupled with his bad mood, would lead to hurt feelings. Letting Raine stay up late was Paula's way of relishing every last minute with his sister. Besides, Raine being tired wasn't so bad. It might prevent her from chatting about her favorite topic—Quinn.

Running late, Eliot hurried Raine through the school doors before the morning buzzer rang. Once inside, he gave her a heartfelt hug and choked back the tears. He didn't doubt the effect his actions would have on her. Ripping her away from Quinn would devastate his little sister. He worried about Raine reverting to the withdrawn little girl he met months ago. Right now, Raine had no idea what he had done and how his actions would impact her life.

Raine's lashes fluttered against his cheek. "I love you, Eliot."

"Back at ya, munchkin," he replied, hoping she wouldn't hate him forever.

****

"What do you mean he's away until next week?" Eliot hollered into the phone at Dr. Momani's receptionist.

"He's on holiday, Mr. Traversini," she responded, her tone wavering between professional and placating. "Dr. Torres is on call. I can schedule you with her," she offered.

"Nah," Eliot grumbled, begrudging his psychiatrist for vacationing. "I'll wait 'til he's back." He hoped the man had gone diving and was being tormented by sharks. Not in open water, but in one of those big cages. The kind that shook and rattled every time a great white bumped into it.

Right. His therapist was more likely sitting poolside, slathered in SPF, and reading about a giant squid's reproductive cycle.

He hung up, disappointed Dr. Momani, who provided no concrete answers, was unavailable. Sure, there was another option. A different psychiatrist. But no way would he relive his humiliating life story with a stranger. And what could a different shrink do other than listen while he rambled about how he screwed up. He didn't need someone with a Ph.D. to confirm what he already knew.

Work sucked. Usually, a distraction from his misery would help take the edge off, but not today. Everything, and everyone, annoyed him, including Omeir's constant cheerful chatter. Having a desk beside Omeir's was like being stranded on a broken Ferris wheel with a sugared-up toddler.

"Omeir," Eliot bellowed, "can't you do your damn job without all the mindless chitchat? For a computer geek, you suck at being an introvert."

Snarking at Omeir was like swiping cotton candy from a kid's hand. The man deserved a better friend.

Most guys would have bellowed back, but Omeir

wheeled his chair to Eliot's desk. "Want to talk about it?"

"Not much to say. I'm just one big hopeless disaster."

Omeir picked up Eliot's jacket and tossed it at him. "We're going out for coffee."

They walked to a nearby café. While gulping bitter java, Eliot unloaded about Runnick Harris and what had transpired with Quinn. Omeir didn't offer advice, but he listened. If the guy wasn't such a brilliant hacker, he could have become a shrink. As Eliot learned from his sessions with Dr. Momani, all that's needed is a degree and intermittent nodding.

"If you're worried about seeing Quinn, come crash at my place," Omeir said.

"Thanks, but I've got Raine."

"Bring her along. My place isn't big, but I can clear out and visit my mom for a few days."

"I'm fine where I'm at. Besides, I'm taking care of Hudson." Quinn never came back for him, and Eliot lacked the courage to return him.

"The offer still stands if you change your mind."

An hour later, Eliot was back at the office. The pit in his stomach was still there, but he ceased stomping around the office like a hungry grizzly.

After a non-productive day, he picked up Raine and headed home. Disappointment rose in his chest upon discovering Hudson still in his apartment. This time, he mustered the gumption and marched across the hall.

"Quinn," he bellowed through the hollow metal door.

After several unsuccessful attempts, his frustration shifted to genuine concern. He returned to his place, gathered Raine, and took Hudson for a walk. He stayed near their building in case Quinn came home. She didn't. Returning home, he clicked on the television for Raine and retreated to the kitchen. He grabbed two frozen food bags and poured the contents onto a cookie sheet. Thirty minutes later, he beckoned Raine to eat.

"Aren't we waiting for Quinn?" Raine asked, staring at the charred chicken nuggets and burned potato patty.

"She's visiting her friend Gabby tonight," he replied, hoping she was indeed safe.

****

He sat in Pratt's office, avoiding his colleagues for the second day. With the lieutenant speaking at a terrorism conference, Eliot convinced his boss's assistant he needed privacy to finish his reports. He usually lagged on paperwork, so the older woman bought his excuse. He suspected Omeir had updated Safia on his personal problems as she stayed clear. He didn't mind. Omeir's big mouth saved him from grouching at her. Being miserable to Omeir was one thing, but Safia wouldn't tolerate his pissy attitude.

He was reviewing one of his embarrassingly subpar reports when he heard a loud knock.

"Pratt's not here," he yelled. "Come back tomorrow."

Another knock sounded, this time even louder. Eliot got up, expecting Pratt's assistant. He figured she was too timid to barge in but wanted to ensure he hadn't moved the boss's golden hammer ornament. He swung the door open. *Oh crap.*

Chapter Thirty-Six

"What are you doing here?" Eliot demanded of the uninvited visitor.

Gabby brushed him aside and marched into his boss's office. "I've met a few boneheads, even dated a couple, but you, you big lug, are a total dipshit."

"Where's Quinn?" He assumed she had gone to Gabby's place, but now he wondered if she had left the city.

Gabby plopped onto Pratt's chair, taking over the weathered desk. "I liked you, Eliot. I thought you were good for Quinn, even bordering on worthy. I didn't even say that about Chad when he was doing and saying all the right things. There was something about him—too perfect, perhaps. You're far from perfect, but I didn't fathom you being such a jackass."

"I don't expect you to get it."

"Why? Do you think you have a monopoly on shitty relatives? Newsflash, the world is full of crappy parents. Granted, your father is particularly detestable, but that's why he's in jail."

Quinn had told her. He wasn't upset that she did, but he was surprised Gabby was hounding him knowing the truth. "This isn't your business."

"You must have some smarts in your neanderthal skull to tie your shoelaces. So how can you believe you're like your father? I've seen you with your sister.

And if you doubt how genetics work, consider Raine. You don't believe she's like your mother. Or do you? Do you presume she's going to grow up like Carly? Full of hate and anger?"

He ignored the barb. Her insults and belittling him were irrelevant to what really mattered. "Dammit, Gabby, where's Quinn?"

"At my apartment, crying her eyes out over a first-class jerk who doesn't deserve her."

"You left her alone?"

"Of course not. Kiefer's there. And his buddy Cody's coming over later. Did I mention he's a model?"

He gritted his teeth. From what he had heard from Quinn, pretty boy had the personality of a cardboard box. "What are you doing here?"

"I told you. I wanted to see the dipshit who broke my friend's heart—to face the selfish bastard."

"I'm not arguing with you. I deserve your contempt. I didn't want to end the engagement. I love Quinn." His voice crackled. "I love her so damn much."

"Of course. Why else would you send her packing?"

"C'mon. This isn't easy for me."

"And it is for Quinn?" Gabby snarled.

"No. I know she's…"

"She's devastated, you idiot. You gave her a ring, made a promise to her, had her rearrange her entire life, and then tore her dreams to shreds."

Even if his throat hadn't constricted, he couldn't respond. Gabby's comments were true.

"So your old man's a scumbag rapist and criminal?"

It felt like an interrogation from a budget movie that lacked sufficient funds to cast a good cop opposite the bad one. He exhaled. How much more salt could she pour on his gaping wounds?

She spun a full rotation on the office chair before pushing back from the desk. She marched over to Eliot and glared. Gabby wore outrage like a superhero wore a cape. She was an aspiring actress, but this outburst was not a performance. She was truly pissed.

He could have hauled her ass out of his boss's office. She didn't belong here. How she found him was troubling. The civilian woman waltzed into the lieutenant's office, past a slew of undercover police officers. Quinn must have told her he was with the NYPD. But there were numerous precincts, so how had she selected this one?

"I appreciate your loyalty to Quinn, but you shouldn't be here. This leads me to ask—?"

She stabbed her finger into his chest. "You don't get to ask questions. Your job is to listen."

Pushy, opinionated, and an immense pain in the ass, Gabby reminded him of Safia. God forbid if the two of them ever became allies. *Best for everyone's sake that they never meet.*

He considered moving away from her and her pointy digit, but he didn't dare. His battered ego refused to be outmaneuvered by a civilian.

"You know Quinn's life wasn't all great. Sure, she had wonderful parents, but she lost her mother. Cancer sucks, lover boy. And then there was Chad. He was a piece of shit. Oh, but not at first. He was tooth-destroying sweet in the beginning. I guess you can relate."

Gabby's verbal dagger pierced him. *She's no longer satisfied with flesh wounds. She's aiming to leave me in a pool of blood.* Normally, he would have walked away, but this was his workplace. Abandoning an angry civilian in his lieutenant's office would be foolhardy. He'd be investigated for compromising national security and risk losing the sheriff's job.

He noticed her lifting her finger and stepped aside. Tackling the air, she swung her hand back and rested it on her hip. She wasn't finished yet.

"Oh," she said as though she remembered something else. "Before Chad, there was Michael. Did she tell you about him? What he did?"

Hearing the creep's name sickened Eliot. "Her history. My background. Our families. They're total opposites," he replied. Don't you get it? That's why I can't allow her to marry me."

Gabby's nostrils flared. "Allow?" she hissed. "Well, Mr. Teacher. Oh, sorry, that's not right. It's Mr. Detective, isn't it?"

He knew better than to respond to her rhetorical question.

"Quinn told me the truth when I asked why you were moving to Baxley. We're best friends. She tells me a lot of things. But back to my point. You figure every time she looks at you, she won't get past your father?"

"I'm not saying every time, but a day will come when how I came into this world and who brought me here will matter."

"And you love her? You love Quinn?" This time her voice softened.

"I do. More than I ever believed was possible. But love isn't enough. She deserves someone—"

"Shut the hell up, Eliot," she snapped. "You don't know Quinn. You don't know jack. Before you screw everything up, providing it's not too late, go see her. Talk to her about Michael. Maybe you'll learn something about Quinn."

She stepped around him and marched to the door. Though annoyed, frustrated, and a bit terrified, Eliot admired Gabby's gumption.

She squeezed the doorknob and spun around. "It's chocolate, by the way."

"I have no idea what you're talking about."

"In case you're wondering what comforts a lactose-intolerant girl when a guy breaks her heart."

"Huh?" *Did all that chair spinning cause her hamster to tumble off the wheel?*

"Think, you big lug. Quinn can't drown her sorrows with ice cream. So don't go bringing her Rocky Road. And no roses. It's way too cliché, and they wilt fast. Bring her chocolate. And not milk chocolate, but the dark stuff. Splurge and go to a European shop."

"I can't fix this with chocolate."

"Don't be stupid. You can't live without Quinn." Gabby let out a dramatic sigh. "You're not a total douchebag. You're scared. I don't like what you've done, but I can't hate you. So grab a set of balls and work this out before it's too late. Cody has a massive crush and will act if you don't."

"He's not her type," he muttered.

"Yeah, and she once said the same thing about you, lover boy."

****

"Who's that?" Safia asked Eliot, pointing to Gabby, who smiled at Omeir before the elevator door closed.

Eliot glared at Omeir.

Safia swatted his arm. "Who's the blonde?"

"Gabby," Eliot replied.

Safia clicked her pen. "The name's not familiar."

Omeir wore a subtle smirk. He had likely misinterpreted Safia's annoyance for jealousy. His buddy spent years deciphering their female colleague's words, body language, and sideways glances. Never did he get it right.

"She came to see Omeir?" Safia whispered.

This time Eliot detected concern.

"No, she paid me an unannounced visit. She's Quinn's friend."

"How did she get past the guys downstairs?"

"Good question," Eliot shouted, getting Omeir's attention. "I would love to know how Gabby found me. Any ideas, Omeir?"

"I got a hold of her and asked her to come by," Omeir replied. He didn't seem the least embarrassed about his underhanded tactics.

Safia moved to Omeir's desk. "Why'd you do that?" Her voice was loud enough for Eliot to hear. "You said we shouldn't interfere."

"I know. But as I told you yesterday, Scorp had a fight with Quinn, and I…I figured…" Omeir stuttered at Safia's intense stare. She hadn't a clue how leaning over his desk affected him. Months ago, Eliot would have considered Omeir pathetic, but now his friend's reaction came across as sweet.

"What, you're playing Cupid now?" Safia snapped.

Eliot heard every word but stayed quiet, curious about how this would end. Just because he screwed up didn't mean others couldn't find love.

"No…umm, not exactly," Omeir replied.

"You know more than you let on," Safia said.

Eliot doubted Omeir would cave and give the details. His friend chattered incessantly, but he didn't gossip. Eliot noticed Omeir peering at his screen and ignoring Safia's comment. *Bad move, bro.*

Safia spun the laptop away from Omeir.

"Hey, I'm working," he protested.

"This fight he had with Quinn, it's a big deal, isn't it?"

"Come on, Safia, you know Scorp and I talk, but I don't feel right about disclosing his business, even to you."

Eliot would have found his friends' conversation amusing if he had been in a better mood. They were so focused on each other they forgot he was within earshot. An eighty-year-old man full of ear wax could hear them.

"I called Gabby hoping to help Scorp with his relationship," Omeir explained. "I suspect Quinn's his first."

"What?" Safia hollered all too loud.

Thankfully, most fellow officers had gone for lunch and weren't around to weigh in on his sex life.

Omeir's face reddened. "Not a first, first, but I don't think he's ever been in a relationship before."

"Go on."

"When it's your first love, you think…"

"Great," Eliot muttered. *Did everyone have to be a fricking psychiatrist?*

"Think what?" Safia asked.

"It's reasonable for Scorp to believe he doesn't deserve her because she's too perfect."

Eliot's annoyance dissolved, realizing Omeir was referring to his own feelings toward Safia.

"She's not perfect," Safia snapped. "Nobody is."

"Isn't Scorp driving you crazy with his brooding?" Omeir asked. "He's miserable and dragging the rest of us down. He's crazy in love with Quinn and I'm trying to steer them back together. Wouldn't you want a friend to help you if you were being ridiculous?"

Having spent the morning being berated by Gabby, he didn't like Omeir calling him ridiculous. He didn't have a spat with the high school cheerleader over pink-streaked hair. These were real problems among grown-ups.

He was about to shut up his colleagues when Safia said, "You called Quinn's friend to straighten Scorp out?"

"Kind of," Omeir replied.

"That's incredibly sweet."

Eliot glanced at Omeir. His friend had a goofy grin on his face. He was clueless about acting cool.

"I guess if it works," Omeir replied to Safia. "Otherwise, I've awakened the beast."

Eliot let Omeir's comment slide. His friend meant well, even though his actions were misguided and futile.

****

When Paula called, asking about taking Raine to the movies, Eliot said yes.

"If you want, she can stay over, and you can take her to school in the morning," he encouraged.

Eliot had been called stupid, idiotic, ridiculous, and several other colorful adjectives—and all by people who liked him. He tried to curtail his grouchiness but failed with Omeir. His sister was better off staying with the Wilsons.

Arriving home, Eliot found Hudson waiting by the door. "Sorry, bud. I thought she would have picked you up." He leashed the anxious dog and led him outside. As the crisp wind struck his face, Eliot quickened his stride, going over his conversation with Quinn's BFF.

Is Gabby right? Quinn won't care about who my parents are. Perhaps regarding Carly, but Runnick Harris was a different story.

And what about that Michael creep? Why should I learn more about the man who tried to rape Quinn? How the hell is that relevant?

Eliot hated having more questions than answers.

"Dammit," he grumbled, unsure of anything except that he would pound Dr. Momani's door on Monday morning. He soured, picturing the doctor wearing socks with sandals and drinking mango juice at an expensive resort. Resenting the man for taking time off was selfish, but Eliot had become a miserable asshole. Maybe the good old shrink would help him. Or at least shove him down the right path. Perhaps the situation wasn't all doom and gloom. Maybe he had a chance for a normal life.

Returning to his apartment, Eliot decided to call Zak Ahmadi. The former detective understood self-loathing. Eliot picked up his phone. He considered texting Quinn for a second, but what would he type? He ached to hear from her. Hell, he'd be happy if she sent a middle-finger emoji. He pushed the careless notion aside and scrolled his phone contacts for Ahmadi.

A deep bark startled him.

"What's up, bud?" He glanced, looking for what had riled the big clump of fur. He hoped it wasn't a mouse. Raine would go ballistic if he had to trap the furry little critter. She had a fondness for all creatures, including the disease-carrying varmints. He remembered how he found one in the kitchen a few months back and smacked the little bugger with a broom. Raine hollered for him to stop, which he did. Then he spent two hours encouraging the rodent into a glass bowl. After capturing the mouse, Eliot freed it outside. Now he wondered if the little rascal, tired of scavenging food in the wilds of Brooklyn, had snuck back in. Lounging in a warm kitchen, eating fallen scraps from a five-year-old was a far better life.

Hudson let out three loud woofs and then trotted away. Eliot followed him. Inside the kitchen, Hudson nudged his nose against an empty dish. He wasn't barking at an intruder rodent. He was hungry.

"Okay, boy, I'll get you your dinner." He tugged the kitchen drawers, searching for kibble. Quinn habitually left freezer bags of dog food at his place. Last week, he told her more baggies weren't needed. He had enough to last several days. And that was…

Shit. It was days ago.

As a last resort, he opened the fridge and checked the lettuce crisper. There was no hidden stash.

A sad whimper emanated from Hudson.

He stroked the animal's fur. "It'll be fine, Huds. I won't let you starve."

Eliot returned to the cupboards. "I have kiddy cereal, crackers shaped like giraffes, and oatmeal cookies." Any one of them would work until he purchased dog food. He reached for the crackers and remembered Quinn telling him about Hudson's allergies. *Beef…chicken…gluten?* He wasn't sure. The last thing he needed was Hudson to be sick. He'd never forgive himself if something happened to Quinn's beloved pet.

"Dammit." He should have taken the apartment key Quinn had offered, but he saw no need. Picking the lock wasn't an option. Quinn used to have a cheap lock on her door, one where the cylinders easily tumbled. But after she gave him the serpent picture, he insisted on doing something nice for her. A normal man would have cooked her a meal, but being a cop, he installed an impossible-to-pick disk-blocking lock. Besides axing down the door, there was now only one way to get inside Quinn's home.

****

"Call her and ask what to feed the dog. Better yet, tell her to collect her animal," the voice on the phone demanded.

"Don't you think I tried?" He heaved in frustration at Safia, whom he had reluctantly dialed. "She won't pick up. She's…" He was unsure how to respond.

"She's what?"

"She's too pissed to talk to me."

"What did you do?"

"It doesn't matter."

"It does if you want my help."

"It's complicated."

"Complicated?" she screeched. "I'll tell you what's complicated. Getting investigated by internal affairs for breaking into a woman's home."

"Please," he sighed. "I don't know what to do."

"I hope you're talking about your relationship. Feeding a dog isn't difficult."

"Huds has allergies. He needs a particular type of food. I have no idea what it is. He's whining. It's breaking my heart." Eliot's heart was broken long before he placed the call. It shattered when he pushed Quinn away.

"I'll come over, but I'm not entering her apartment unless you tell me what happened. All of it."

"Fine, but let's talk after you get me into her place.

Huds is starving."

"No. I need to know what's going on before I commit a felony. Keep trying to get a hold of Quinn and, in the meantime, feed the thing a carrot."

"What if he's allergic to vegetables?"

"He's a dog, not a toddler."

Safia made no sense, but Eliot wasn't surprised by her lack of knowledge. She destroyed Omeir's office plant last year when he went on holiday. How the hell could you kill a cactus?

****

Eliot glared at the coffee cup in Safia's hand. What part of urgent did she not understand?

She peered past Eliot into his apartment. "The dog looks energetic," she snarked.

"One carrot isn't gonna get him through the day." At this moment, a bull in a rodeo chute had more patience.

"So, what's really going on between you and Quinn?"

"Fine," he grumbled and moved aside for her to enter. "I never went to Raine's school."

Her eyes widened, and her mouth fell flat. "But that's what you told me."

In hindsight, confessing he lied about meeting his sister's teacher was not the best way to start the conversation. But when he revealed where he had gone, Safia softened.

"I had no idea about your father."

"Until the other day, no one did. And how could I not tell Quinn, especially considering what she's been through?"

"For what it's worth, you made the right choice. And

you may not want to hear it, but you're better off without her."

"What are you talking about?" he snapped. "Quinn's amazing."

"She's punishing you for your father's actions. I don't see why you're not outraged."

"She's not punishing me."

"Punishing. Judging. Whatever. It's all the same. Quinn broke off the engagement because you didn't come from a so-called perfect family."

"I terminated the relationship." The ache in his chest hardened.

"Because of something Quinn said, right?"

In a hurry to move Safia past the shocking revelation about his dad being a rapist, Eliot had omitted a few details. Among these was the fact that the breakup was his fault.

"Quinn tried to convince me it doesn't matter that my father's a monster. I'm sure she might believe it, but she'll think differently a year or even a month down the road. Quinn's a good person—more than I'm worthy of. I can't give her the life she deserves. Who my father is and what he did will always haunt me. I can't put Quinn through that."

Safia muttered in Arabic. Eliot dropped his head.

Safia continued, "You're a great colleague, a wonderful friend, but you're acting like such a—"

"—Asshole."

"I was going to say *man*, but your term is accurate. Do you know why I supported you when you joined our team? Why I befriended you when Zak and Omeir wanted nothing to do with you?"

He suspected she wanted to piss off her father, a

high-ranking official within the NYPD. Her interest in the department's bad boy would make Daddy Dearest flip.

"Despite your hard drinking and womanizing ways, I knew you would have my back."

"And how did you know that?"

"It doesn't matter because it's true."

"You sound like an overpaid motivational speaker. Give me one example."

"You showed me you're a team player. You stepped up when Zak got stabbed. You didn't do the obligatory *I'm here for you* nonsense. No, you stayed in touch with Zak and called him even when he told you to get lost. You traveled to Baxley and made sure he was okay. And you still check up on him."

"It doesn't make me a hero. You and Omeir were there for him too."

"You're right. Caring about a friend doesn't make you a hero, but it makes you a good man. Omeir, Zak, and I go way back, but you hardly knew him. And you've done an amazing job with your sister. She worships you. Regarding Quinn, I admit I was skeptical of the whole relationship you started. But then I saw you guys together, how you started as friends, how you cared about her, and how you respected her. I'm not a dreamy-eyed girl, but seeing you fall in love with Quinn was so sweet, my icy heart thawed."

"Safia, you're not as cold as you pretend."

"Neither are you."

"But I can't make all this shit I feel about myself disappear."

"Go back into counseling."

Omeir must have blabbed about the sessions with

Dr. Momani. He bit his lip and let her comment go. His life had been on full display for months now. He spent years avoiding overly dramatic people, and here he was, a guy in constant crisis mode.

"But before you visit the departmental psychiatrist," she said, "you best grovel for that good woman to take you back. There's no use going to Baxley if she isn't with you. You'll wind up a bitter, cranky sheriff."

She was right. Yes, someone blocked his happiness, but that person wasn't his mother or his father. It was him. He spent his entire life on the fringe. The Wilsons tried including him, but he never fully accepted their generosity. He was afraid if he considered them family, they would be taken from him. But when Raine came along, he no longer remained detached. He dove right into being a big brother. Eliot loved his sister with all his heart and fought when Carly threatened her safety. He battled as hard as he could.

Shamefully, he didn't do the same with Quinn.

Instead of stepping into the ring and fighting, he retreated like a coward. Frightened about the future, he abandoned a woman who consistently went the distance for Raine and him. He blamed his father for messing up his life. And although the man ruined many lives, it wasn't Runnick Harris's fault this time.

Chapter Thirty-Seven

Quinn glanced at the phone message. Her father had texted, letting her know he was at O'Hare airport. He was en route to Los Angeles. A simple phone call and he'd cancel his business trip, but crying on his shoulder would make her feel powerless. She spent years regaining her confidence. The last thing she wanted was to fall apart and have her father coddle her. She'd refused her father's money for that exact reason, and it was also why she didn't tell Eliot about Michael. As a natural protector, he would shield her excessively. He fussed enough over his kid sister. If left unchallenged, Eliot would only have her walk Hudson during daylight hours. He constantly snuck out the door with Hudson at night, claiming he needed to stretch his legs.

She texted her dad back. *—Have a great trip. Love you—* She'd wait until he returned to tell him the engagement was off. If she told him now, he'd head straight to New York or insist she meet him in Los Angeles. She loved the warm California sunshine but wasn't ready to rehash why she and Eliot had split.

Having control over her life was how she healed. Running off wouldn't nullify the pain. Besides, she couldn't leave Hudson for days on end. She knew Eliot would take good care of her beloved pet. Even though he broke her heart, he was still the same man she fell in love with. The breakup with Eliot hurt far more than the one with Chad, even though Chad had done far worse and for selfish reasons.

She missed her fun times with Eliot—teasing him about his frilly sofa cushions, their competitive bantering at the gym, and watching those boring baseball games. And most of all, she missed lying in his arms. Her cheeks grew wet with tears. Gone were narrating bedtime stories and giggling at Eliot's barnyard noises.

She glanced at the time. "Do you know when Gabby will be home?"

"She didn't say," Kiefer said.

Just as well. It would be easier to do this without Gabby around. Quinn pulled out an envelope from her purse. "Can you give this to her when she gets home?"

Kiefer backed away.

"It's a thank you letter," she clarified, realizing he thought it was a suicide note. "I appreciate you both allowing me to stay, but it's time I return to my apartment." She also included some money for the food she had eaten.

He took the envelope. "I'm sorry it didn't work out, Quinn. I mean with Eliot. Not you staying here. You're welcome to come back if you need to."

Though she no longer resented Kiefer, hugging him didn't feel right. "Thanks," she mumbled and left. She loved Gabby for being supportive and letting her crash, but her friend had her own life. A life that led her to leave abruptly yesterday afternoon when they had plans to go shoe shopping. Quinn didn't care Gabby had bailed on the shopping excursion. Floral ankle boots weren't going to mend a broken heart. Not even country musicians believed this. But she wanted someone to talk to, someone who would tell her it was all right, even if it wasn't. Instead, she ended up conversing with Kiefer. He surprised her. He listened to her babble for hours, and he was genuinely worried about the note she had just handed him.

Arriving in front of her apartment building, she paused. This was where it all started—where she met Eliot and fell in love. She took a breath, peeked inside, and raced up the stairs. She'd do her best to avoid Eliot. Her heart couldn't handle running into him.

A pang of pain hit her. In a few weeks, he would be gone. Tears trickled her face. Her heart broke. She loved not only Eliot but his kid sister. Not being part of their life would hurt. She hoped one day Eliot would view things differently, but by then, she'd be a stranger to Raine.

She unlocked her apartment door. The usually sticky lock was smooth, turning without a tug. She figured the constant use had loosened it. She set her keys on the entryway table. Her gaze fell to the boxes in the living room. She'd spent hours packing for the move to Baxley. Now the cardboard cartons were a taunting and painful reminder of her profound loneliness.

She entered the kitchen. An enormous gift basket sat on the counter. Through the colored cellophane, she noticed an assortment of chocolates. She was about to read the attached card when a knock sounded at the door.

She peeped through the hole. "Did you break into my apartment?" she hollered, her tone more accusatory than intended.

"Technically, no, but I'm responsible."

Exasperated by the bizarre response, she rubbed her brow line.

"The particulars aren't as important as why I did it,"

he said.

"You could have left the basket outside the door, or better yet, you could have given the chocolates to Raine."

"I got into your apartment to feed Huds. The poor guy was whining from hunger pains."

She threw the door open. "Is Hudson okay?"

"He's fine. I'll bring him over later." He placed his foot in the doorway. "Can I come in and talk?"

"Haven't you said enough?"

"I'm not here to argue. I'd like the chance to…um…Can I come in?"

Exhausted, she stepped aside.

He walked into the living room and sat on the apartment size sofa, his body overwhelming the furniture. "I brought you a gift basket. It's dark chocolate, not milk chocolate."

"I saw it." Eliot had devastated her by ending their engagement, yet he seemed more concerned about her inability to digest dairy.

"Umm, did you read the card?" he asked.

"I didn't get a chance."

"It's the last basket of chocolate I will ever give you."

Pain stabbed her chest. "I don't want a farewell gift." Receiving a consolation goody basket for being dumped was upsetting and weird. "Look, I'll say goodbye to Raine before you head to Baxley, but not now. I'm too emotional."

"I didn't mean… He rubbed his knuckles. Gabby suggested the chocolate."

She straightened. "You talked to Gabby?"

"Yeah, she showed up at the precinct and verbally

walloped my ass. Quite the devoted friend you have."

"I'm sorry, I had no idea. I assumed she went to a rehearsal."

"It's not your fault. Besides, Gabby made sense, and so did Safia.

"Safia knows?"

"I mistakenly trusted Omeir, who blabbed to Safia. I've been knighted a total dipshit by your friend, and I suspect Safia called me something similar but in a different language. But it doesn't matter. What I did to you, and to *us*, was wrong."

"Until the other day, when you treated me like a child, nothing was wrong with you or us." She sat down. She didn't want to do this, but she couldn't let him go without attempting to persuade him one last time. "It's about you, Eliot, not your mother or father. It's frustrating you don't understand this, but I can't change how you feel. I'm without options here. I can't make you stay, and I can't make myself stop loving you. You keep telling me you're powerless, but you're the only one with a choice."

He muttered what sounded like *I know.*

Just because Eliot likely acknowledged she was right didn't mean he would do anything about it.

"I don't want to lose you, Sprinkles. I do want to marry you. I want you with me when I head to Baxley with Raine, but…."

"But you can't," she said, finishing his sentence.

"I'm afraid…No, I'm terrified you'll wake up one day and feel different."

"I appreciate your honesty, but I'm livid. You and I have been through so much, yet you don't know who I am. I'm trying not to make myself the victim. The last thing you need is more guilt, but what you're doing makes no sense. You don't hesitate to put yourself in harm's way for your job but won't take a leap of faith regarding me?"

"I'm not trying to hurt you."

"I know." She didn't doubt he loved her. "I wish you would realize I won't ever judge you by your family. My love for Raine isn't tied to you. I love her because she's a fantastic kid. So why would my love for you be tied to Carly or Runnick? I hate what Carly did to you, what she did to Raine, and I hate everything your father represents, but it doesn't make me love you *or* Raine any less. My heart doesn't work that way."

"I want to believe you, Sprinkles, but what if one day—"

"It won't." She grabbed his hand and let out a heavy sigh. "I know because of what happened with Michael."

He stared at her.

"Michael's sister didn't tell you?"

"Michael? The creep who tried to rape you?"

"Yes, but I'm talking about his sister now."

"What sister?"

"The one who visited you."

"Are you saying—"

"Gabby is Michael's sister."

"But she's your friend. Your best friend," he said.

"Yes, and she bears a strong resemblance to Michael. She has the same pale blue eyes, the same blood type pumping through her veins, and the same two parents as Michael. Did you know the DNA percentage between siblings is the same as between a father and son? I'm not a geneticist, but it's scientifically proven that Gabby has approximately fifty percent of the same DNA as her brother, the exact ratio you share with Runnick Harris. So I do know from experience how I'd react, not only today but years from now. I know because I have never once felt anything but love for Gabby. She's not blood, but she's my sister in every other sense. Gabby is the reason Michael never raped me. She heard my screams and came rushing into my dorm. And slamming a two-hundred-pound athlete against the wall was the easy part for Gabby. The worst came later. Campus security wanted to deal with the matter internally and not have the police lay charges, but Gabby encouraged me to go to the authorities. And when the trial began, she testified. The poor girl endured an ugly cross-examination from a highly paid legal team who labeled her a vindictive bitch jealous of her brother's success. And that's not all. Both her parents disowned her for telling the truth. Gabby gave up a trust fund and her entire family to do what was right. Like you, she's a pain in the ass who thinks she knows what's best for me, but I wouldn't have survived without her."

"Why didn't you tell me?"

"Because it shouldn't matter. Besides, Gabby and I never discuss Michael. The past is the past. She can't change who she's related to any more than you can. And that's okay because it's irrelevant to who you are, to the man I fell in love with, and who I will never stop loving."

He pulled her into his arms and kissed her. "How did I ever get this lucky?" he whispered.

"No," she corrected, "we're both fortunate."

Epilogue

Eliot sat on the deck, savoring his morning coffee and enjoying mother nature. Life in Baxley was serene. Even the birds chirped harmoniously. He checked his phone's calendar. He had a council meeting tomorrow and wanted to ensure it didn't conflict with parent-teacher interviews. *Good.* He could go with Quinn and meet Raine's teacher, whom his sister adored. He flipped the device over. Checking his emails could wait. Since moving to Baxley, today was the first time he had a day with no appointments.

The screen door flew open, and Raine bustled into the yard. She ran to the swing set he had assembled last night. Eliot waited, thinking she'd ask for a push. She didn't. She was growing up fast and doing more on her own. She was still shy around most adults but had made new friends, and Quinn had scheduled a playdate with the Sanford twins for next week. There'd be a house full of carnage, but seeing Raine happy would mitigate the damage the twins would cause.

The door creaked behind him. A crisp floral fragrance drifted in the air. He wasn't a guy who could tell whether it was lilacs or gardenias. In fact, he had no idea what a gardenia was, but he loved this scent. Warm, smooth arms wrapped around his shoulders. A big grin engulfed his cheeks. He inhaled. Still unable to determine the flower species, he now detected the scent of marshmallows. Was he simply hungry, or had the beauty industry infused food into their products? Good thing she didn't smell of bacon.

Quinn's lips grazed his ear. "I missed you in the shower today."

"Because of a promise I made, I had to deal with an intruder." He had discarded his T-shirt and had unzipped his jeans when Raine barreled up the stairs screaming. It was a high pitch squeal only a young girl could make. The first time she howled like that, he almost went into heart failure, but now, he knew the source of her fright.

"Damn spiders," he groaned. "I know you hate pesticides, but maybe you should reconsider."

She laughed. "I'll google a natural remedy." She handed him his coffee and took the chair beside him.

Quinn's name had been added to Raine's adoption papers. Unfortunately, he'd have to wait until next year before her name went on a marriage certificate.

Though he considered convincing Quinn to seal the deal with a simple justice of the peace ceremony, he didn't. She deserved a wedding with her father escorting her down a church aisle and with Raine as the most adorable flower girl ever. Quinn's opinionated, yet loyal friend had already chosen the bridesmaid dresses. Just as well. Paula would boot his ass if she didn't participate in the special day.

"Don't feel obligated to join us at the gallery in Chicago. I'll understand if you'd rather go fishing with Zak."

He kissed her cheek and inhaled once again. Craving both sex and s'mores was a first. He'd have to take Quinn camping or build a secluded backyard firepit.

"Did you hear me?"

"Zak has other fishing buddies. I'm spending the day with my girls."

"It's a small gallery," she warned.

"Would you rather me not tag along?"

"Course not. But it's an abstract exhibit, and there's no coffee shop."

"Abstract is my favorite."

"Yeah, right."

"I'm serious. I enjoyed the paintings and sculptures that time we visited MoMA with Gabby and Kiefer."

"I figured you preferred it to the alternative. You know? A romance movie."

He leaned across the patio table and brushed his thumb across her lips. "The art museum taught me something. Before meeting you, I wasn't fond of abstract art. I didn't get it. Globs of splattered paint made no sense. I'm a simple man. Trees and sky, I get. But now I understand. I get how special those globs are. It makes me feel…"

"Feel what?"

"Abstract art is so Quinn Merrick."

A crease formed across her forehead.

"You're like those splattered paintings," he said, trying to clarify.

"The ones you said look like a three-year-old painted them?"

"Yes. But I was wrong. They are masterpieces, just like you're my masterpiece. You're not like one of those boring classics with chubby angels or serious faces. You're explosive. You invoke excitement. You're color in a monochrome world. I love that about you. I love it so much that I wish everyone could meet you and discover your greatness. But I also love that I can see in you something others may not. It's like subtle strokes between layers of paint or different colors colliding. It's fine when others realize your beauty, but I don't want them buzzing around and gawking at you. I don't mind if they glance, but they must move on. I should be the only one who spends hours admiring you."

"That was so…"

"Awful?"

"It's weird, but it's also incredibly romantic. Oh, that reminds me. I have something for you."

He glanced at the swing set. "Shouldn't we wait until Raine goes to bed?"

She laughed. "Not what I meant, but keep the thought for later." She kissed him. "Wait here." She ran into the house and returned with a blue gift bag.

He cocked his head. He loved spoiling Quinn and Raine, but receiving presents still made him uneasy. Spotting the bright shiny bag, Raine charged across the yard.

He pulled his chair back, allowing Raine to climb on his lap. "Wanna help me with this?"

She replied by removing the pretty tissue paper.

Astonished by what he held in his hands, he choked up. "How?" he asked Quinn.

"I wanted some baby pictures of Raine, so I asked Alisha if she had any. This was my favorite, so I had it framed. She found several others. "Raine, sweetie, will you go into the spare bedroom and bring me the envelope on the dresser?"

He waited until Raine left, then pointed at the second picture in the frame. "And where did you get this one?" he asked, referencing the photo of a little boy, a toddler with thick dark hair and deep-set dimples.

"I mentioned to Alisha there were probably many kids who never had childhood pictures of themselves. She told me she was one of those kids. It never occurred to me she might have grown up in the system. I felt stupid for bringing it up and was relieved when she handed me Raine's pictures. I hurried out of there, profusely thanking her several times as if gratitude could erase the pain I saw on her face. A few days later, she called wanting to meet. I thought maybe she found more pictures of Raine. She hadn't. But she had gone through archived files. Your file. She found this picture of you as a boy. I'm sorry, it was the only one she had."

"Being able to have one is incredible. Thank you." He leaned over and kissed her.

"You might want to call Alisha and thank her. She spent half a day searching the archived files."

"Yeah, I will."

Raine returned and handed Quinn a large, padded envelope. "Who's that?" she asked, looking at the other photo Quinn had framed.

Quinn touched the picture on the left. "This is your brother when he was young."

Raine glanced at her own baby photo and then at Eliot. "You look like me."

"Yeah, I do, don't I? But you're much cuter," he added.

His sister nodded, making him laugh.

"I always noticed the resemblance, but it's more noticeable in these pictures—especially the dimples," Quinn said.

"Come here, Raine," he shouted as his sister darted to the swing set.

Raine hurried back. Eliot glanced at his sister's baby

picture and then at her face. She, too, had dimples. They weren't as distinct. They were relatively tiny dents and a bit lopsided.

How had he not noticed?

"Can I go now?" Raine asked.

He nodded and went back to the photo. He tried to remember his mother. Not the last time he saw her when her cold blue eyes glowered with disdain, but rather her as a young woman. Finally, a memory came to him. He was around five or six, and Carly had taken him to an amusement park. She abandoned him for a while, likely to score drugs, but she brought him on the Ferris wheel before she took off. He remembered her laughter and the smile that stayed on her face long after the ride had stopped.

"Is Carly in any of the pictures with Raine?" he asked Quinn.

"No, but there is a photo of Carly by herself. Alisha wasn't sure what to do with it. I asked her to add it to the other photos and let you decide. If you rather not see it, I'll turf it before you flip through the others."

"I'd like to see it."

Quinn picked up the envelope and dug through the various photos. "Here," she said, pulling it out.

He took the picture from her hand. Carly must have been no older than eighteen. He would have been a toddler at the time. He had no idea what had transpired before the picture was taken, but Carly was smiling. And within that rare smile were dimples. Carly's were more like Raine's—a subdued indentation.

He returned to the separate photos of him and Raine. He stared at the boy he once was—the boy with dimples. He no longer hated those dimples. He didn't know if he inherited them from Runnick Harris or Carly Traversini, but it no longer mattered. What mattered was the life he had built and the family he now had.

A word about the author…

Gloria Joynt-Lang was born in France and raised in various locales throughout Canada. Before she started writing contemporary romance, she worked in the criminal justice system – technically spending time behind bars. As a Canadian, she's fanatic about hockey, poutine, and apologizing. She currently resides in rural Alberta with her husband and their sassy Yorkie girl. https://www.gloriajoyntlang.com/

Thank you for purchasing
this publication of The Wild Rose Press, Inc.

For questions or more information
contact us at
info@thewildrosepress.com.

The Wild Rose Press, Inc.
www.thewildrosepress.com

www.ingramcontent.com/pod-product-compliance
Lightning Source LLC
LaVergne TN
LVHW020528100826
845148LV00010B/1385

* 9 7 8 1 5 0 9 2 5 3 4 0 1 *